Praise for Baker & Goodman's

The Wake-Up Call

"*The Wake-Up Call* is a fun and engaging novel! Baker and Goodman pull you into Frannie's disasters and make you want to see what she's up to next!"

—C. Gabel

"*The Wake-Up Call* is the nursing world's version of the classic *Traveling Pants* books. Be ready to feel youthful once again, reliving the ups and downs of college life and finding yourself."

—K. Goodman

"You feel for Frannie. You get caught up in her struggles, learning to grow up and be independent, while trying to make new friends. She feels so misunderstood; your heart just goes out to her while also wanting to ring her cute little neck."

—D. Herrington

The Wake-Up Call

Joy Don Baker
&
Terri Goodman

THE WAKE-UP CALL is a work of fiction, Names, characters, places, and incidents either are the product of the authors' imagination or are used fictitiously. Any resemblance to actual persons, living or dead is entirely coincidental.

Copyright © 2018 by Baker & Goodman

All rights reserved. No part of this publication may be reproduced, distributed, or transmitted in any form or by any means, including photocopying, recording, digital scanning, or other electronic or mechanical methods, without the prior written permission of the publisher, except in the case of brief quotations embodied in critical reviews and certain other noncommercial uses permitted by copyright law.

Published 2018
Printed in the United States of America
ISBN: 978-1-7322535-0-6
E-ISBN: 978-1-7322535-1-3
Library of Congress Control Number: 2018905808

Cover design: *Fresh Design*
Interior design: *JETLAUNCH.net*
Author photo: *Kelly Williams Photography*

For information, address: Baker & Goodman
Watauga, TX
admin@bakergoodman.com
www.bakergoodman.com

Table of Contents

Chapter 1 1
Chapter 2 9
Chapter 3 23
Chapter 4 41
Chapter 5 62
Chapter 6 75
Chapter 7 82
Chapter 8 95
Chapter 9 108
Chapter 10 122
Chapter 11 135
Chapter 12 148
Chapter 13 166

Chapter 14 179

Chapter 15 185

Chapter 16 205

Chapter 17 211

Chapter 18 221

Chapter 19 226

Chapter 20 234

Chapter 21 239

Chapter 22 247

Chapter 23 250

Chapter 24 254

Acknowledgments 265

Authors' Note 267

About the Authors.. 269

Chapter 1

The Dallas heat scorched Frannie's lungs, and the humidity plastered her hair to her neck and shoulders. She grabbed her long blonde hair into a ponytail and rummaged in her purse for something to hold it off her neck.

"This weather is something else. I need to get out of this outfit before my nylons melt to my legs."

The cab line at Love Field was short. "It shouldn't take long to get to the university," her father said, "if we can find a cab big enough to hold all that stuff you and your mother insisted you couldn't live without. There aren't enough days in the semester to wear everything you brought."

Three suitcases fit into the back of the Yellow Cab station-wagon with the steamer trunk wedged into the back seat, leaving little space for Frannie. Her cramped position mirrored the tightness in her chest that increased as the cab neared the Crestmont campus. She took a deep breath as they pulled up in front of a four-story, red brick Colonial building set well back from the street.

"I'm Sally Adams," said a young woman, reaching out a hand to help Frannie from the cab. "I'm one of the Resident Assistants here at Hadley Hall. What's your name?"

Frannie took Sally's hand but said nothing.

"I'm Gerhart Braun," Frannie's father filled the void. "This is my daughter, Frannie. She left her voice somewhere between the airport and here."

Embarrassed, Frannie blurted, "I'm Frances Estelle Braun. Please call me Frannie."

Sally nodded. "You're going to love Hadley Hall. Let's get you checked in." At the end of the long walkway, they climbed the wide circular steps to the porch that ran the length of the building. Students and families sat in white rocking chairs and on swings anchored to the high porch roof. Sally pushed open one of the ornate double doors into the formal lobby of Frannie's new home, a large space dotted with comfortable groupings of chairs and sofas.

Sally stopped at the baroque, hotel-style front desk. "Let me introduce you to Mrs. Crandall, our dorm mother." Mrs. Crandall welcomed the Brauns while Sally picked up the keys to Frannie's suite.

"Males are allowed in the suites only on move-in day," Sally explained as they walked toward the end of one first floor wing. She unlocked the suite and handed the key ring to Frannie. Three suitcases sat on the floor of the sitting area by a group of four comfortable chairs with two lamp tables and a coffee table. There was an area to one side for small kitchen appliances, and a Jack and Jill bathroom separated the two bedrooms. "You're the first to arrive," said Sally. "Select the bedroom you like."

Frannie peeked into both rooms. "I like this one," she said, dropping her purse on one of the twin beds. Her father hauled in the suitcases, heaving two of them onto Frannie's bed and the third onto the other.

Sally handed her the room key. "Add this to your keyring. The small key is to your suite's mailbox in the lobby. If you lose a key, replacements cost two dollars." Then she took a document from her pocket and unfolded it on Frannie's desk. "This is a

The Wake-Up Call

campus map," she said. "Hadley Hall's right here on the oval. The building behind us is the Student Union. The cafeteria is on the second floor. The quickest way up are these outside stairs. The Bookstore's on the first floor, and the Game Room is next to it. When we're not in class, most everyone is either in the Student Union or in the Library off to the left of Sheppard Hall at the top of the oval. Across the oval from us is the Simpson Science Center and Thompson Hall where you'll register tomorrow. You'll learn where everything is in no time. If you have questions, stop by the front desk."

"Thanks, I need to get out of this outfit," Frannie announced. "Philly summers are hot, but never this hot!"

As Sally turned to leave, two young men arrived lugging Frannie's trunk. Sally pointed to Frannie's bedroom and they dropped it unceremoniously inside the door.

Mr. Braun said, "Sally, I'll come with you. Frannie, start unpacking while I ask Sally about lunch. We'll have a few hours to visit before my flight home."

Left alone in the suite, Frannie opened the suitcases and stacked piles of clothing onto both beds and both desks, then draped clothes for the closet over both chairs.

Discarding her favorite travel outfit on the floor, she toweled herself dry, then put on a pink mini skirt and a white peasant blouse. She traded her stacked heels for strappy white sandals that she dug out of the trunk, then slid a beaded bracelet onto her wrist. She smiled at her blue-eyed reflection in the mirror. "Cool!"

She began with the closet but quickly ran out of hangers. She opened all four drawers of her dresser, then sighed. "*I don't know where to begin… Mom would know. Good Lord, I have more stuff than will fit in these drawers!*"

"We have reservations for lunch," her father announced as he crossed the sitting room. Sally recommended a Mexican restaurant just a short walk from here." He stood in the doorway, hands on hips, head shaking side to side, "You haven't made a dent in this mess. Twitch your nose like Samantha on *Bewitched*. We should go now, you'll have to do this later.."

Frannie sighed, "I wish it were that easy."

"Learning to do for yourself is one of the reasons we agreed on a college away from home," her father reminded her. "Your mother can't take care of you forever."

"Maybe I should have listened to her and stayed in Philly," Frannie pouted. I could have gone to Temple and lived at home, and all this stuff would still be in my drawers and closets where it belongs. What was I thinking?"

"You can settle in later. I see you've changed, and I am not taking another step outside in this jacket." He removed his tie, folded it into his jacket pocket, then searched in vain for a hanger. He settled for looping the jacket over the closet doorknob, then rolled his shirt sleeves to the elbow. "Not the look I usually go for," he grinned, "but this is Dallas and I don't plan to die of heat exhaustion."

Frannie grinned at the reprieve and searched for her purse, tipping several piles of clothing onto the floor in the process. "Here it is," she cried as she spied the strap peeking from beneath a pile of folded sweaters. They tumbled in disarray as she pulled the purse free. With a shrug at the mess, she followed her father out of the suite.

"This is an attractive campus," her father said. "It's big enough, but not too big."

La Cantina was a busy place, with Mexican tiled floors and a brightly colored mural featuring dancing señoritas and guitar-playing señores. The hostess led Frannie and her father to a table for two by the windows and handed them menus.

"Looks like we'll have to order from the pictures," Gerhart said. "I don't recognize a single dish. What would you like?"

Frannie pointed to a picture that looked a bit like Philly cheese steak, her all-time favorite. Her father chose something completely unfamiliar. "This might as well be an adventure for both of us. Crestmont was the right decision, Frannie. You'll learn to take care of yourself. Your mom's a fantastic homemaker, but it's time you started managing the things she's always done for you."

"I know you're right, Dad, but I don't know where to start."

"Well, organizing your things will be a good beginning. After all, they are *your things*. I know I'm repeating myself, but you and I chose Crestmont because we knew it would give you the opportunity to succeed on your own."

"I know I wanted to come here," Frannie sighed, "but Mom was so sure it would be best for me to stay home."

"Success for your mother is being an excellent homemaker, but that's not enough for women today. Besides, one salary no longer provides everything a family wants and needs. Crestmont will prepare you for whatever life has in store."

"I'm going to be a nurse. I'll be able to contribute if I have to."

"That's true, but at the same time, you'll be responsible for managing your household, cooking, cleaning, laundry, and putting things where they belong. Frannie, homes and dorm rooms don't just take care of themselves."

"I know. I know." Frannie looked defeated.

"You're not a child. You're a bright young woman and you need to act like one. You have the opportunity to learn and grow, and it's up to you to take advantage of it."

"I will, Dad, I promise. I wish you didn't have to go back so soon."

"You'll be fine," her father reassured her. "I know you'll enjoy your classes because you've always done well in school. Time will fly and the holidays will be here before you know it."

Frannie squeezed her Dad's hand and prayed that she'd made the right choice."

They returned to Hadley Hall together to retrieve Gerhart's coat and tie while Mrs. Crandall called a taxi. Frannie and her father waited together at the curb, then shared a long goodbye hug. "You'll be fine, Frannie," he assured her. "Crestmont is a wonderful opportunity for you." He climbed into the cab and Frannie stood waving, not bothering to wipe away the tears streaming down her cheeks. She felt a stab of anxiety when the Yellow Cab turned at the end of the oval and disappeared.

She stood for several minutes, then swiped at the tears. *"I can do this!"* She turned toward the dorm, then stopped, unable to face the confusion in her room. She pulled the map from her pocket. *"I can check out the Student Union, just long enough to get my bearings and maybe meet a good-looking guy. That would be cool."*

The Student Union clock showed 2:45. *"I can take an hour and still have time to unpack before dinner."* She wandered about, peeking into the bookstore and glancing at students and their families seated in the conversation areas. She climbed the stairs and found the cafeteria. The cavernous room took up half of the second floor. It was empty, but the *Beach Boys* blared from a boom box in the kitchen. Alone and overwhelmed, she understood how Alice must have felt as she spiraled down the rabbit hole.

"You new?" The voice startled her. Frannie turned to see a tall, good-looking young man leaning against the wall, grinning and drinking in the full length of her. His straight black hair was not quite shoulder length and he sported a two-day beard. He wore tight faded bell-bottom jeans and an untucked cowboy shirt with the top three pearl snaps undone. "You're cute," he commented. "Want me to show you around? The action is downstairs."

Frannie took a breath, a bit less anxious now that someone was talking to her. She looked him up and down slowly, just to let him know she'd noticed. "I'd love a tour." Then she added with a coy smile, "You're not bad-looking either."

"Stephen Barton," he said, reaching out a hand, "from Midland. I'm a sophomore, Liberal Arts."

"Frannie Braun," she said, "from Philadelphia. Is Midland in Texas?"

"Yep and the best view of Midland is in your rear-view mirror."

Frannie grinned, positive that he'd said that a million times before. Stephen threw an arm around her shoulders and pulled her along, pointing out the large ballroom that occupied the other half of the second floor. Downstairs they passed an open area with study carrels and the bookstore, then stopped at the

The Wake-Up Call

Game Room. "C'mon in," he said, propelling her across the room toward a group of boys playing darts. They watched several games, Frannie enjoying Stephen's arm draped across her shoulders. Then he stepped in to play, winning four games in a row with Frannie cheering each victory.

He invited her to play and beat her handily. "I need to get a lot better at this to give you a run for your money," she said, then spotted the clock. "Oh no, it CAN'T be after five! Stephen, I have to go. Thanks for the tour, and for the games. I hope we'll run into each other again." She hurried out of the Game Room and ran to Hadley Hall.

※

Sally ushered Robin into the suite. "Your other suitemates, Leslie Bleu and Katie Grayfox, have taken that room, so you'll be sharing this one with Frannie Braun."

Robin pushed the door open and gasped, "What the hell!" There was no one inside, but clothing covered every piece of furniture and most of the floor. "Shit!" She turned to Sally, "There isn't a square inch left in this room for my stuff. I don't even have a bed! Leave it to some rich bitch to think she owns the whole world."

Embarrassed, Sally set Robin's suitcase on the floor and shrugged, not knowing what to say.

With a wicked smirk, Robin said, "No problem. I can take care of this." She scooped up everything from one bed and threw it onto the other, creating an untidy mountain of clothing. Sally backed out of the room. Robin cleared her dresser, desk, and chair in the same manner. She stood back, inspecting her side of the room. She lifted one of her suitcases onto her bed, opened it, and draped several items over her arm. When she walked into the closet, she found one short section of rod empty of clothing, suitcases on the floor below, and not a hanger in sight.

Robin shouted, "You've gotta be shittin' me!" She stood glaring into the full closet.

Frannie stepped into the doorway and stopped short, her eyes wide and mouth moving like a fish out of water. "Hey! You took my bed!"

Behind Frannie, Leslie and Katie entered the suite. Frannie's exclamation stopped them in their tracks.

"I WHAT?" Robin yelled, glaring at Frannie. "Both beds were covered with crap! ONE of them HAD to be mine, and neither of them had your name on it."

Frannie stammered, "I meant to be back earlier. My father took me to lunch and…"

"Who the hell ARE you? Some rich kid with MAIDS?"

"I was hanging clothes, but I ran out of hangers… and Dad made lunch reservations, so I had to leave. I… I thought I would be back earlier."

"Look. I don't give a damn! Just get hangers! Then get enough stuff outa this closet so half of it can be mine. Find somewhere else for your suitcases, like under your bed, or out in street for all I care!"

Noticing the two girls standing mute outside the bedroom door, Robin shrugged. "Obviously, she thinks she owns the place. She's claimed the whole room for herself. What did she expect me to do, set up camp in the bathroom? Oh, of course not, cuz that's full of her crap, too."

Frannie insisted, "I was going to leave you half. I just didn't know where to put everything."

The tall brunette entered the room one step ahead of the second girl who was the image of an Indian princess. "I'm Leslie Bleu and this is Katie Grayfox. We're your suitemates."

"I'm Robin Hart, and I have no idea who *she* is." Robin jerked her thumb toward Frannie.

"My name is Frannie, Frannie Braun… and I'm not rich and I'm definitely not what you called me earlier."

"Well, glad to meet both of you." Looking to Katie for support, Leslie continued, "We're finished unpacking, so we can help you two get settled if you'd like? Frannie, how 'bout we go to the front desk and check out options for hangers? I could use a few myself."

Chapter 2

Frannie, red-faced from the encounter with Robin, followed Leslie out of the suite. "How did things get so crazy in such a short time?" she mumbled. "Who does that witch think she is talking to me that way?"

Leslie asked at the front desk, "Are there extra hangers somewhere?"

Sally pointed across the lobby to a door under an EXIT sign. "That door will take you downstairs to the laundry. You'll find loads of hangers. Help yourselves."

On the way downstairs, Leslie reassured Frannie, "I'm sure Robin will calm down. After all, you couldn't really expect her to feel welcomed by the mess you left her."

"But..." Frannie stammered. "I didn't know where to put everything and my dad made lunch reservations."

"But you didn't come back. Katie and I would have helped you get settled."

"I just didn't know what to do."

"Well, let's find the hangers and try to get things back on track."

They entered a room lit by bare bulbs dangling from the ceiling. A bank of washing machines flanked by three dryers created a workspace with a rolling clothes rack full of hangers.

Leslie said "I'm so glad the washing machines don't require coins. It looks like all we have to do is push START. These folding tables are great. We won't have to cram our clean laundry into a basket. You'd be surprised how fast, dry clothes get wrinkled."

"Really?"

Wide-eyed, Leslie asked, "You *have* done laundry before, right?"

"Wellll, Mom generally does it Can't be too hard, can it?" Plopping onto a chrome chair, Frannie said, "Leslie, these chairs look like they came from a 1950's *Leave it to Beaver* episode. I'm glad the furniture in our suite is nicer than this."

Leslie chuckled, then sat by her. "It does look pretty ancient. Imagine coming down here at night by yourself. How spooky would that be?"

Frannie shivered at the creepy thought.

"What kept you so long after lunch with your Dad?" Leslie asked.

"I didn't want to be alone, so I went to check out the Student Union. I planned to look around for a bit, them come right back and put my things away. I never dreamed that I would wind up with such a nasty roommate. She's mean! She had no right to talk like that. Besides, I'm not rich!"

"Be fair, Frannie. You can't expect your roommate to be happy with the mess you left. By the way, what did you do in the Student Union all that time?"

"I met this guy, Stephen Barton. He started flirting with me. He's a sophomore, and he was soooo gorgeous. He knew everything about the campus. We went to the Game Room to meet his friends. That's what took so long."

"Are you going to meet him again?" Leslie asked.

"I hope so," she replied dreamily.

"Frannie, what's your major?"

"Nursing, what's yours?"

The Wake-Up Call

"I'm in nursing, too. I have an athletic scholarship, and I'm not at all certain how school and sports are going to mesh but I have to make it work. I've always wanted to be a nurse, and I need my scholarship to stay here.

"Do you have brothers or sisters?"

"Yes, two of each and I'm the oldest. My mother would probably count Paul, my boyfriend because he spends more time at our house than his."

"WOW, you have a boyfriend. Is he at Crestmont? We could double date," Frannie chirped.

"Paul didn't get a scholarship, so he's still at home. I don't think he knows what he wants to do. One thing for sure is that he isn't happy about my coming to Crestmont. He thinks I should have chosen a college closer to Abita Springs."

"Where's Abita Springs?"

"It's a little town with maybe 2,000 people just across Lake Pontchartrain from New Orleans. That's Cajun country. Where are you from?"

"Philadelphia. My dad and I selected Crestmont because it has a good nursing program and a Christian background. Mom insisted I go to college in Philly and live at home, but I need to be on my own. At home, Mom takes care of everything and Dad says I need to learn to do all that by myself. So here I am, and I've already met Stephen."

"Your dad has a point. We all have to start managing ourselves and things we've always taken for granted."

"I wonder what's back there," Frannie mused, pointing to the black hole behind the laundry?"

They rose to explore and found a light switch that revealed long hallways lined with padlocked chicken wire storage cages that held bicycles, suitcases, trunks, boxes, and sports equipment. There were racks in some with overstuffed garment bags.

Frannie read the labels above the doors on her left. "These labels match suite numbers. Let's see if we can find ours." They searched until they found the cage for their suite. "Leslie, this is marvelous. I can store my luggage and even some of my clothes if

I can find a clothes rack. That wicked witch won't have anything else to complain about."

"I might have brought a few more things if I'd known there'd be storage. But then, I don't know where one more thing would have fit in either Nellie or my parent's car.

"Nellie?"

"Oh yeah, Leslie chuckled, "Nellie is my '56 blue Chevy, kinda like *Herbie* in the movie *Love Bug*. I named her right after Mama and Daddy gave her to me on my sixteenth birthday. Even my high school friends and my family call her Nellie."

"That is just toooo funny."

"I could store my bicycle here. I might bring it back the next time I go home

They grabbed hangers, then ran up the steps to ask about a key to storage at the desk."

Out of breath and excited, both girls started talking at once.

Sally held up both hands. "One at a time. One at a time." She pointed at Frannie. "You first."

Frannie gasped, "wire cages… with numbers… Are they for us to store things? Will our suite key open them?"

Sally replied, "Yes, each suite in Hadley Hall has a storage area with its own key. There is a $10 key deposit that you get back when you return it. Suitemates usually share one key."

"Cool." Frannie and Leslie said in unison and rushed off to the suite armed with hangers.

⚜

"Guess I need to start *somewhere*." Robin sighed. She turned from the closet and surveyed the piles of Frannie's belongings. "All this stuff for one person."

"Let me help," Katie offered. "I'll hand you clothes and you can decide where you want them to live. Things to hang in the closet can go on your chair until Leslie and Frannie get back with hangers."

The Wake-Up Call

"Thanks," Robin smiled. "I can use the help. My inconsiderate roommate didn't make it easy."

"I imagine that finding the room like you did was disappointing, but I don't think Frannie intended to be selfish. I think she got distracted and didn't realize how long she'd been gone. She seems more overwhelmed than spiteful to me.

"In my book, she's a thoughtless bitch!"

Katie shook her head. "That's a bit harsh She looked bewildered when she told us that she looked at her clothes and didn't know where to put anything. I don't think she's had much experience taking care of herself. I'm guessing that her mother took care of the laundry and housekeeping and didn't expect Frannie to help. She's probably more sheltered than rich."

"Yeah. Well, I hope she's not expecting me to be her friggin' maid!"

"I doubt that," mused Katie. "I think she just needs some time to settle in and get a handle on her new world. She seems lost. We need to give her the benefit of the doubt."

"Maybe..." Robin conceded. She had to admit that she felt a bit lost herself. She'd never been completely on her own before either. Robin yanked open the top dresser drawer and dumped in an armload of underwear and socks. Katie passed folded clothes to Robin who shoved them into the next drawer.

"You might have to wear those things at some point," Katie said, laughing.

Robin glared at Katie, then laughed, too. "Just taking my frustration out, I guess. I'll try to give the little bi..., my roommate the benefit of the doubt. You heard me say *TRY*, didn't you? Patience is definitely not my strong suit." She rearranged her clothing and filled the remaining drawers.

"Do you want your shoes on the floor under your clothes or on the shelf above? Katie asked.

"On the floor, I think," Robin replied. "I only have three pairs, plus tennis shoes."

Katie asked, "What's your major? I'm in nursing."

"I am, too. I settled on nursing rather than teaching a long time ago. I can't picture myself keeping my cool in a classroom full of brats. The idea of bringing healthcare to folks who don't have easy access is more enticing. But the first thing I have to do is get a job. Or… I could cozy up to my rich bitch roommate…" Holding up her hands, "Just kidding."

"Do you have a job in mind already?" asked Katie. "If not, the counseling center would be a good place to start. Mom and Dad want me to stay focused on school and not think about a job, but I'd like to keep my options open, just in case. They have campus jobs in the cafeteria, the bookstore, and the library."

"I looked for restaurants nearby on the cab ride in from the airport. I like waitressing because of the tips but working late could get difficult with our curfew. I expect campus jobs would accommodate class schedules and study requirements, but I don't expect they'd pay well."

"Maybe I'll go with you to the counseling center. It wouldn't hurt to learn what's available in case I decide to work, too."

"What made you decide to become a nurse?" Robin asked. "None of my friends at home care much about a career, and not one of them is going to college."

"Well, I'm a farm girl, and I love taking care of the animals. Mom always said I'd be a wonderful nurse. In high school, I thought about becoming a vet, but, when I saw how long it would take, I knew that we didn't have enough money for all those years of school. I never told anyone about that dream except my best friend, John.

"There's an Indian clinic in Atoka where I live that might be an awesome place to work. My family is American Indian and we respect health and well-being, but the older folks often mistrust White medicine. When I'm a nurse, the People, that's what we call our native tribe, will trust me. I'd like to think that I will be able to help them choose the best of both options. My family has been saving my whole life to send me and my younger sister to college. I'm the first in my family to go."

The Wake-Up Call

"Me, too," remarked Robin. Gram always proclaimed that education was the way to get ahead in this world. Not counting my poor excuse for a boozer father and my mother, the mouse, there's just Gram and me. When I was five or six, the bastard started coming on to me, and Gram rescued me from that hellhole."

"In high school, I hung around with some real losers. It wasn't until today that I realized how right she was about them. This very morning, when I went to say goodbye, my friggin' boyfriend stole a carton of cigarettes right in front of me. If a cop had been there, my whole life would have been ruined. There wasn't time to tell Gram how sorry I am for all the grief I've caused her. So, here I am." Robin said. "In this room, you have the rich, sheltered bitch, and the poor kid who grew up in a hurry and owes Gram an apology."

"Hmmm...," Katie pondered, "I guess that's one way to look at it, but how about this? In this room, we have the sheltered kid who needs help developing some independence and the autonomous roommate who can help her get there?"

Robin grinned. "How do you manage to turn every crappy situation into something workable? Don't you ever get upset about anything?"

"Farm people learn that there are things you can't control… like the weather, market prices, and other people. So, you do the best you can with what you've got and hope for the best. Frannie is what we've got, so we should do the best we can with her."

※

"Look what we got," Frannie exclaimed as she dropped her armful of hangers on top of the clothes on her bed. "And guess what we discovered?"

Robin wasn't ready to hear about Frannie's adventure, but before she could unload another barrage of verbal abuse, Katie stepped in. "What did you discover, Frannie?"

"We found a locked wire storage cage in the basement that all of us can share. There's a ten-dollar key deposit that we get back. If we split the cost, that's only $2.50 each. The cage will accommodate all our luggage, and stuff we don't need right now, like winter coats. If we want to hang anything up, we'll need a clothes rack with a cover to keep everything clean."

Katie suggested, "Let's concentrate on getting the room straightened up first. We can arrange for a key on our way to dinner. We still need to get to the cafeteria before it closes."

Frannie sighed, deflated, and disappointed that her suitemates, particularly her roommate, were not excited about stopping to explore the basement gold mine. Moving into the closet, Frannie began to take winter clothing off the rod. "This can go into the storage unit. That will leave plenty of room for your clothes, Robin."

Robin snorted but forced a smile when Katie caught her eye. "Thanks, Frannie," she said.

Katie winked her approval. "Frannie, when you're done hanging stuff, we can organize the dresser, and whatever's left we can store in your suitcases."

The four got to work, Katie hanging what Robin handed to her, and Leslie helping Frannie sort clothes into the closet, dresser, and suitcases.

They were nearly done when Robin announced, "Guys, it's almost time for the cafeteria to close. I'm starving and don't want to miss dinner. Let's get that key on the way back."

***

The clock read 6:45 when the girls hurried into the cafeteria. "We made it with fifteen minutes to spare," Leslie said, relieved. "With luck, they'll still have some food for us."

Grabbing trays, they eyed the limited selection in the nearly empty serving containers. "I'll have filet mignon," Robin announced, grinning at the student on the serving line.

The server obviously appreciated the bit of humor so near the end of her shift. "Well, Ma'am. It just happens that we're plumb out of filets tonight. Can I interest you in what's left of

The Wake-Up Call

the chicken tetrazzini? To go with that, we have wilted salad and overcooked peas and carrots."

Robin shrugged. "Whatever you have left, just give me lots of it. I'm hungry enough to eat almost anything."

"I would have thought the school would have healthy food," Katie commented. "There's more sauce than chicken, and the vegetables are swimming in grease. They could do with my Mom in the kitchen. She's absolutely the best cook. You need to taste her cornbread and stew."

"If this is what we get to eat all the time," complained Frannie, "I'll turn into a blimp and none of my clothes will fit."

"Or, maybe you'll just waste away to nothing," Robin muttered.

They pushed their trays down the line toward the desserts. "Jell-O." snarled Robin. Can you believe that's the only dessert left? I hate Jell-O."

Disappointed, each of the girls placed a bowl of the jiggling dessert on her tray, then scanned the room to find four seats together. "Over there," Katie pointed to four students who were gathering their trays to leave.

Settled into their seats, the girls eyed their trays. "From now on, we're getting here at the *start* of the service," Katie said with determination.

As they ate, they scanned the cafeteria. Frannie spotted Stephen killing time with two other guys and three girls several tables away. Stephen's arms were draped across the shoulders of the girls on either side of him. He was talking; the others were laughing. "Look," Frannie exclaimed, pointing in his direction. "That's the guy I met today. Isn't he gorgeous? He gave me a tour of the Student Union and we played darts in the Game Room."

The girls followed Frannie's gaze. "Hmmm," nodded Robin with a knowing expression. "He might be gorgeous but look how he's dressed… that slouch…and the way he's holding court at the table… he's the spittin' image of the loser I left behind in Chicago. He thinks he's hot shit, but what he is, is *Trouble!*"

"You don't even *know* him," Frannie stammered, wondering if there were anything at all that she could say or do that Robin wouldn't criticize. "How can you say he's awful when you're looking at him for the first time… and from a distance?"

"Are you blind? Mark my words, he's bad news."

"He *is* good-looking…" Katie commented. "Frannie, take some time to get to know him and you'll figure out what kind of person he is."

"I just don't see how anyone can tell who's a good person or a bad person from just seeing them from a distance," Frannie grumbled. "I think he's cute, and he was nice to me today. He liked me, and I just think it's wrong to make snap judgments like that."

"And thinking he's terrific isn't a snap judgment?" Robin countered. When Frannie opened her mouth to reply, Robin interrupted. "No problem. I won't say *I told you so* when he breaks your heart… or worse."

"But…" Frannie started to protest.

Leslie interrupted. "Let's wait and see. He *is* good-looking from a distance. I'll say that much for him. It's OK to start out thinking everyone's nice. You can always change your mind if they don't live up to your expectations."

Frannie nodded, grateful for Leslie's support.

"Frannie, what is your major?" Katie asked, changing the subject.

"I'm in the nursing program."

"Then all four of us are future nurses," Katie said. "We can study together and help each other out. I've heard that even the first two years of the nursing program are demanding, with all the science and math prerequisites. It didn't sound like there would be time for much of a social life."

Frannie responded without hesitation. "Of course, there will. I got straights A's in high school and I had plenty of time to spend with my friends.

Katie turned to Leslie. "I meant to thank you for how gracious your parents were today. I could tell they were surprised when I arrived with my family. They couldn't have been expecting your roommate to be anything but White."

Leslie shrugged. "You look like an Indian princess. That's a *good* thing... at least in my book." She frowned, "My folks are dead set against treating some folks different from others. They've always said that it's what you say and do, not where you come from, that matters."

All three nodded in agreement. "So how about you, Leslie? Why nursing?"

"I got into sports in junior high and learned how important staying healthy is to an athlete's career. Nursing was a natural choice. A nurse should never have trouble getting a job."

Frannie chimed in, "I've wanted to be a nurse since I was little, so I could help my mother take care of Nana. My grandmother has lived with us since I was tiny and she's my best friend. She used to be able to get around better, but she has multiple sclerosis and now she can't walk at all. Nana says when I'm a nurse, I can take care of her, and my kids, of course."

Robin sneered, "So you're here for an MRS degree. That explains why you're so anxious to believe that loser is your Prince Charming."

After a few seconds of uneasy silence, Leslie groaned, "Hungry as I thought I was, I don't think I can finish this stuff. It is worse than it looks. I could sit on this Jell-O without squashing it. We might have to keep food in the room... to keep us all from starving.

"I hope the cafeteria isn't the only job the counseling center has available," Robin said to Katie. *They couldn't pay me enough to stand there for hours and stare at this garbage.*

"Let's get back," Katie suggested. *We need to truck our luggage down to the cages, and Frannie needs help getting the rest of her stuff put away.*

"We also need to figure out how we're going to handle orientation tomorrow," said Katie.

Frannie gazed across the room at Stephen, wondering when she'd hook up with him again. During the entire meal, he had never once glanced in her direction.

The girls stopped by the desk for a key to their storage locker, then made several trips to stow Frannie's full suitcases and everyone else's empty ones.

"Let's decide how to handle the bathroom in the morning," Leslie suggested, once they'd settled in the sitting room. We can't all be in there at the same time. "I don't need more than 20 minutes, just time to jump in the shower and brush my teeth. I'm not shy. The locker room pretty much takes the *modest* out of you, so, if you need in the bathroom while I am in there, be my guest. What about you guys?"

Katie said, "We have to be in Blakemore Chapel for orientation at eight. Seems early. I kinda like sleeping in, so I wouldn't mind going last in the shower. I must admit that I'm a little shy. As long as I have my panties and bra on, I'm fine with company."

Frannie jumped in with, "I'll go first. It takes me about an hour to get ready and you could all sleep a bit later."

Robin nodded. "Sounds like a plan. Leslie, you want to go second or third?"

"I'll go third," Leslie answered. "It will take us about 10 minutes to get breakfast, maybe 20 minutes to eat, then another 10 minutes to get to Blakemore. We need to leave here about seven. That means Frannie gets the bathroom from five to six, then 20 minutes each for the three of us, and we are out the door."

"I'm glad you're the one getting up early, Frannie," Katie said. "I am *not* a morning person, even living on a farm my whole life."

"Piece of cake. We're going to have such fun together." Frannie said.

Robin rolled her eyes, then waved goodnight and headed to the bedroom.

Leslie searched for a station with popular music on the small transistor radio she'd brought from home. "I LOVE this song." She said, recognizing Simon and Garfunkel's *Bridge over Troubled Waters*.

"Me, too," Frannie chimed in.

"Me three," Katie agreed, and they sang along, swaying to the music.

At the end of the song, Frannie whispered, "I am a little afraid of Robin and I have to go in there with her."

"Frannie, Robin's okay," Katie assured her. "I think that she was a little taken aback when she saw how you left the room earlier."

Changing the subject, Frannie turned to Leslie. "Tell us more about your boyfriend Paul."

"Well, we grew up together and started dating in high school. In our senior year, he was captain of the football team and I was captain of girls' basketball. We were king and queen of our senior prom. He and I drove up here in Nellie and my whole family followed in our family car."

"Oh, how exciting that Paul got to come here with you" Frannie exclaimed.

"I wish he'd decide to go to college. Otherwise, he might get drafted and wind up in Vietnam," said Leslie.

"That would just be awful," Frannie blurted. "My brother, Petey, is in the Army and thank goodness he's in intelligence and won't have to go to Vietnam. I would absolutely die if anything happened to him. He's the best brother in the world!" she said, fingering the locket that never left her neck.

"Going over there would be terrible…" pondered Leslie, staring at the carpet as if it were a crystal ball.

Katie glanced at the clock. "It's late. Frannie, you're the one who needs to get up at five, remember? Don't forget to set your alarm."

Frannie found Robin asleep. She dropped her clothes on the floor and rummaged through drawers as quietly as she could, looking for pajamas, fearing she would wake the sleeping beast.

From Robin's bed came a tired voice, "Go to bed! You have to get up at five. Set your alarm and don't wake me until you're done in the bathroom."

"I am trying to find my alarm clock and I need to turn on my night light."

"YOUR WHAT? You're shittin' me! I can't believe a grown woman is afraid of the dark. Just make sure I can't see it."

"I'll put it in the bathroom and leave the door open a little in case I need to go in the middle of the night."

"Fine. Just be quiet, will you?"

Chapter 3

Frannie's alarm rang at 5 am, just as they'd planned. Robin pulled the covers over her head. The alarm continued to ring. Robin opened her eyes and peeked at Frannie's bed. The hump under the covers didn't move. "Frannie! Turn your damned alarm off." she hissed. There was no response.

Robin raised her voice. "Dammit, shut off you're friggin' alarm!"

No response. Robin sat up and threw her pillow at Frannie, scoring a direct hit.

An arm snaked out from beneath the covers and pushed the pillow onto the floor. "Not yet, Mom. Just a few more minutes." The hand disappeared under the covers and Frannie lay still, her breathing regular.

"I'm not your mom, you spoiled brat," Robin hissed. "Get up NOW!"

Frannie didn't stir. Robin, pissed off and wide awake, climbed out of bed and turned off the alarm. "OK, you pampered little shit, I'll take your bathroom slot and you can sleep all day for all I care."

Robin yawned and stretched and made as much noise as possible collecting her toiletries and a towel. She eased the bathroom door to Leslie and Katie's room shut. In fifteen minutes, wrapped in a towel and ready to dress she cracked open the door to Katie and Leslie's room and found them awake and talking. Robin described how her morning had begun and announced that the bathroom was available.

"It's 5:35," said Leslie. Wake Frannie and let's hope she can get finished in time for me to take your 6:20 slot."

"Forget that." retorted Robin. "I'm not her mother. She slept through her turn. She can wait for the rest of us to finish. Then she can take as long as she likes. You go ahead, Leslie."

Leslie gathered her things and Robin returned to her room and slammed the door. Frannie didn't stir. Robin dressed and went into the sitting room to look over her orientation materials. At 6:20, Katie and Leslie joined Robin. Frannie still hadn't stirred.

Katie suggested, "Why don't I wake Frannie? Then we can get an early start on breakfast. It will be nice to get to the cafeteria while there are still choices. Frannie can meet up with us there."

"Suit yourself," retorted Robin. "I don't care if she sleeps all day."

Katie shook Frannie's shoulder. "Frannie, you need to wake up if you're going to make it to Orientation. We're leaving for breakfast. Meet us there." Frannie opened her eyes but didn't say anything. Katie repeated her suggestion, then left to join the others.

Frannie's eyes closed and she drifted back to sleep. At 7:00, she awoke with a start. No alarm. Eyes wide, she took in the empty room and Robin's made bed. *"How could they let me sleep? Mom always made sure I was up on time. What do I do now?"* She looked at the clock again, then tore through the room, a tornado of activity, vainly attempting to snuff the burn of disappointment.

Frannie grabbed her purse and orientation materials and hurried out of the room at 7:45, leaving her bed unmade and the bathroom a mess. Rushing along the path, she pulled the campus map from her orientation packet. Blakemore Chapel

The Wake-Up Call

was somewhere past the Student Union, but she didn't know where. Walking fast, her eyes searching the map, she ran headlong into Stephen Barton. Startled she gasped, "OH!" and dropped everything.

"Whoa! Slow down. Can't imagine anything going on here that's worth being in that big a hurry." Stephen grinned and stepped back so Frannie could pick up her purse and the scattered orientation packet.

Frannie stammered, "Oh... hi, Stephen. I... I need to be in Blakemore Chapel at eight."

"What was your name again?"

"Frannie. Frannie Braun."

"Well, Frannie, you're on the right track. Blakemore is that building right there with the bell tower," he said, pointing to the chapel 50 yards further down the path on the right. "See ya around."

Frannie watched him walk away. *He didn't offer to pick up my things or even remember my name. He must have been in a hurry, too.* She gathered her things and hurried toward the chapel, arriving just before the program began. The large chapel was crowded. "Excuse me," she said as she climbed over several pairs of legs, reaching the empty seat she had spotted in the second row from the back.

"Is this seat saved?" she asked the pretty brunette in the next seat.

"No, Sugar, it's yours if you want it. I'm Missy, by the way. And you are?"

"Frannie. Thanks. I nearly didn't make it."

"You don't sound like you're from around here. That's a Yankee accent if I've ever heard one. You're rushing around like a Yankee, too. You can slow down and take it easy. This is the *South*, ya know, not New York." Frannie sat and arranged the orientation packet on her lap.

"I'm from Philadelphia, not New York, but from down here, I guess it's hard to tell the difference," Frannie grinned. "Are you from Dallas?"

"Heavens, no, I'm from Baton Rouge, Loooosiana. That's the *real* South. My family's been coming to Crestmont University for ages... ever since it was Crestmont College. My mother, grandmother, and two aunts... and every one of them is a Theta Rho Xi. I can't wait to pledge. You're going out for a sorority, of course."

Not wanting to sound ignorant, Frannie replied, "Well... I haven't quite made up my mind."

"Oh, you must," Missy insisted. "Your sorority sisters are your best friends, and it's a great way to meet *guys*. I can't imagine being at Crestmont and not being part of Theta Rho Xi. You get to live on the sorority floor in the upper-class women's dorm your sophomore year. It's the one social scene that counts."

Awesome" Frannie said. "*So...maybe it doesn't matter that my roommate is awful. When I'm in a sorority, I'll spend all my time with my sorority sisters and I won't be in the suite except to sleep. Who knows, I might just meet Mr. Perfect my freshman year. Then I wouldn't have to worry about anything ever again.*"

Amplified noise interrupted Frannie's thoughts when the speaker tapped the microphone to bring the room to order. Missy whispered, "Let's have lunch together. I'll tell you all about Theta Rho."

Frannie missed most of the presentation lost in thoughts about sorority life and meeting guys. The purple and gold freshman beanie captured her attention. She whispered to Missy, "I have a couple of outfits that will go with these colors. It's one of the things that made me choose Crestmont. I like the Crestmont Coyote, too. He's like a dog, and that's so much nicer than a toad, a gator, or a roadrunner."

The two girls whispered back and forth during the three-and-a-half-hour program, then hurried together to the cafeteria. After meeting Missy, Frannie hadn't thought once about how the morning had begun.

Moving through the tray line, Frannie and Missy grimaced at the gray food on their plates. "Ooohh, this looks disgusting. I'd give anything for a good ole juicy, Philly cheese steak," Frannie said. "That is my favorite food in the whole wide world. Just thinking about it makes my taste buds tingle. I can smell the onions sizzling." Her stomach produced an unladylike growl. "Oh, sorry, Missy. I missed breakfast this morning and I am major starving."

"Me too, let's find a place to sit. This place is a madhouse. My mom always says, *breakfast is the most important meal of the day*, but I like sleeping in more than eating."

"Oh, you are soooo right, Girlfriend." Frannie agreed.

Frannie spotted her roommates sitting at a table in the far corner of the room, enjoying the panoramic view of the university through the plate glass wall of the cafeteria. "*I don't want to sit with them anyway. Robin didn't bother to wake me and neither did Katie or Leslie. Well, all the better for me because I have Missy to myself. Missy seems to know so much about campus life, especially sororities.*"

Frannie spied two empty chairs at a table out of view of her roommates, and she and Missy rushed to grab the seats. "Missy, tell me about orientation week? Do they plan things so that we can meet people before classes start?"

"Ooohh yes, I have a schedule in my bag," Missy reached past her striped bell bottom pants leg into her large, bright pink and orange bag and pulled out a few sheets of paper. "The next thing on our agenda is getting registered for classes."

"I hope there's free time for us to see what fun stuff there is to do on campus."

"Let's drop all this stuff off at the dorm before we register," Missy suggested.

"Sure thing. I thought they'd never stop handing out those monster packets of junk this morning. Why would we read all that stuff on the history of the school? It isn't going to be on any tests."

"Ah, Sugar, I figure all we need is to be able to recite the school song and the school chant in case an upperclassman stops us.

I'm not sure what would happen if we couldn't, but I do know that I don't want to test the limits of possibility on that score."

Frannie pointed, "Oh, Missy, look. Do you see that good-looking tall guy in the blue and white shirt and blue jeans standing with those other boys? I met him the other day and he toured me around the student union. Isn't he just dreamy?"

"WOW! He *is* mighty hot... What's his name?"

"Stephen Barton, and a he's a sophomore. He's so cool. Do you know any boys on campus yet? Do you have a boyfriend?"

"Whoooaa girl, slow down. You Yankees just rattle way too fast. Remember this is *Texas*, so one question at a time. No, I don't have a boyfriend, but maybe this Stephen will know some other good-lookin' guys. I just got here yesterday, so, I haven't met anyone except my roommates. They're nice but they didn't seem interested in pledging a sorority, so I won't be spending much time with them anyhow. By the way, what is your major?"

"Nursing kinda fits with raising a family, don't you think. But I wouldn't have to work at all if my husband were rich and handsome," she said, bouncing her eyebrows towards Stephen.

"Yeah, I know what you mean. I am taking all the required freshman courses. I haven't quite decided on a major, you know?"

They took their empty trays to the conveyor belt, then set off for Hadley Hall. "Missy, those are great looking hip huggers. They go super with that top."

"Thanks. Mom and I came in a little early so we could shop at Dillard's. I got a new pair of shoes, and this outfit. I'm glad you like it. It is super comfortable and it's wash and wear, so no ironing. I just hate ironing."

"I understand that," said Frannie, though she wouldn't know what to do with an iron.

At the dorm, they separated to drop off their things. Frannie prayed, *"I hope no one's in the room right now. The last thing I want is to talk to any of them, especially Robin. All of them just let me sleep this morning. Robin could have at least tried to wake me."*

"Whew," Frannie sighed when she found the suite empty. She dropped her armload of papers onto her desk, ignoring the ones that fell to the floor. She brushed her teeth, then hustled to meet up with Missy.

"Let's pick up the pace," Missy said, beginning to jog. "We're running a bit late."

They approached the end of a long line snaking down the steps from the double doors of Thompson Hall and stretching a block down the sidewalk. "Well," sighed Frannie." I guess we didn't have to hurry. This may take all afternoon. I hope they don't close the doors before we get to register, and I hope I don't melt before we're done."

"Mom told me the line is always long and the doors stay open until everyone is registered."

An upper-class woman interrupted their conversation. "You two!"

Startled, Frannie and Missy, spun toward the unpleasant voice.

"Yes, BOTH of you! Your beanies are crooked. The purple strip with the coyote goes in the front, not in the back," pointing to Frannie, "or on the side," pointing to Missy.

Both girls blushed crimson as everyone nearby turned to enjoy the confrontation. Other freshmen tried to remain invisible in the crowd. Frannie and Missy repositioned their beanies while the upperclassman glared. "Don't let it happen again," she barked and strode across the oval towards the Coyote fountain.

Missy drawled, "Wellllll nooow, wasn't *she* just a royal bitch," and the crowd around them snickered.

※

Just as they reached the base of the wide stone steps, Robin, Katie, and Leslie came through the double doors looking fresh and cool. Spotting Frannie, Leslie called, "We've been keeping an eye out for you all day. Did you make it to Orientation OK?"

"Yep. Missed breakfast but got to Orientation on time. I sat with Missy. Missy, these are my suitemates. She's from Baton Rouge and her whole family went to Crestmont." Frannie turned to Missy, "My word, we've spent most of the day together, and I don't even know your last name."

"Hi, everyone. It's Broussard. My whole name is Millicent Broussard, but I've been Missy my whole life. I wouldn't think to answer if someone called me *Millicent*."

"Then *Missy* it is. Nice to meet you," Katie said. "I'm Katie Grayfox."

"I'm Leslie Bleu."

"I'm Robin. Robin Hart."

"Robin and I are going to meet with a campus jobs counselor," said Katie. "Leslie's going to the stadium. What are you two planning to do?"

"If we ever make it through registration, Missy and I are going to get our books. What was registration like once you got in there?"

Robin replied, "It goes pretty quick once you check in. It shouldn't take more than 20 minutes if you don't have to change any courses. Then there's another line to get your ID card made.

The girls had been sidestepping up the stairs while they talked. When they reached the double doors, Leslie said, "I have to get on over to Owen Field to meet the coaches. If I have enough time after that, I'll pick up my books and catch up with you guys for dinner."

Katie," Robin said, "You and I had better hurry or we won't be able to get back here for our meeting with the work counselor. Nice to meet you, Missy. See you later."

Missy said, "They seem nice."

"Katie and Leslie are nice, but Robin and I got off on the wrong foot. She was royally pissed that I hadn't gotten my stuff put away when she got to the room."

"That sounds a bit rude," Missy offered. "Why was that a problem?"

"Well, I kinda left my stuff all over the room and she came before I got back from the Student Union. I didn't leave any place for her to put her stuff, but she coulda been a lot nicer about it. She didn't have to call me names. I'm not rich and I'm not the word that rhymes with rich, and starts with a B, either."

The two girls finished with registration and reluctantly traded the air-conditioning for the oven outside. Frannie said, "Let's get our books and how about afterward we go for a tour around campus. I haven't checked everything out yet, have you?"

"Not yet, let's get a coke at the *SnaKbaR* in the Student Union and cool off before we go to the bookstore. Then we can drop off our books off at Hadley and scope out the Library and the rest of the buildings. My mom says there are some really neat places on campus."

In the *SnaKbaR*, they each got a *Dr. Pepper* from the machine, then compared schedules. Disappointed, Frannie said, "The only course we have together is Old Testament.

"Bummer, but we have the same English and Math courses, but we're in different sections. It would be cool if we have the same professors; then we could study together."

"On the bright side," Frannie chimed in, "We have most afternoons free and there will be plenty of time for fun."

They sat sipping their drinks, cooling off, and checking out every boy who walked by. "That one is a zero, for sure," Missy giggled, pointing to a nerdy looking young man with pimples. "Zero is a definite loser. Four is date material." What do you give that one?" she asked, pointing to a short, nice-looking boy.

"Two," Frannie said without hesitation. He's cute, but he's short and he looks like he's 12. I'm short, but I like tall guys, and I don't want my date to look like my little brother."

"I'm on board with that, Girlfriend," Missy giggled.

"Let's get the bookstore out of the way," Missy suggested. Leave your stuff here on the shelf. You can only take your wallet and the list of textbooks you need."

The girls passed through the turnstile and looked around the large store. "There," Frannie said, pointing to a sign that read *Freshman Courses*. "Look at all of those books. I'm glad they labeled the shelves with course numbers or we'd be here all day. Wait. Let's check out that coyote paraphernalia. I would love a t-shirt or a nightshirt with the school logo. Books can wait."

They prowled through the displays. Frannie squealed, "Missy look at this! Isn't it just FAB?" She held up a scooped neck, girlie t-shirt sporting a Lady Coyote.

"You'll look way cool in that," Missy said. "Besides Girl, it will show off what you have," cupping her hands under her breasts. "You can wear your new shirt on our tour of the campus."

"It just might do its magic if we run into Stephen," Frannie winked.

"Right on Foxy Mama"

Frannie hugged her treasure as they made their way to the freshman books.

"That shirt's super cool," Missy said as they left Hadley Hall for the Library.

Frannie picked up a map just inside the library doors. They walked past the front desk and through a set of double doors.

"This must be where folks study," Missy surmised, eyeing the tables scattered about the large area. "It's neat to be here when it's empty. We can talk without people *shushing* us. Look up; that balcony runs all the way around. What a great place to hang out and people watch. We can rank all the guys and pick out the best ones." Missy bounced her eyebrows.

"Let's go up there and look around," Frannie said, indicating stairs at the far side of the room. "The stacks seem to go on forever. What an awesome place for a private rendezvous."

"Let's see what's on the upper floors."

"All study tables," Frannie said, looking around the third-floor space. "Let's go up one more."

On the fourth floor, they found glassed-in rooms, each with a table and chairs. Missy read a note taped to the glass. "Rooms may be reserved for three or more people. That's pretty neat." With a wink, she said, "I wonder if they care what the people *do* in the rooms… but then, three would definitely be a crowd."

The Wake-Up Call

"Well, I've seen all I need to see here. What about you?" Frannie asked.

"Yep. My mother says there's cool stuff on the roof of Simpson Hall. Wanna check it out?"

"Awesome. Let's bug out of here."

They left the library and walked around the oval, passing students still in line to register. "Let's take these stairs," Missy suggested, pointing to a stairway at the side of Simpson Hall. The observatory might be restricted, and we stand a better chance of not being stopped if we take these straight to the roof. Besides, this way we'll avoid the stinky labs on the science floors.

They reached the roof and gaped at a large, ornate gazebo. "It's a building on top of a building," Frannie exclaimed, "a glass hexagon with a roof and invisible walls. Wouldn't this be perfect for a spring wedding?"

"Perfect... and a great place to do a little star gazing with a handsome guy," said Missy, as enchanted as Frannie. "Mom was right. This is a special place. Can't you just see women in long dresses and men in tuxes dancing under the stars? It reminds me of the *Sound of Music*. I can almost hear the music and see Liesl and Rolfe dancing."

"Look there," Frannie pointed. "Bushes and trees are growing up here. It's like a fairyland in the sky. Geez, it's hot up here!"

"Boy, you do talk fast. I think the telescope is behind those tall shrubs. Plants grow anywhere in the South, as long as there's water."

"WOW!" The two girls peeked around the tall shrubs at the huge telescope mounted on a revolving platform that provided an unobstructed view of the sky in every direction.

"I hope they have some special event up here when it is cooler. Frannie said. "This could be major fun."

"Me, too," Missy agreed. "I wish we could stay, but we need time to clean up for dinner. It's going to take more than toweling dry to make me feel human again."

"Yeah, my new t-shirt is soaked. Do you want to join my suitemates and me for dinner tonight?"

"I already told my roommates I would meet up with them. It's hard to find a table for eight in the cafeteria, so if we don't connect tonight, we'll hook up tomorrow.

"There should be a good job on this list somewhere," Katie said as she and Robin walked from the counseling center toward the Bookstore. "Look there." Katie pointed ahead. I wonder who that is with Leslie." Leslie, wait up."

The girls turned at the sound of Katie's voice, and Leslie exclaimed, "Cool, Barb, you get to meet two of my suitemates." When Robin and Katie had caught up, Leslie continued, "Hey, you two, meet Barb Phillips. She's in the athletic program with me. We're going to get a coke since she doesn't have to be at work until 4:30. Join us."

"Nice to meet you, Barb. We were just going to check out the bookstore. I want to get an idea of how much our books will cost, and if they have used books available." Katie pulled out her printed schedule with the textbooks for each class.

"Great idea, Barb said, I didn't expect to have any free time between practice and work. Let's have a coke, then I'll go to the bookstore with you. I can't remember what's required for my classes, but they're bound to have a list in there somewhere."

"Wow, The *SnaKbaR* is crowded," Leslie noted. "Let's get in line for cokes or we'll die of thirst before we get our books. Those girls are leaving. I'll grab their table. Would you get me a *Dr. Pepper?* Leslie asked, handing Barb a dime.

"These beanies sure make you stand out in a crowd," Barb said as she, Robin, and Katie carried drinks and joined Leslie. "I, for one, will be glad when orientation week is over. I have never understood the pleasure some people get from harassing others who can't fight back. What's even more confusing is that a university is a place where you're supposed to learn to be an adult, but at the same time, they encourage *un-adult* behavior."

Katie nodded, but countered, "I'll bet it's a *Catch 22* for the university. They need to have structure, but if they're too strict, it's like prep school, and we're too old for that level of discipline. I think a university tries to be more like the world *out there* with all kinds of challenges, and we get to figure out how to cope. I agree with you though, about picking on vulnerable people. When I'm an upperclassman, I can't imagine that lording my superiority over some poor freshman would make me feel good. I know what it feels like to get picked on, and I wouldn't do it to someone else."

"Initiation rituals have been around forever," Robin mused. "Think about the horrible *coming of age* stuff that tribal kids had to do to become adults. Even the Army seems to believe that you can't be a good soldier if you can't survive that boot camp shit. Compared to that, we freshman are pretty lucky."

"So, Barb," Leslie turned to her new friend, "you're the expert… tell us what Dallas is like. Do you live near here?"

Barb tilted her head, deciding which of Leslie's questions to answer first. "Well, the answer to the last question is, I don't live too far from here. My dad's store and our house are on the same block a little less than a mile north of the campus, this side of Central." Noting their quizzical looks, she explained, "Central Expressway… It's the north/south highway that divides Dallas into East and West. We see a lot of CU students in *The Market* since it's the closest grocery to the school. A mile isn't too far to walk when you want something to eat."

"Is there anything to do off campus?" asked Leslie.

"Of course, there is," Barb said. "Dallas is the second largest city in Texas."

"I need to get a job," Robin chimed in. Katie and I checked out campus jobs, but the hours are restricted and the pay is awful low. "I think that waitressing is the way to go… I could study during the day and work in the evening. Tips could add up if I do a good job, but that means I have to work somewhere that doesn't cater to students… most students are broke." She rummaged among her things, then placed the list she'd gotten in the counseling center in front of Barb. "These places are supposed to hire students. Any suggestions?"

Barb looked down the list, then pointed to *Rob Rory's Steakhauz*. "This one… Rob Rory's. Rory is Mr. Davis and Rob is Roberta, his wife. I've been eating there all my life. The food is good and the place is always full, and it's close to campus. I don't expect the tips would be ginormous, but I do expect that families understand that students work hard and need the money."

"Thanks," Robin said. "I hope they have an opening. I'll stop by tomorrow. Keep your fingers crossed for me."

Barb took a pen out of her bag and pointed to the restaurant list. "Can I write on this?" Robin looked puzzled but nodded.

"This is my address and phone. I was thinking that I could pick you all up on Saturday and show you downtown. Dad has help in the store on Saturday. Call me if you're interested. I'm so glad we met and got to know each other a little. I've got to git, cuz Dad's expecting me. I've played a little too long so, I'll stop by the bookstore tomorrow."

"We'd love to go exploring with you on Saturday," smiled Leslie.

"Our own private orientation," exclaimed Katie.

"Thanks again for suggesting Rob Rory's," Robin said.

Barb waved as she made her way out through the crowd.

"Has either of you seen Frannie since registration?" asked Robin. "I can't believe that I'm even thinking about that twit. First, I think how nice it is that she's somewhere else, then I wonder why I haven't seen her. How's that for weird?"

"Robin," Katie said with a broad smile, "you're a tough cookie outside and a marshmallow inside. Frannie's lucky to have you as her roommate. She just doesn't know it yet."

Flustered, Robin couldn't think of a thing to say.

Katie smiled. "I hope there's a good selection of used books," she said to let Robin off the hook. "I don't mind benefiting from someone else's hard work, as long as they underlined neatly and didn't scribble illegible gibberish in the margins."

The Wake-Up Call

"My scholarship includes books," Robin said. "If there's anything we can share, let me get it."

After scouring row after row of books in search of new and used texts, they checked out and hurried to the dorm. Peeking into her empty bedroom, Robin said, "No Frannie," then collapsed with the others into chairs in the sitting room.

"Let's try to get to dinner early tonight," suggested Leslie. It would be nice if we didn't have to eat the dregs two nights in a row."

"Sounds like a plan," Robin remarked. "We need to tell Frannie that she can have the bathroom last since she can't seem to get up on her own."

"Maybe it would be good for all of us if we gave her another chance," said Katie. "If she goes first, we all get to sleep later."

"Good point. OK, one last chance," Robin agreed. "But I am *not* going to be her alarm clock. She'll learn to wake up when she's supposed to or can sleep all day. I don't care."

"I did feel bad about leaving her this morning," said Katie, "but I agree that she has to learn to take care of herself."

Robin added, "If we take over her mother's role, she'll never develop any responsibility. It might take being late a few times for her to learn her lesson."

"I'm excited about classes," said Katie. "I'm going to try to get some reading done before they start. I like staying ahead of the assignments. I understand lectures better when I've read the material first, and I'm not one of those students who learns best under stress."

"Me either," Leslie agreed. "I've always had to study hard for my grades. I envy those students who can just open a book and osmose the material. My folks keep reminding me that you appreciate most what you work hard for."

"Those are wise words," Robin said. "Gram has the same philosophy. *Success requires hard work and a good education.* I've always done well in school and I think it's because Gram never let me play before my homework was done."

Moments later, Frannie sailed in, her t-shirt plastered to her body and talking before the door closed. "Hey, guys, I had the *best* afternoon," she bubbled. "It feels good in here. It's ungodly HOT outside. Missy and I explored the campus. She's nice. She has the most gorgeous clothes. We can share, but she's two inches taller, so length might be a problem. Her whole family went to school here. We checked out the library. It's huge. You wouldn't believe the roof of Simpson Hall. There's a telescope up there. It would be a great place to go with a date… dark, and quiet, and so close to the stars." Her words trailed off as she realized that all three of her suitemates were staring at her, and no one had said a word.

"Slow down," Robin commanded. "Stories make more sense when they start at the beginning. So, start at the beginning? What telescope?"

A bit deflated, Frannie continued "The telescope's not all, there is an amazing gazebo, too. The walls are glass and they open, like a fairytale ballroom in the sky."

"I wonder what it's for," Leslie wondered.

"Hmmm… I don't know," replied Frannie. "It was just so cool. It would be a great place to get married."

"I'm interested in the library," said Katie. "Did you scope it out?"

"Well, it has four levels. The card catalog takes up one whole wall of the first floor and the rest is current books and periodicals. The second floor is a balcony with tables for studying and stacks. The third floor is all study tables and stacks, but the fourth floor has little glassed-in conference rooms. There's a sign that says you can reserve them at the front desk for three or more students."

"That sounds perfect for us," Katie said, looking at Robin and Leslie. "We'll be able to study together without disturbing other students. Thanks, Frannie."

Frannie interrupted, "Missy told me that there's a Tug of War at nine tomorrow morning. Her mom said it's a fun event. They put the freshmen on teams with a few upperclassmen to help out. I keep changing my mind about what to wear. I want to dress up to make a good first impression, but you can get muddy, so I'm not sure what I should wear."

Robin rolled her eyes. "It's a good thing I don't have that many clothes. For me, picking an outfit doesn't take time away from important things… say, like getting up on time, or leaving the room in decent shape so my roommate doesn't trip over the clothes on the floor. By the way, did you and Missy talk about anything but clothes and boys?"

Frannie sat speechless, without a clue how to respond to Robin. *How did we get from the Tug of War to tripping over my clothes? Does she have to make every conversation about how much she doesn't like me? What did she expect we'd be talking about? Classes haven't even started yet.*

"Frannie." Katie's voice snapped Frannie out of her reverie. "The tug of war sounds like fun. Let's all go. We also have a tea tomorrow afternoon at 2:00 in the fourth-floor lounge. I'd like to know how we're expected to dress for it. Let's stop by the desk on the way to dinner and ask."

They stood to leave. Robin glanced at the papers Frannie had dropped on the floor before leaving with Missy, looked up at Katie, and managed to hold her tongue.

"Frannie, you might want to pick up your things and put them on your desk," suggested Katie. "There might be important information that you wouldn't want thrown away."

Without hesitation, Frannie turned back and gathered her things.

Robin shook her head in resignation.

"Well, the food was better than last night," exclaimed Frannie as the girls settled into the sitting area after dinner to listen to music. "Leslie had the right idea about getting to the cafeteria early."

"It's been a pretty cool day," Leslie commented. "I enjoyed meeting Barb. It will be nice to have a friend who knows her way around Dallas. I hope she was serious about taking us out and about on Saturday."

"Me, too," Katie added.

"Barb made it sound like Rob Rory's is just what I need. I can't wait to check it out," Robin said. "I hope they have an opening for me."

"What tour?" Frannie asked.

"Oh, Barb offered to show us around Dallas on Saturday, and maybe a little shopping," Leslie said.

"Cool. Shopping. Count me in." chirped Frannie.

They spent the evening talking about Frannie's and Missy's exploration of the campus and the activities planned for their first week at Crestmont. At 9:45, Katie said," We get to sleep in a bit tomorrow, but I'm still ready for bed. The Tug of War doesn't start until nine. Let's plan on breakfast at eight. Frannie, how much time do you need to get ready and what time do you want the bathroom?"

"Well, if you three take an hour altogether, that's seven to eight, so I need to get up at six," Frannie calculated.

"Don't forget to set your alarm, then," Katie reminded her. "Good night, guys."

In their room, Frannie selected several outfits. "What do you think of this, pink shorts and halter top for the Tug of War?"

Robin shrugged, "Frannie, does it matter what you wear?"

"Of course, it does," Frannie replied. My mother said that I always need to dress to make a good impression." Her final decision was a pair of hemmed cutoff jeans with a peasant blouse. "I love the way the neckline sets off my locket." She fingered the gold heart that never left her neck. "Petey gave it to me for my sixteenth birthday."

"I'm not waking you in the morning," Robin reminded Frannie. "You can sleep all day if you don't get up when your alarm goes off."

Frannie adjusted her alarm clock and turned out the light, checking to be sure that her night light was on in the bathroom. *"What's with her anyway? The alarm will ring; I'll turn it off; I'll get up. I do miss you, Nana. You'd know how I should handle Robin."*

Chapter 4

Frannie woke with a start at 8:15 to find the suite empty. "Oh, no! They left me again! Why is it so much trouble for Robin to wake me up?"

"Drats! I'll be lucky to get to the Tug of War on time. Maybe a quick stop by the *SnaKbaR* for a pop and a package of those powdered sugar donuts. I can get ready fast, but there's just no way to shorten the time it takes to put on makeup."

Frannie stuffed coins in the pocket of her cutoffs so she wouldn't have to carry a purse and took the shortcut to the Student Union through the hedge behind the dorm.

Frannie scarfed down the donuts on her way to the field and sipped *Dr. Pepper*, her favorite pop. "At least I got here in time. I can get where I need to be without their help. Robin will figure that out soon enough."

An upperclassman handed her a yellow card with a large purple eight. "Welcome to the Coyote Challenge Tug of War. Your team has the flag with that number. There will be two people with shirts like ours to help you get organized," said the upperclassman, pointing to his white shirt with a purple and gold coyote. The girl standing next to him wore a purple shirt with a gold and white coyote.

"I didn't see those shirts in the Bookstore yesterday. They're cute, but I like the one I bought better."

She spotted her three suitemates on three separate teams, but not one on Team 8. She found the right flag and was elated to see Missy on her team, and the upperclassman squatting down re-tying his shoe was Stephen. *"I couldn't have planned this better!"*

Stephen glanced at her without recognition. Missy nudged Frannie and whispered, "There's your dreamboat, our coach for the day and you are dressed to kill."

The microphone blared, silencing the crowd. "Good morning and welcome, everyone, to the Annual Crestmont University Coyote Tug of War. I'm Joan Jenkins, president of the Coyote Campus Student Club. Freshman, for the duration of orientation week, you will be known as Coyote Babies or Cubs or Cubbies. The Tug of War is a challenge between Coyote Babies and the Coyote Royals, all upperclassmen. It is your one chance for a position of superiority during orientation week. Listen carefully while I explain the rules.

"Two Coyote Royals are assigned to organize each team. The winners of the first heat will play against one another until there is one Coyote Baby team standing undefeated. That team will then have the honor of taking on the Coyote Royals team. The winning team rules Orientation Week.

"There is a purple flag tied to the rope in front of the first person on each team. To win, a team must pull the opponent's purple flag across the center line of the mud pit. One Coyote Royal judge in a purple and gold golf shirt will stand on each side of the pit to determine when a purple flag crosses the center. Spectators, please do not bump the judges when rooting for your teams.

"Freshmen, pay attention! If the Coyote Babies win, all upperclassmen will wear this badge." A Coyote Royal held up a large poster of a purple coyote in a diaper standing in victory over a small, defeated gold coyote. "However, if the Coyote Royals win,

The Wake-Up Call

this is the badge the freshmen will wear." This poster featured the same diapered purple coyote under a banner that read, *I am a lowly coyote baby who lost to the Coyote Royals.*

"The sign to my left shows you the order for the first heat. You will have 10-minutes to organize before we start. When you hear this whistle…" Joan blew a shrill blast… "the first heat will begin. The judges will blow their whistles when a purple flag crosses the center line to end a match. Coyote Babies, you have a lot at stake. Listen to your coaches and do your best."

"Team 8, listen up. I'm Stephen Barton and my partner is Tess Aikens. We are your coaches and cheerleaders, that is, until the last round when we intend to squash you like the little babies you are."

"Plan on getting royally dirty," Tess warned the group. "Just go with it and have fun."

Frannie and Missy eyed the pit. "That's real mud," Frannie said. "If they put us at the back of the line, maybe we won't get too dirty."

Missy replied, "My mom told me just to enjoy it because there's no way to stay clean."

Stephen and Tess put the strongest freshmen at the end of the rope. "Those two guys at the end look like football players. Maybe we have a chance," Frannie said from the third spot behind the flag, right behind Missy.

Frannie's and Leslie's teams won the first heat. Robin and Katie met up on the sidelines to cheer, after losing their matches.

In the second heat, Frannie's and Leslie's teams lined up on opposite ends of the rope. Robin cheered from the sidelines, *"Come on, Leslie and Frannie! One of you is gonna save us."*

The two teams were evenly matched, and the struggle lasted longer than the previous set. Frannie and Missy were splattered with mud, but both were still on their feet when they pulled Leslie's team's flag across the center line. "I can't believe I beat you in a sport," Frannie laughed as she and Missy hugged Leslie after the match. "This day will go down in history." Leslie laughed with her, then made their way over to Robin and Katie to watch the remainder of the matches.

At the end of the final heat, it was Frannie's team that shouldered the burden of protecting the freshman from the Coyote Royals' claim of supremacy. "Can you believe this?" Frannie exclaimed to Missy when the freshman winning team was announced. "We gotta do this."

"It would be fantastic if we saved the freshman class," Missy marveled. "My mom would be the proudest Alum in Crestmont history. Let's do it!"

On the sidelines, Leslie commented, with a wry smile, "This game is rigged, you know. That upper-class team hasn't broken a sweat. They're fresh and strong and Frannie's team was exhausted from winning four straight matches."

Katie said. "I thought about that but figured it's all in good fun."

Robin snorted, "Setting anyone up for failure doesn't sound like fun to me. I know we've talked about it before, but it's childish and I don't think we should be forced to participate just because we're freshmen. Those who think it's fun can enjoy themselves, but I'd rather put my energy into doing something meaningful… like working, or studying, or spending quality time with my friends."

Katie laughed out loud. "Girlfriend, we may need to grow Frannie up, but we need to put some *child* in you!"

Robin grinned but had no idea what to say.

The Cubs and Royals lined up for the final match. Like Frannie, Stephen was third from the flag on his team. *"Maybe that's a good sign,"* she mused. *"It could mean that we're destined to be together."*

The whistle blew and the struggle began. Frannie was excited and tugged as hard as her tired arms permitted. Her team pulled the opponent's flag toward them early, but the Coyote Royals were fresh and inched their flag in the other direction. Frannie could hear her roommates screaming, "Frannie, hang in there!" "Frannie, pull!" "Frannie, you can do it!"

The purple flags moved back and forth. Frannie leaned back, pulling with all her might. Her feet dug for purchase in the slippery mud. She was nearly sitting on the ground, gooey mud coating the back of her legs. *"I'm having too much fun to care,"* she realized, surprised at herself. Watching Stephen get muddier and muddier lifted her spirits. *"If getting muddy is what it takes to have fun with Stephen, then how bad can getting muddy be?"*

It was obvious that Frannie's team was tiring. Their purple flag crept toward the centerline. With a loud Coyote yell, the Royals pulled the Babies' purple flag across the center line, plunging Frannie face first into the mud. "*Noooo*," she screamed silently.

Frannie struggled to her knees and scraped mud from her face. She blinked to clear her blurry vision. "You're pretty cute covered in mud." Stephen loomed above her, not as muddy and bedraggled as she was.

"Not my best look, I'm afraid."

He reached for her hand and helped her up, "Want to meet me in the Game Room for some fun?"

"Sounds like a date. I promise I'll wear something nicer than mud for the occasion. What time should we meet?"

"How about after dinner? 6:45."

Before she could answer, he walked off. "Okay," she replied to his retreating figure.

"Hey there, Girlfriend," called Leslie. "Good try! For a minute I thought you might whup their butts." Leslie, Katie, and Robin encircled Frannie. "You did a great job. No one can call you a pipsqueak after *that* performance."

"I've gotta get cleaned up." Frannie spread her arms to display her mud-covered body.

Robin added, "Me, too, and I have to get rolling on my job hunt." She turned to follow Frannie, then laughed at the trail of mud clods dropping as she walked. "You are a sight," she called to Frannie. "I wish I had a camera!"

"Robin, before you leave for your interviews try a little bit of this lipstick." Frannie handed her roommate a lipstick tube with a shy smile. "I think you'll like it."

"Yes, do," agreed Katie. "It will dress up your outfit a bit and don't forget to smile. People like waitresses who smile."

"Uh, thanks, Frannie." Robin hesitated, then reached for the lipstick. "That's nice of you, and Katie, thanks for the reminder. I guess smiling isn't my natural facial expression."

"I think Rob Rory's will be the best choice, but I won't know for sure unless I check out the other options. I'll be back in time for the tea and let you know how things turn out."

As soon as Robin left, Leslie said, "I'll jump in the shower if that's okay. I'll be quick."

"Fine, Frannie do you want to shower after Leslie?" Katie asked. "You can't go anywhere looking like a mud puppy."

"This morning was major cool beans." Frannie gushed. "I have a date with Stephen this evening after dinner. I'm so excited, I have goosebumps all over."

"Hold that thought, Frannie. I'm going to get a towel to sit on so I don't get any more mud on the floor. I'll get one for you, too," said Katie. "Then you can tell me all about the plans for your date."

Frannie settled herself carefully onto her towel. "After the last match, Stephen picked me up out of the mud and asked me to meet him in the Game Room for some fun after dinner."

"Is it a date or will others be joining you?"

"Oh, it has to be a date. We set up a time and everything." insisted Frannie.

"Shower's free," Leslie called from her bedroom.

"Katie, you go ahead, I need to think about what I am going to wear tonight."

"You might want to plan your outfit for the tea first. You can probably wear the same thing on your date?"

"Oh no, my tea clothes would never do for my date."

"Then, tea outfit first, date clothes later." Katie gathered her muddy towel by the corners. "I'll shake this into the commode. You can dump yours as soon as I'm done in the bathroom."

The Wake-Up Call

Frannie got up and shook her clothing to make sure that all the loose dirt fell onto the towel before she walked into her room.

"So, what should I wear tonight? I want to look fantastic for Stephen. I wonder why Katie thought it might not be a date. If a guy asks a girl out, it's a date!"

Leslie called from her room, "Frannie, what are you wearing to the tea?"

"Not sure," Frannie answered, thinking, *"I guess I'd better do that first. Picking out what I wear tonight will have to wait."*

※

"Hey guys, I'm home," Robin sang out. "Good news all around!"

"Do tell," Katie said joining her in the sitting room. "Give us the quick version, then you can fill in the details when we're all ready for the tea."

"So… I got the job. It took me less than 15 minutes to walk back from Rob Rory's, and I start work at five on Friday. I need to change. I'll be ready in a jiffy."

Robin chose a dark skirt and white blouse and slid her feet into her Capezios, the only "dressy" shoes she owned. "Ready," she announced as she joined Katie and Leslie in the sitting room.

"I hope this is dressy enough for this to-do," Robin said. "Frilly isn't my style."

"I expect we'll see everything from dressed-to-the-teeth to casual," Leslie volunteered. "I doubt anyone who's met Mrs. Crandall would have the nerve to wear shorts or jeans. I'm a plain dresser, too, Robin. It's slacks and blouses for me; there's hardly a dress in my closet. Let's get upstairs and find out what we're in for. Frannie, five minutes, no more."

Frannie bounced in at five minutes to two. "Do I look OK?" she asked, pirouetting for them to inspect her short purple and gold plaid skirt and gold blouse. "I thought this outfit would be perfect. I bought it for rallies, but it seems right for today, too."

"You look just fine," Katie agreed.

Robin rolled her eyes.

"Do you want to use my lipstick again, Robin?" asked Frannie. "I'll get it for you. It's right on the sink."

"That's sweet, Frannie," Katie said before Robin could decline.

Robin applied a touch. "Thank you, Frannie. It was nice of you to offer."

Frannie smiled, pleased with Robin's kind words.

The girls entered the social hall on the fourth floor, Frannie in the lead, twirling her skirt. "Leslie was right about all different kind of outfits," she said. "I'm glad I dressed up. Mom always tells me to look my best, especially when I'm meeting people for the first time. I'm sure she'd like this outfit."

"The room looks tremendous with the furniture rearranged," Robin exclaimed. I wouldn't have thought it could hold this many people. I wonder what they did with the ping pong table?"

Katie surveyed the noisy room and pointed, "Do you want to sit over there in those chairs, or stand at that cocktail table near the front? It looks like those might be our only options."

"The chairs," said Frannie. "Who wants to stand when you can sit?"

"I'll go sit and save seats while you three get food," Katie offered. "But, please hurry. I don't want to keep saying, *Sorry, these seats are taken*."

Tea and cookies balanced on their laps, the four chatted and surveyed the room. Leslie commented, "You can sure tell the Resident Assistants from the freshman. They're so comfortable and confident in dresses and heels. Just think, that could be us in a year or two. I wonder what benefits there are and how you get to be one."

"Good question for Mrs. Crandall," Robin said.

An amplified voice interrupted the chatter. "Good afternoon, young ladies. Welcome to Hadley Hall." Necks craned to locate the source of the voice. Mrs. Crandall, in a dress, nylons, and heels like the RAs, stood beside the tea service. She held the microphone to her chin. "We have lots of information to share with you."

The Wake-Up Call

She introduced the RAs assigned to each floor. Frannie whispered, "Sally's our RA. That's cool. I like her."

"We think of Hadley Hall residents as a family. Our mission is to keep you safe and promote your success at Crestmont University. While there are ample opportunities for social activity, your academic success is primary. After all, that is what keeps you here. Even though you think you are prepared, you will be surprised at how different college is from high school. At home, your parents and your teachers took some responsibility for your activities; here no one will ask if you've done your homework, suggest that you study, or review your work. In college, *you*, and only you are responsible for your success."

Frannie's shoulders slumped. *"THAT has been made crystal clear. My roommate doesn't help me with ANYTHING!"*

"With that in mind, we have rules at Hadley Hall to help achieve our mission to protect you and to facilitate your success. You'll find them in your orientation packet. I encourage you to read them and discuss any questions with your RA. We give demerits for abusing the rules to remind you of your responsibilities. If your behavior continues to earn demerits, we will ask you to leave Hadley Hall.

"For your safety, we lock the exterior doors at 10:00 pm Sunday through Thursday and open them at 6:30 am. We expect you to be in the dorm during those hours. Friday and Saturday the doors close at 11:00 pm. If you return after the doors are locked, you will have to ring the bell. We may excuse extenuating circumstances, but we don't tolerate disregard for dorm rules. We permit visitors only between 6:30 am and 10:00 pm. We do not allow overnight guests. Only females may visit your suite. We do not intend the rules to be punitive; they are in place to encourage behavior that leads to success."

"The RAs have walked in your shoes. They will understand your challenges and will do everything they can to help you. However, if you have difficulty with another student, I expect that you will try to resolve the conflict with that individual before seeking help from your RA or from me. Our first question will be *Have you discussed the situation with her?*"

"Your suites do not have kitchenettes, but you may bring in small appliances for preparing and storing food. Take care not to prepare food whose odor escapes your suite. It is essential that you have respect for others."

"Before we break into groups, does anyone have questions for me?"

"How do we get our mail?" asked someone near the front.

"Each suite has an assigned mailbox at the front desk. If you receive a package that will not fit, we will place a notice in your box. Just stop by the desk and ask for it. The postman comes at nine each morning. Drop your outgoing mail in the slot labeled *MAIL*. Anything else?"

A hand waved for attention. "Are there any rules about using the telephones?"

"The telephone in your suites permits unlimited campus and local calls. You may make only collect calls to long-distance numbers through the campus operator. There are two pay phones in the center landing on each floor. We have a ten-minute limit on conversations if someone is waiting."

Mrs. Crandall looked around and saw no more raised hands. "Let's break into groups by floor. Find your RA and you can begin to get to know them and your neighbors. You may freshen your tea and get more cookies on your way."

With full teacups and plates of cookies to share, the four girls squeezed onto a sofa and Sally perched on the arm of a chair. "First, let's meet one another," she said. "When I call your name, tell us where you're from and what you'll be studying."

When Sally called her name, Leslie levered herself off the couch. "My name is Leslie Jean Bleu. That's spelled B-L-E U, not like the color. I'm in the nursing program. I'm here on an athletic scholarship, and I'm on the basketball team. It would be great if I made varsity my first year, but that's not likely to happen. I'm from Abita Springs, Louisiana. That's just north of New Orleans."

The Wake-Up Call

Frannie scooched to the edge of her seat while two more girls introduced themselves, then jumped up when Sally called, "Frances Braun."

"I'm Frannie and I'm from Philadelphia. I'm going to be a nurse. I'll help mom take care of Nana, and I'll know what to do when my children get sick." The girls waited for more, but Frannie shrugged, said, "That's all," and sat down.

"Sara Grayfox," called Sally after several more girls had introduced themselves.

"Officially, it's Sara Katherine," said Katie, rising, "but I've always been Katie. I'm from Atoka, Oklahoma, and I'm also in the nursing program." She smiled and sat down.

"Jennifer Hart." Sally was met with silence. Frowning, she repeated, "Jennifer Hart…?"

Robin's eyes widened with recognition and she jumped up. "Oh, that's me! Sorry. I go by Robin. No one's called me Jennifer for years. When I was little, my grandmother said my red hair was just the color of a robin's breast, and I've been Robin ever since. I'm from Chicago and I'm in the nursing program, too. Sally, I have a question. I'm going to be working evening shifts at Rob Rory's SteakHauz. If I work until 10 or later, how can I get back into the dorm without earning demerits?"

"I can help you with that, Jen… uh… Robin," said Sally, making a note of the name Robin preferred.

When everyone had spoken, Sally introduced herself. "I'm Sally Adams. I'm a junior in the nursing program. I'm from Weatherford, Texas, about an hour due west of Crestmont. I want to warn you nursing majors that the program is NOT for sissies. It has a great reputation. Nearly 100% of our nursing graduates have passed their State Board exam on the first try, and the reason for that is the program is tough and the professors hold us accountable." She looked at the group and smiled. "Those of you who chose nursing because you couldn't think of anything better to do might want to consider other options." Everyone giggled.

No one spoke up when Sally asked for questions. "Well then, you girls stay and get to know one another. Remember that you can come to me any time you need help."

Frannie pondered, *"I wonder if she was talking to me when she said that about considering something besides nursing. Of course, I want to be a nurse. What else would I want to be."*

Frannie trailed behind her three suitemates, thinking about her date with Stephen. She quickened her pace to catch up, then thought better of it. *"Every time I mention having fun, they look disappointed. What could be so wrong with my wanting to have fun? I got good grades in high school and I hardly studied at all."* She shrugged, *"I don't care what they think. I have a date with Stephen tonight and I'll have more fun than all three of them put together."*

Robin, Katie, and Leslie settled into their sitting area. Frannie hesitated, not sure whether to join them or get ready for her date. When all three looked up at her expectantly, she brightened at what felt like an invitation and dropped into a chair. "That was fun. Did you see the gorgeous outfit the girl sitting next to you had on, Katie? It looked fantastic, dressy, and comfortable all at the same time. I think I'll look for something like that when we go shopping." Robin rolled her eyes and Katie and Leslie said nothing.

Katie turned to Robin, "So, you're gonna work at the SteakHauz. Fill us in on the details."

Robin leaned forward. "First, I checked out some of the counselor's, recommendations, but they weren't what I had in mind. Then I got to Rob Rory's and the hostess turned out to be the owner's daughter, Maddie, who's a Crestmont graduate. But get this. When I introduced myself to Mr. Rory Davis, one of the owners, he said, *Robin… I was expecting you.* It turns out Barb and her dad had dinner there last night and Barb recommended me. Can you believe that? I can't wait to thank her.

The Wake-Up Call

Anyhow, they have a great system. Everyone learns to do everything so if someone can't make it to work, we all pitch in and keep the customers satisfied. Mr. Davis considers his employees a family; we pool all our tips so that you get tips even when you're not serving customers."

"That sounds so perfect," Leslie exclaimed. "When do you start?"

"Friday at five. Oh, and if I can get a shift early, I can eat there for nothing. Beats the heck out of cafeteria food."

Frannie chimed in, "Maybe Stephen and I will have dinner at your restaurant and we'll sit at your table. I'll make sure he leaves a good tip." She stood. "I need to get changed. Stephen and I have a date tonight, and it never hurts for a girl to look her best."

"Frannie, be careful. I was serious about that guy." Robin said. "He's no good... Mark my words!" She stopped talking when Katie put a hand on her arm.

When Frannie's door closed, Katie whispered, "I agree with you. I think he's a loser, but Frannie's like a little kid. The more you say against him, the more she'll defend him. She's got to figure Stephen out for herself. I hope, she'll get the picture *before* she gets hurt."

"I wouldn't count on that," Robin replied. "That loser will take as much advantage as possible. If she kisses him, he'll be demanding the whole enchilada. I'd bet on it." She sighed, "I don't know why I give a damn what happens to her, but I do. He's so obvious. If she weren't batting her eyelids and fawning over him, he wouldn't give her the time of day. He makes me think of Jake, my loser ex-boyfriend, and thinking about Jake makes my blood boil."

"I just thought of something," Leslie remarked, surprise in her voice. "I've not given Paul a single thought these last two days. It's weird, everything is happening so fast that I haven't missed him at all. Maybe it's because ever since I got my scholarship, and he didn't get one he's done nothing but complain."

"If he can't be happy for you, you *should* be moving on." Robin proclaimed.

Katie intervened. "You might invite him up for something like Homecoming. That would give him an opportunity to fit in with your college self."

Frannie came out of her room, sporting a mini skirt and white go-go boots, and fresh makeup in place. "How do I look?" She glanced at each of the girls, settling her attention on Katie. "I want to look good for my first date with Stephen."

Robin couldn't hold her tongue. "If all you do is think about dating… especially if you concentrate on losers… you won't be around long. You'll flunk out before you ever get into the nursing program, where you just might have found a handsome doctor to marry."

"Oh!" stammered Frannie. "Why would you say that? I got nearly straight A's all through high school, and I didn't have to study or give up my social life."

"You're not in Kansas anymore, Dorothy!" Robin said "You should have listened to what Sally said.

Leslie interrupted, "Come on. We agreed to get to dinner early. Let's go."

Frannie followed them to the cafeteria, wondering what their problem was with having fun.

"WOW, getting here early pays off," Leslie exclaimed. "The food selection actually looks appetizing. Here's another suite rule: *early to meals*." They had no trouble finding a table for four.

They enjoyed dinner and lingered over dessert. Frannie scanned the room and stood abruptly. "I have to get to the Game Room for my date. I thought that Stephen would be here for dinner and we'd go together, but I suppose he's already there."

Robin shook her head as the girls watched her go.

⁂

In the Game Room, Frannie spotted Stephen watching a foosball game, with his arm draped around Tess's shoulders. "*If Tess is his girlfriend, why would he ask me out?*

"I play the winner," he announced.

The Wake-Up Call

"This isn't right" Frannie decided. *"He hasn't once looked to see if I'm here. We have a date, so why is he getting ready to play another game?"*

Frannie strode toward Stephen, who glanced up without expression. Then recognition crept across his face. "Hey, Cubby. C'mon over and join the fun."

Stephen encircled her shoulders with his free arm and continued to concentrate on the foosball game, one arm around Tess and the other holding Frannie. *"I have no idea what to do,"* Frannie admitted to herself. *"He's so cute and he obviously likes me. Somehow, I have to let him know that I hate being called "Cubby" and when we have a date, he should spend his time with me."*

Frannie's beanie was the only one among Stephen's friends, as was her *loser* pin from the Tug of War. *"I'm either the only freshman in this group, or I'm the only one following the rules,"* she thought, feeling conspicuous.

"Guys, Cubby was on the last freshman team standing this morning. Actually, she wasn't standing. I pulled this coyote baby from the mud."

"She cleans up pretty good," commented Stephen's crony, Greg, giving Frannie a thorough once over.

"My turn!" Stephen called out as Greg scored the winning goal. He released Tess and Frannie and moved in to play.

"I remember you from the Tug of War team this morning," Tess said to Frannie, leading her away from the table. You played a great game. How do you like Crestmont so far?"

"It's cool. I love the school colors and the coyote, but I'll be glad when Orientation Week is over. I met Stephen the first day I was here. He toured me around the Student Union. He asked me out for tonight after the Tug of War this morning."

"Really?" Tess sounded skeptical. "Where's he taking you?"

"He said to meet him here. He's dreamy. I'm glad he likes me."

"Hmmm," Tess replied, eyeing Stephen. "He didn't say anything about leaving. Do you like games?"

"I like ping pong and *Scrabble* and *Monopoly*, and we play *Risk* at home."

"I like board games, too, but these guys have more brawn than brains. They pretty much stick to table games and darts. Stephen is the reigning foosball champion. Once he starts playing, it's hard to get him away from the table."

Stephen won the game and James got up to take Greg's place. Stephen never once looked in Frannie's direction. *"Is he going to play all night? I wish he'd ask ME to play something, like ping pong or darts. I wasn't expecting to spend my whole evening with Stephen just standing around watching him play."*

"Hey Stephen," Tess called out. "If you win, I'll take over for you. You can't hog the table all night." She winked at Frannie. "Besides, Frannie here might be able to whup your butt in ping pong or darts." Frannie shot her a grateful look.

Stephen looked up, surprised. "Oh, yeah OK. I'll win this game in a heartbeat.

Relieved, she settled in wait, grateful for Tess's smooth move.

"You've met Tess. Let me introduce you to the rest of the guys," Stephen said, as he stepped back from the table. "The one she's gonna crush is James." James winced, then leered at Frannie. "That one waiting in line to get clobbered is Greg." Greg waved at her and winked. "Those two hot babes coming in are Sharon and Marilyn. They're both sophomores. Marilyn's our ping pong champ, and Sharon's not so bad at the dart board. Hey everyone, this is Cubby. You can take it from me, she's a knockout when she's covered in mud."

Greg called out, "Go, Cubby!"

Frannie winced, then frowned when Stephen threw one arm around Marilyn and the other around Sharon, pulling them in for a quick hug. Then he put his hands on Frannie's shoulders, looked her up and down, and chuckled "You clean up pretty well considering what you looked like the last time I saw you! Hey, a ping pong table just opened. Tess says you might wanna whup my butt. You do know that I'm the Ping-Pong King at Crestmont?"

"We'll see about that." Frannie smiled at her change of fortune. "I'm pretty good myself. Besides, Tess told me that Marilyn is the reigning ping pong champ."

The Wake-Up Call

Stephen shot a glance at Tess. "Naaah," he shook his head. "Marilyn beats me once in a while. Lemme show you."

Frannie picked up her paddle, thinking, *"This is fantastic, I have him to myself."*

"I'll take it easy on you the first round, Cubby, but then you gotta stand on your own two feet." They played a game and, keeping his word, he went easy on her and beat her by just two points. "Okay, now that we are all warmed up, we can play ping pong."

Pleased that she'd held her own in the first game, Frannie replied, "I can take you, Big Boy! Bring on your best game."

"You got it, Cubby!" With a smug look, he slammed her first serve off the left corner and her second off the right corner, scoring the first two points. He beat her 21-7. "Another game?" he asked with a wicked smile

"I want you to put your arms around me, not pummel me with ping pong balls."

Tess walked up with Greg. "How about Greg and I get the table and you and Frannie play darts?" Frannie gave her another grateful look.

Stephen's reply disappointed Frannie. "You can play the winner, Tess," he said. "C'mon, Frannie, show me what you got."

With little enthusiasm, Frannie picked up her paddle. Then a new thought occurred to her. *"He wants me to get to know his friends. That's kind of nice. He is a guy, after all. He wants me to see how good he is at games."*

Greg reached for her paddle as soon as Frannie lost the game. "Here," she said. "Give him a run for his money." She moved to Tess's side and watched Stephen beat Greg 21-11. He was sweating, and Frannie thought he looked manly.

"Cubby," he called, pulling a few coins from his pocket, and holding them out to her, "How about you get me a *Coke* and get one for yourself, too."

Flummoxed at the unexpected command, she reached for the coins. "Ssssure," she stammered.

Tess scowled at Stephen. "I'll go with you," she said to Frannie. "Anyone else need a drink?" The others shook their heads.

Other than Tess, no one seemed at all surprised at Stephen's behavior. *"I've got a lot to learn about college,"* Frannie thought. *"People behave differently at home."*

She and Tess returned with the drinks, a *Coke* for Stephen, and a *Dr. Pepper* for her. Taking the can that Frannie held out to him, Stephen said, "Thanks Cubby, I needed this. I'm kickin' ass, but I need a break. Wanna play something else?"

"Let's try foosball," Frannie replied. *"I thought I was good at ping pong and he clobbered me. I guess not being good at foosball won't be a big surprise."*

The gang, as Stephen called them, drifted over to watch them play. *"Heavens, with everyone looking over my shoulder, I'll be lucky to do anything right."*

"Wow," Stephen exclaimed at the end of their first game. He had beaten her, but she had played better foosball than she'd expected. "You're sure better at foosball than ping pong."

"Hey, Dude," Greg said. "The pool table just freed up. You owe me from last night. Get over here so I can take you on."

"Yeah, sure, nothing better to do," Stephen replied, and headed for the pool table without a word to Frannie.

"Did he just say nothing better to do? I certainly have something better in mind."

By the time Stephen had beaten Greg three out of five games, it was nearing 9:00. *"How can I get him to pay attention to me before I have to be back in the dorm? Oh, well, what do I have to lose?"*

"Stephen," she said, "come for a walk with me."

Startled, he looked as if he'd forgotten she was there. "Sorry, Cubby, I'm on a roll. Stay and watch if you want. Can't leave while I'm winning."

It was 9:30 when Stephen lost to Greg. Frannie grabbed his arm before he could begin another game. "I need to go back to the dorm," she said.

"You turning into a pumpkin? There's plenty of time before curfew."

"We could walk and talk a bit."

Greg and James followed their conversation with wide grins Greg winked at Stephen. "Go on, Man. I haven't whupped James' ass for a while and your little cubby wants you to spend time with her."

Tess scowled.

Stephen nodded to his friends, then said to Frannie, "Wait for me by the door and I'll walk you back to the dorm."

"Finally, we'll be alone. He DOES want to spend time with me." Frannie said goodbye to Tess and moved toward the door to wait for Stephen.

She fidgeted as Stephen, Greg, and James huddled, whispering, and laughing.

"Let's walk the long way around the oval and check out the fountain," he suggested. "We'll be at the dorm in plenty of time for curfew."

"That sounds nice", Frannie smiled up at him as he pulled her close. They walked slowly around the top of the oval and stopped to watch the fountain. They spoke little, but Frannie was content to have his arm around her. "I enjoyed being with you tonight, Stephen."

"If you want to meet up again, I'm always in the Game Room. Come by anytime."

They walked up the steps to the porch of Hadley Hall. "Nite, Cubby. See you around," he said, then bounded down the steps.

Frannie watched him leave. *"It was too soon for a kiss goodnight, I suppose."* She hurried to her suite to tell her suitemates what a wonderful time she'd had and that Stephen had asked her out on another date.

❦

"We're in here, Frannie," called Katie from her bedroom. "Come tell us about your evening."

Frannie kicked off her boots and climbed onto Leslie's bed. "I met lots of Stephen's friends. Tess Aikens was there. She was the other coach of my Tug of War team this morning. There were two more girls and two guys. Stephen said I looked nice. He's a great ping pong player. I'm going to have to practice if I want to keep up with him. He beat every one of the guys. He beat them at foosball, too. He's good at all the games. Then, we had a *pop* and he walked me home the long way by the fountain. He even asked me out again."

"Anything happen on the walk home?" asked Robin.

"Well, he had his arm around me, but he didn't kiss me if that's what you mean. He was a perfect gentleman."

"Glad to hear that," Robin said, "but you be careful. I have a gut feeling he's up to something."

Katie broke in. "We're glad you enjoyed your evening, Frannie. Robin's just reminding you to take your time getting to know new people. Anyway, we've been talking about tomorrow. It's our first day of classes and the three of us have the same schedule. What does your schedule look like?"

"I can't remember," said Frannie, "realizing that she hadn't given classes a thought since she was in the bookstore with Missy. "Let me get my schedule." She hesitated, trying to remember where she'd put her things.

"You picked your orientation materials up off the floor and put them somewhere in your room," Katie reminded her."

Frannie disappeared into her bedroom. "I've got it," she exclaimed. "Monday, Wednesday, and Friday I have English at eight, Old Testament at nine, and Math at eleven. On Wednesday, there's Chapel at ten." She looked at the others.

"Cool! Your schedule is the same as ours," Leslie said. We're going to breakfast at 7:15, and then to class. We want to get there early enough to sit together. If you want to go with us, we can try the same bathroom schedule.

"Far out!" Frannie agreed. "I'll set my alarm for 5:15 and pick out my clothes for tomorrow. I want to look good for the first day."

Robin rolled her eyes. Frannie selected and discarded several outfits. "Shouldn't you hang up the ones you're not going to wear?" Robin suggested, frowning at the growing pile of clothing on Frannie's chair. "They'll be too wrinkled to wear if you just leave them there."

The scolding aggravated Frannie, but she had to admit that Robin had a point."

"Bathroom's all yours," said Robin. "I assume you want to brush your teeth."

"Was that a suggestion or a snotty comment?" Frannie wondered.

"Frannie," called Katie. "Don't forget to set your alarm. It's up to you to get up when it goes off."

"OK," Frannie called back, then glanced at Robin in time to see her roll her eyes and shake her head.

"What's with her? The alarm will ring; I'll turn it off; I'll get up and shower. How complicated is that?"

Chapter 5

Frannie's alarm rang at 5:15 am… and rang… and rang. Robin opened one eye and lay in bed, fuming. There was no sound other than the irritating buzz *"I'd let that thing ring until the cows come home but it'll wake Katie and Leslie before Frannie ever hears it. No need for them to be up this early."* She threw back the covers in frustration, swung her feet to the floor, and silenced the alarm.

"Amazing." she thought. *"She hasn't moved a muscle. Well, it's obvious that we need a Plan B. There's no reason the rest of us have to be up this early. It's Frannie's problem. Let her figure it out."*

Robin crawled back under the covers, intending to sleep until her 6:15 bathroom slot. She repositioned her pillow and burrowed deeper into the cocoon of covers, but she was wide awake. *"What an inconsiderate little SHIT! How can someone from a nice family grow up without developing any common courtesy?*

"It's interesting, though… She's always surprised by the reactions she gets from her thoughtless actions." Robin thought. *"I'll be damned if I'm going to be her mother. I learned to take care of myself; she sure as hell can learn to do the same."*

The Wake-Up Call

At 5:30, Robin disappeared into the bathroom. By the time she had brushed her teeth, showered, dried her hair, and dressed, there was still no sound from Frannie. She could hear the pattering of feet in Katie and Leslie's room. Robin knocked on the door.

"Come on in, we're both up," said Katie.

"Can I assume that sleeping beauty's prince hasn't yet arrived?" Leslie asked with a grimace.

"I don't think her current prince has given her a single thought," Robin retorted. "I doubt he'd notice if *Sleeping Beauty* slept for the whole 100 years. I let the alarm ring until I realized that it would wake you two before it woke her. Then I couldn't get back to sleep, so... who wants the bathroom next?"

Leslie took the next slot and Katie finished in the bathroom at 6:30. Wrapped in her towel, Katie stopped in to shake Frannie's shoulder. Frannie repositioned herself but slept on. "Frannie!" Katie's voice was sharp. "Wake up. If you get up now, you can still make it to class on time. You might even have a few minutes to catch breakfast."

Frannie opened her eyes and stared at Katie, slowly registering recognition, followed by surprise and dismay. Her mouth gaped as she looked at the silent alarm clock on her desk. "But... what happened to my alarm? Why didn't it go off?"

Katie shook her head, realizing that Frannie's transition from pampered child to self-sufficient adult wasn't going to be easy. "It rang until Robin was afraid it would wake Leslie and me. As soon as I'm dressed, the three of us are going to get breakfast. We'll stay in the cafeteria until 7:40, then we're leaving for class so we can get there early enough to sit together. If you get up now, you won't be late."

Frannie nodded, holding back her tears. "Katie, why didn't Robin just wake me up? I don't understand why she needs to be mean to me. My mother never had any trouble getting me up on time."

Katie considered her response. "Frannie, Robin *did* try to wake you. She shook you, spoke to you, and let the alarm continue to ring." Frannie started to protest, but Katie interrupted, her expression stern. "No, Frannie, it's not Robin's job to wake you. We're all living away from home for the first time, and we're all realizing how much more responsibility we have for ourselves."

A tear slipped down Frannie's cheek. Katie pulled her gently to her feet. "Get up and get ready. I doubt that you need a whole hour in the bathroom. Hurry, and if there's time, meet us in the cafeteria and we'll all go to class together. Otherwise, we'll save you a seat."

Katie went to dress. Frannie found her towel under some clothes on her chair and went into the bathroom. *"If Katie were my roommate, she wouldn't have let me sleep so late. Robin just hates me."*

Katie, hearing nothing from the bathroom, called through the door. "Frannie, don't just stand there. I meant it when I said that we are all learning what it means to be on our own." As if Katie were a mind-reader, she continued, "Robin doesn't hate you. I would have let you sleep, too. You'll never be OK on your own if you have to count on someone else to look out for you."

Frannie couldn't believe her ears. *"Do Indians have special powers?"* She stammered, "I'll get ready as fast as I can and meet you in the cafeteria. Oh, and thanks for getting me up. I'll try harder tomorrow." As she brushed her teeth, she pondered, *"How does someone just wake up when they're supposed to? I hope Katie can teach me the trick."* She rinsed her mouth and stepped into the shower.

※

"Whew! I made it!" Frannie met up with her suitemates as they dropped off their empty trays.

"Here," Katie handed Frannie a napkin-wrapped package. Don't expect take-out every day. Tomorrow you'll be up in time to eat with us."

"Thanks, Katie," Frannie said as she uncovered a scrambled egg sandwich. "Katie," Frannie said, "will you help me figure out how to make myself hear my alarm?" Robin rolled her eyes and bit back a stinging retort.

"It's a good thing we don't have Old Testament first," Robin commented. "I'd be tempted to sleep through Frannie's alarm. I'm glad we start with English. I like reading, writing, and even grammar. It was diagramming sentences that showed me how to choose between *who* and *whom*. Maybe I'll be a novelist instead of a nurse. She looked thoughtful. "Maybe not. I'm looking forward to nursing more than I thought. I'm certain I couldn't spend a whole day pecking away at a typewriter."

"I wonder if Old Testament will be like Sunday school," Leslie mused. "If so, that should be an easy *A,* I've been going to Sunday school since I was born."

"What I know about the Old Testament I could write in large letters on a postage stamp" Robin admitted. "We've never been a church-going family. Come to think of it, church might have done my worthless parents some good."

Katie put her hand on Frannie's arm and shook her head when it looked like Frannie was about to ask Robin what she meant. "Not now," she said.

Frannie looked surprised. *"Katie is looking out for me. She just kept me from saying something that would set Robin off. I do think she can read my mind."*

Katie and Leslie took seats in front of Robin and Frannie. "I hope they let us keep these seats," Katie said. "My teachers made us sit alphabetically so that they could learn our names."

Robin leaned over and replied, "College is going to be an interesting change of pace. I don't think they'll try too hard to learn our names."

A tall, stern woman strode to the front of the class. "Good morning ladies and gentlemen. Welcome to Freshman English. I'm Dr. Gladys Bennett. I teach English at all four levels, so we might have the pleasure of being together again after this semester. With that in mind, let me share my expectations.

"First, you will submit your assignments complete and on time. Responsibility is as important to your success as intelligence."

Frannie winced. "All of you are intelligent, or you wouldn't be here. Those of you who breezed through high school without lifting a finger might find yourselves challenged for the first time."

Frannie shifted in her seat. *Why does everyone keep saying that?*

"Second, I expect original work. Integrity and accountability are also prerequisites for success. I love the English language and will do my part to help you speak and write well. Please understand that my corrections and comments are intended to stimulate improvement. The course is not difficult if you apply yourself. This class will be both a learning opportunity and a chance to express yourself. Perhaps you will even get to know yourselves a little better.

"Your first assignment is to tell me in up to three pages, using your best grammar and sentence structure, a bit about yourselves and what brings you to Crestmont University. I'll be doing the assignment with you. On Friday, I'll read my essay to you, then I'll read some of yours, with permission, of course.

"Questions?" Mrs. Bennett surveyed the room. "Okay then, begin writing. Don't be too hasty. There is time for you to recopy your essay to be sure that I get the cleanest, best-prepared work that you can produce. When you finish, you may leave.

Frannie was the first of the suitemates to complete her paper. She glanced at her suitemates. Katie was copying her essay over. Frannie scanned her essay. *Just a few strikeouts... not enough to recopy the whole thing. I'm outa here. There might be some cute boys wandering around.*

With that pleasant thought, she gathered her things, handed her essay to Mrs. Bennett, and left to wait outside for her suitemates. Mrs. Bennett looked at the time: 20 minutes of class time left. She shrugged and began to read Frannie's essay.

A hurried five-minute walk took them to Old Testament in the huge auditorium beneath the chapel. They climbed over legs and

The Wake-Up Call

bags and dropped into four seats about ten rows from the front. An electronic squeal silenced several hundred student voices, followed by an amplified staccato rapping as a small, lean man tapped the microphone.

"Welcome to Old Testament. If Old Testament is not your final destination, you might consider taking a different flight." A swell of laughter signaled the students' appreciation for the casual welcome and the hope that Old Testament might not be a *heavy* class after all.

"Old Testament is a required course for all students at Crestmont University. I can imagine that's the only reason most of you are here, so I want to assure you that you won't be sorry. The Old Testament is rich in history and wisdom that can be fascinating and meaningful, regardless of your religious convictions. I am Dr. Ethan Creighton, and it will be my pleasure to bring the Old Testament to life for you. I am also privileged to be the first chapel speaker for the semester."

※

"Well *that* was a refreshing surprise," Robin exclaimed, as they climbed the stairs to the chapel. "This could turn out to be my favorite class. I might just change my major from nursing to religious studies." She grinned at her suitemates' wide-eyed stares. "Guys, I'm just kidding. I can't believe you took me seriously. An hour ago, I said I might become a writer."

"I enjoyed our English class," said Katie.

"Me too," added Frannie. "Today's assignment was really easy. It didn't take any time at all."

"I'm not so sure about Mrs. Bennett," Robin warned. "She has pretty high expectations. We'll just have to see what she says about our essays."

"Fair enough," agreed Leslie. "So far the semester is shaping up well. Chapel might just be a good break between classes. If Math turns out to be OK, all we have left to worry about is Chemistry."

The 50-minute chapel service proved to be a pleasant interlude. Dr. Creighton's talk focused on the promise the freshman year held for each student. He spoke of developing independence and responsibility as well as preparing for a career. "College is a gift to young people. It's the first time most of you will be responsible to and for yourselves, and you still get summer vacations. Once you graduate, you'll have obligations to others, such as an employer, a spouse, a family. You have duties from which you can't take a vacation any time you'd like. Make the most of your college years," he told them. "Work hard and play hard; enjoy your investment in the life for which you are preparing." When he finished, the room remained quiet for a few moments before the students began gathering their belongings.

"Hmmm," Robin commented as the girls headed for Math. "Creighton made good points. Frannie, I hope you were listening."

At Robin's comment, Frannie dropped back a few steps, and Katie slowed to walk beside her. "You did hear him, didn't you? Everyone is reminding us that college is a transition between childhood and adulthood and that we have to become responsible and independent. Leslie, Robin, and I need you to understand that we can't be responsible for you. Taking care of ourselves is challenge enough. Robin's comments can be rough, but she's right to remind you that you need to grow up. We all do." She patted Frannie's shoulder, then hurried ahead to catch up with Robin and Leslie.

Frannie squared her shoulders. *"I'm as grown up as they are. I'll bet none of them did as well in high school as I did. They think I can't have fun and get good grades, too. Well, they're wrong. I've always had fun and I've always gotten good grades. They'll see. And what's the big deal about waking me up? Mom wakes Dad up, and HE'S an adult!"* She lifted her chin and caught up with the girls. She would show them that she would be just fine.

Their algebra professor, Mr. Elderwood, was tall, handsome, and looked too young to be a college professor. Frannie's suitemates were attentive as he outlined the course and explained his expectations. Frannie thought, *"That's the problem! They're all too serious. They don't know how to relax and have fun. They never heard the wise words, all work and no play... isn't a good thing."*

Frannie passed the class daydreaming about Stephen. *"What do I have to do to make him pay more attention to me. He always has his arm around someone... and I want that someone to be me."*

Robin's "Come on, Frannie," interrupted her daydream. Walking to the cafeteria, Frannie said, "I hate Math, but Mr. Elderwood is cute. If I didn't already have Stephen, I would seriously consider dating him."

Robin groaned, "Good grief Frannie, get real. He's twice our age and probably married with six kids. But you have a point; he's a much better choice than Stephen, that's for sure."

Frannie sighed. "I'm supposed to connect with Missy for lunch. She's going to fill me in on sorority rush. I'll hook up with you at Freshman Seminar.

❦

"I'm excited about Sorority Rush," Missy said, as Frannie set her tray down. "I just know I'll get into Theta Rho Xi. My mother is still an active alum, and that matters a lot."

"Do you think I can get into Theta Rho Xi without any family history?"

"Of course, you can. Someone has to be first in their family to pledge."

"So, tell me what happens during Rush."

"Wellll... this afternoon, everyone interested in pledging meets in the auditorium in Simpson Hall. If you're not in a sorority by your sophomore year, it's pretty much too late. Someone from the Crestmont Sorority Council explains how they enrich your life and contribute to the college. Then everyone breaks into small groups to tour all the houses with a student guide. Our campus is too small for sorority houses. Here, each sorority has its own wing in the upper-class dorm. I think it would be so much more exciting to live in a sorority house than in the dorm."

"I'd like that, too," Frannie agreed. "I wouldn't have to live with someone who picks on me all the time. We'd have a real kitchen and wouldn't be stuck with cafeteria food; home cooking is always better."

Missy rummaged in her constant companion, her dazzling pink and orange bag. "I have the schedule. We register at 2:30 and orientation starts at 3:00."

"I have Freshman Nursing Seminar at 1:00. I hope I'll have time to run back to the dorm and change," said Frannie. "I need to look my best."

<hr />

Frannie caught up with her suitemates and the four set off for Montgomery Hall and the Freshman Nursing Seminar. "I wonder what the seminar is all about." Frannie mused.

"I bet we'll find out when we get there," Robin retorted.

Frannie reminded herself that Robin's problem was that she just didn't know how to have fun.

"I'm kinda looking forward to this," Robin said. "It will be our first peek at the nursing program. I hope it gives us an idea of what it's going to be like. Since it is pass/fail, I hope that means no homework.

"*This could be a good thing for me,*" thought Frannie. *"I've always said I want to be a nurse, but I've never given it much thought. I might learn enough to help me decide one way or the other."*

"Come on in and have a seat." A tall woman greeted the students at the door. "We sit in a circle so that we can engage with one another. I'm Dr. Freda Nunley, Dean of the Crestmont School of Nursing. Welcome to the School of Nursing. My office is on the fourth floor of this building, and my door is always open. To schedule an appointment, call my secretary at extension 400. Do you have any questions for me?"

No hands were raised.

"Then, please meet Ms. Pamela Reynolds, the faculty facilitator for your weekly seminar. She is also the lead professor for the Medical-Surgical Nursing course in the junior year. Before coming to Crestmont, Ms. Reynolds was an intensive care nurse in two of the largest hospitals in Dallas. She has clinical expertise in addition to academic credentials. You'll also meet other nursing faculty throughout the semester. I'll let you get back to your class. I look forward to working with you as you progress in the program." She waved to the students as she left the classroom.

"Good afternoon and welcome to the Freshman Nursing Seminar," began Ms. Reynolds. "We will meet from 1-2 each Wednesday. Each week, we will have a discussion topic. When there is a writing component, I will review it and comment, but I will not grade them. This is a pass/fail course. Your grade will depend upon submitting all your assignments on time and participating in discussions and projects.

"Today our discussion topic will be *you*. Each of you will introduce yourself, tell us where you're from, and why you've chosen the nursing program."

Leslie was the first of the suitemates to speak. "My name is Leslie Jean Bleu. Nurses help others and I like to help people. I chose nursing because it is a profession that will give me a variety of options. I don't know yet if I'm interested in clinical practice or in nursing management, but I'm going to be good at whatever I do. I'm here on an athletic scholarship so I'll have athletic commitments along with my nursing courses. I expect it's going to be a challenging four years."

Frannie leaned toward Leslie and whispered, "You never stop moving your hands when you talk. I think that is just too funny."

"I know. I do it all the time and don't even notice it." Leslie replied. "I'd have to sit on my hands to keep them still."

Robin spoke next. "My name is Robin Hart. I'm from a long line of red-headed Irish immigrants. I want to be a nurse because I have seen so much unhealthy living in the poorer neighborhoods of Chicago, my hometown. I am positive that better healthcare options would make a difference in the community."

Katie stood. "I am Katie Grayfox, from Atoka, Oklahoma. I want to bring better healthcare to the Indian People. I have seen older members of the Choctaw tribe refuse healthcare because they don't trust White doctors and nurses. I hope that more of them will use the clinic when one of their own is a nurse there."

Frannie sat forward in her chair. "My name is Frannie Braun. I'm from Philadelphia. My Nana has multiple sclerosis and I want to be a nurse so that I can help my mom take care of her. Also, when I get married, I will be able to keep my children healthy and take care of them when they get sick." She dropped back in her chair. She didn't hear another word until a male voice interrupted her reverie.

The voice belonged to a tall, stocky young man with a broad smile. "Hi, my name is James Robert Johnson. Everyone calls me J.R."

"He's a teddy bear," Frannie whispered to Katie.

J.R. continued, "I've wanted to be a nurse ever since my younger brother got hit by a car when we were riding our bicycles. A nurse who was driving through Arp, that's the little town in Texas where I'm from, stopped and tried to save his life. A helicopter took him to a Fort Worth hospital, but he didn't survive the trip. No one in my family wanted me to go into nursing, but I know that it's the right thing for me to do."

"I've never known a guy who was interested in nursing," Frannie whispered. "He's such a BIG guy. I'll bet he'll be a great nurse."

The introductions complete, Ms. Reynolds rose. "Thank you, everyone, for sharing a little about yourselves. "Our topic for discussion next week will be *What makes nursing a profession?* I'll see you on Wednesday at 1 pm sharp. Have a good week."

⁕

Frannie and Missy arrived on time to register for sorority orientation. Each of them received a colored card with a number, then sat together in the auditorium, waiting for the meeting to begin at 2:30 among a sea of purple and gold beanies bobbing throughout the room. "Look, Missy, isn't it interesting that most

The Wake-Up Call

of the beanies don't have the coyote facing front? I think that girl picked on us for nothing yesterday."

The sound system boomed, "Welcome Ladies." The student at the podium adjusted the volume. "Welcome, I'm the chair of the Crestmont Sorority Council. The Council manages Sorority Rush. We," motioning to girls standing along the wall on either side of the auditorium, "represent all the sororities on campus. These Council members will be your tour guides. Each sorority is unique, but all sororities encourage academic excellence and active participation in campus events. During Rush, you'll visit each sorority to determine, which one best suits you."

"Some of us already know, which one fits best," Missy whispered to Frannie, "but visiting all of the sororities will be fun."

"Gather your things and find the tour guide with the number that matches the card you were given at registration."

"Later, Gator," Missy said. "I'll try to catch up with you at dinner. I want to hear all about your tour."

Frannie joined seven other girls and followed their guide to a classroom.

"Please take a seat. I'm Cathy Johnson, Cathy with a C. We'll visit all five Crestmont sororities in Kirkwood Hall. A House Guide will provide information about her sorority's history, its focus, and what distinguishes it from the others. I encourage you to ask questions and visit with other sorority sisters. We have 30 minutes for each visit, so make good use of your time.

"Pass these around" Cathy instructed, handing Frannie eight copies of their tour schedule with the name of the House Guide for each sorority. "After our last visit, you'll complete a card indicating your top three sorority preferences. The Selection Committee will compare your selections to the choices they have made to determine your schedule. Tomorrow, stop by the registration table at 2:30 to pick up the tour schedule for the sororities that invite you back. Are there any questions?" No one raised a hand, so Cathy stood. "Then let's get started."

On the way to Kirkwood Hall, the girls chatted among themselves. "I know, which sorority I want," Frannie said. "My friend is going to pledge Theta Ro Xi. Her mother is a Theta Ro alum."

"I've heard that each sorority is considered either social, academic, or service," one girl stated with authority. "Zeta Sigma Upsilon is a party sorority and Phi Zeta Alpha is for nerds."

"I thought that Phi Zeta Alpha was for education majors. I wouldn't call teachers *nerds*."

"That's what the speaker at the orientation meant when she said that each sorority is different," Cathy reminded them. "While you're visiting, be sure to find out what the members themselves think makes their sorority unique. That's as important as what you hear from other people. Remember, a sorority isn't a club you belong to for a little while. For most sorority members, it's a lifetime commitment. For example, once a Theta Rho always a Theta Rho."

Cathy added, "You'll want to make a good impression. While you are interviewing the sorority sisters, they will be assessing you. Ask relevant questions and answer their questions politely. Sororities are picky because they have a limited number of rooms available for new sisters."

"*Of course, Theta Rho Xi is my first choice,*" thought Frannie. *I so want to be with Missy, and she's a shoe-in.*"

Frannie made her choices without hesitation. "*First choice, Theta Rho Xi, of course. Second is Zeta Sigma Upsilon because they have great parties and third is Phi Zeta Alpha because it's the only one left since I'm not interested in a career in music or in being a missionary. Not that #2 or #3 matter, because I want to be a Theta Rho with Missy.*"

Chapter 6

Frannie and Missy made it back to the dorm just in time to join Frannie's suitemates for dinner. "C'mon you two," Robin said. "If we don't leave now, we'll have to stand in line forever, and there won't be a table left with five seats together"

"I'm ready," Frannie replied, stealing one last look in the mirror. Missy, there's a guy in our Freshman Nursing Seminar. It never occurred to me that a guy might want to be a nurse."

"Hmmm… is he gay?" asked Missy.

"I don't know. He didn't say."

Missy said, "Well he wouldn't just come out and *say* it, would he? Did he act gay?" She flipped her wrist and waggled her eyebrows.

Robin whirled on Missy. "Does it matter if he is gay? A person's sexuality is his own business and shouldn't be an issue for other people. Nursing is about taking care of people and he seemed capable of doing that!" She turned around and marched ahead, leaving Frannie and Missy, gaping like fish gulping air.

"What was *that* all about?" Missy asked. "Is it a crime to ask a question?"

"Now you see what I mean? She gets snotty about every little thing I say. The minute I mentioned Stephen, she started in on what a bad person he is." Frannie shrugged her shoulders. "How can you dislike someone you've never even met?"

Carrying their full trays, the five scanned the cafeteria for a table where they could sit together. "Look there," Robin pointed. "Everyone's leaving but Tess and that other girl."

Katie reached the table first. "Mind if we join you?" she asked.

"By all means," Tess replied. "Sam and I are just chatting. We'd love the company. I'm Tess Aikens, a sophomore biology major, and this is Sam Kensington. She's a junior in the nursing program. Sam and I went to high school together in San Antonio."

Leslie said, "That's awesome! It's nice to meet you two. Sam, we haven't met any upperclassmen in the nursing program, except Sally Adams. She's our RA in the dorm. I didn't know you were a science major, Tess. That didn't exactly come up during the Tug of War."

Everyone laughed, then Katie asked, "Sam, what do you find most interesting about the nursing program?"

"I'm excited about taking care of real patients this semester in clinicals. We didn't have much patient contact during the first two years, except for a bit of hands-on care in a nursing home in our sophomore year. We made beds with patients in them. That was a challenge. I bathed a frail, old lady who was very ill. It took me forever, but she was quite tolerant of me. I think she was lonely, and it made me feel especially good that our visit seemed to brighten her day. This year all our classes include clinicals and we'll be in the hospital most of the time. I'm looking forward to the operating room, and maybe a little nervous about it too. We'll spend half days there for two whole weeks."

Robin asked, "Any words of wisdom about our science courses? We have general chemistry this semester and organic next."

"I love chemistry," said Tess. "The sciences are foundational to everything. Chemistry makes sense of how things interact with one another and human biology is a phenomenal exploration. I'm a lab assistant for freshman chem."

The Wake-Up Call

"I have another question for you, Sam," said Leslie "I heard there is a student nurses' organization. I think I'd like to get involved in that."

"It's called TSNA, the Texas Student Nurses Association. The Crestmont University chapter is CU-SNA. Our first meeting is a week from Monday at 1 o'clock. You all should come and check it out. It is a great organization, and I'm secretary this year. Last year the National Student Nurses Association, or NSNA, met in Austin at the same time as the National League of Nurses, the NLN. Being around so many nursing professionals was an amazing experience. The educational sessions were eye-openers. When I'm an RN, I plan to go every year. Keeping up with education and being involved professionally is what makes nursing a career and not just a job.

"Interesting," said Leslie. "I'm positive that I want to belong to CU-SNA, but it's going to be a challenge. I have athletic commitments every afternoon but Wednesday, and they're not negotiable. Can I participate if I can't make the meetings?"

"I can't imagine CU-SNA turning away anyone interested," Sam said. "We'll figure something out. I have to be at the hospital by seven tomorrow morning for my first clinical rotation, and I need to get back and press my uniform. Nice to meet you and see ya 'round campus."

"Frannie, do you want to pop into the Game Room after dinner?" asked Missy.

"Sure. Do any of you want to come with us?" There were no takers.

Tess held Frannie back as the others left to drop off their trays. "I know you like Stephen," she said. "I want you to know that I have no interest in him. Quite honestly, he's not my type. You need to be careful. Get to know him, and don't let his looks fool you. He has a reputation for being a *love 'em and leave 'em* kind of guy, if you know what I mean. You seem like a nice girl, so be careful."

"Uh, OK. Thanks, Tess," was the best Frannie could manage.

"What was that about?" asked Missy.

"Oh, nothing. She just wanted me to know that she wasn't interested in Stephen."

"That's good to know."

Frannie and Missy looked through the window into the Game Room. Frannie pointed to Stephen who was standing with his arms around the shoulders of two girls she didn't recognize. "There he is, Missy. Isn't he just delicious?"

Missy followed her gaze and wondered aloud, "Yes, he's a hunk. Who are those girls with him?"

Frannie said, "I don't know. Probably just friends."

"Ladies first," said J.R., coming up behind them

"Why, thank you," Missy smiled. "Such a gentleman."

"J.R.!" exclaimed Frannie, pulling her eyes from Stephen. "Missy, this is J.R., the guy in our nursing class I told you about. He's from some little town in Texas. J.R., this is Missy. She's from Baton Rouge."

"This is my roommate, Mike Hampton," J.R. offered.

Mike held out a hand. "Nice to meet you," he said, then followed J.R. to the ping pong table.

Missy whispered, "Why don't we hang with them a bit. J.R. is nothing like I imagined. He's a big teddy bear."

Frannie giggled. "That's what I thought when I first saw him, too."

"I love teddy bears," Missy added.

"I'm going to talk with Stephen and check out the action at the dart board. Wanna come?"

"Sure, I'll go with you. You can introduce me to Stephen and his gang. I'll check out J.R. later."

"The one throwing the darts is James. The other one is Greg. I met them the other night."

"Greg is cute."

"Hi, Stephen," Frannie called as they approached.

The Wake-Up Call

"Oh, hey," he replied, his arms still encircling a girl on each side. "Who's this fine Cubby with you?" He looked Missy up and down. He released both girls and put one arm around Frannie and the other around Missy. He winked at Greg.

"Stephen Barton, meet my friend Missy Broussard."

Stephen squeezed Missy's shoulders. "Nice to meet you, Cubby." He maneuvered them all to face the dart board.

Frannie was grateful when Missy wiggled out of Stephen's grasp for a better view of the game. Stephen slid his arm down to Frannie's waist and pulled her in closer.

Frannie was disappointed when Stephen dropped his arm from her waist. "Tough luck, Loser," he said to Greg. "It's you and me for the last round, James. Consider yourself *toast*."

"Frannie," Missy startled her from her fantasies. "I'm going to go check out J.R. Do you want to meet up in about an hour and walk back to the dorm together?"

Frannie answered, "Sure. That would be cool. Come get me when you're ready."

"Wanna play one?" Stephen asked when James walked off, soundly beaten and there was no one left play.

"I haven't played darts much, so other than throwing the dart at that circle, is there anything I should know?"

Stephen stepped behind Frannie and turned her to face the dart board. "Are you right handed or left handed?"

"Right-handed." He placed a dart in her right hand. He stood close enough for her to feel the heat from his body. When he pushed her right hip with his to line her up with the target, it took her breath away.

"Stay focused on the center of the target." He whispered in her ear. He then grasped her right wrist and moved it rhythmically back and forth. "Keep your wrist flexible. Instead of throwing straight at the board, relax your hand and make an arc with the dart so it goes up a bit and comes down to hit the center of the dartboard.

The dart hit the board. Not the wall. Not the floor. Not the ceiling. "Amazing," she said. She was disappointed to hear Stephen say, "That'll do. Let's play." She had hoped that they could stand close to one another a while longer.

Smiling at the memory of his touch, she faced the board, moved her arm back and forth, and let the dart fly. It landed close to the first one. She beamed at her success.

Her smile faded as Stephen moved up, without comment, and announced, "My turn." He threw three darts in rapid succession into the circle adjacent to the center. "That's how you do it, Cubby!" he smirked.

Frannie's next three throws were better than her first three, though Stephen made no comment. Each time Stephen got close enough, she snuggled up to him. Greg and James kept their distance but winked each time they caught Stephen's eye.

Missy approached just as Frannie threw her last dart. "Wow," Missy said. "Not bad! I'm heading back, Frannie. You ready?"

"Well," Frannie hesitated.

Stephen interrupted, "Why don't I walk you both back to Hadley?" Stephen said, "I need to shove off as well."

"Awesome," said Missy, and waved to J.R.

The three left the Game Room, Stephen between the two girls, holding hands with both. Frannie squeezed his hand and moved closer as they walked to Hadley Hall.

On the porch, Missy pulled away. "Thanks, Stephen, she said, then walked to the door.

Frannie stood expectantly, then Stephen leaned down, kissed her lightly on the lips, and bounded down the steps. He called over his shoulder, "See you around, Cubby."

Concentrating on the kiss rather than the departure, Frannie floated over to Missy.

"Oh, Girl, he kissed you!

"Yeeesss, he did," Frannie sighed.

"You two looked like vertical sexy dancers by the dart board. He is pretty hot."

"I had a hard time catching my breath a few times. It was marvelous. That cologne he wears is absolutely intoxicating."

"I expected you two to spend a little more time on the porch. There wasn't anyone else out there, and it's nowhere close to curfew," Missy commented.

"I thought he would stay a little longer, too."

"By the way, Girlfriend, J.R. is a super nice guy. I sure wouldn't mind cuddling up to that teddy bear. Thanks for introducing us."

"For sure," Frannie said, distracted, reliving Stephen's kiss.

Chapter 7

Thursday morning, the four suitemates entered the crowded classroom in Simpson Science Center. "Look there, four empty seats," Leslie pointed toward the back of the room. "Hurry, or we won't get to sit together."

"I've always loved science," Robin commented, settling in between Katie and Leslie, "but teachers can make a huge difference. In high school, I thought biology would be my favorite, but my chemistry teacher was fantastic and my biology teacher turned out to be boring as hell. Thank heaven the boring old bag's tests came straight from the text. Let's hope Dr. Phelps turns out to be interesting."

"I love science too," Leslie volunteered, "but I'm a terrible test-taker. I hope he lets us know what to study."

"We're in this together," Katie said. "We'll study together and we'll all do fine."

Frannie leaned forward in her chair for a better view of a guy she thought might be Stephen sitting near the front of the room. He was engaged in an animated conversation with the girls sitting on either side of him. The buzz of conversation faded as a man in baggy pants and a tweed jacket with suede elbow patches approached the lectern. "Good morning. Welcome to Chemistry 101. I'm Dr. Leroy Phelps, and we're going to have a good time this semester."

"He's old!" Frannie whispered to Leslie, "and he looks like the absent-minded professor from that movie."

Leslie nodded at Frannie's observation, and whispered, "Shhhh, Frannie. Let's just hope he's a good teacher."

"You will need these two textbooks," Dr. Phelps said, holding up *General Chemistry*, a thick book with a red cover, and a smaller text with a soft cover intended for their lab. "There will be a reading assignment for each class. Come prepared so that we can discuss the material. You will have four exams and a final. In lab, you will submit a report on each experiment. There will be three lab exams and a lab final. Your lab reports and all of the tests will comprise your final grade. Do you have any questions?"

For a few moments, the room remained quiet. Dr. Phelps surveyed the room, looking for raised hands. The group of students around the guy Frannie had been watching began talking among themselves.

Dr. Phelps looked in their direction and asked, "Is there something you want to ask?"

"Yes, my roommate told me that you restored a classic Jaguar." Frannie recognized Stephen's voice. "I saw one parked in the faculty lot yesterday, and it was amazing. Is that yours? You actually drive it?"

"Yes, yes, it is. It's a 1951 XK120 Roadster." Dr. Phelps responded. "When I bought it, it was just a memory of the magnificent vehicle it had once been. I've been restoring it for years. All the parts are original, and the upholstery and steering wheel are hand-crafted. I drove it the day it became road-worthy, and I haven't been behind the wheel of another car since. That Jag should last longer than I will."

"Where did you find the parts to restore it?" someone Frannie couldn't see called out.

Dr. Phelps, replied, "Good question. You'd be amazed how hard it is to find original Jaguar parts." The rest of the class fidgeted, wondering how long it would take him to get his class back on track.

After several minutes of animated conversation about the restored Jaguar, Dr. Phelps moved back to the lectern and faced the class. "Well, now, let's get to your first assignment. Read Chapters one and two for next Tuesday's class. Chapter One covers the nature and properties of matter, and Chapter Two covers atomic and molecular structure. On Tuesday, we'll begin with your questions, then proceed with my lecture."

Leslie whispered, "I'm glad he's got the class back on track. I couldn't be less interested in his Jag."

At that moment, Stephen asked, "How long did it take to get the Jag roadworthy?" enticing Dr. Phelps into another lengthy conversation about the restored Jag.

When class was over, Leslie said, "Based on my calculations Dr. Phelps spent half of our lecture time on his stupid Jag. This is going to be a disaster."

Frannie gathered her belongings, intending to catch up with Stephen, but his seat was empty. She sighed and followed her suitemates to lunch. She caught sight of him climbing the steps to the cafeteria, his arms around the two girls who had been sitting beside him in class.

※

"Do you believe that Leeee-Roy Phelps?" Robin said. "I think some of those guys have had him in a course or two before and know just how to get him side-tracked onto that dammed Jag. Chemistry is one of our foundational courses, according to Sam and Tess, and I damn sure don't need it to be hijacked by a friggin' toy car."

Frannie interrupted, "He was kinda cute when he got so excited about his car, like a kid in a candy store. Besides, when he talks about his Jag, we don't have to take notes."

"You just don't get it, you dimwit!" Robin glared at Frannie. "We were in there for two friggin' hours and I have half a page of notes. We have to pass five tests in that class, and I don't think the material is gonna be all that easy to understand on our own. If all he talks about is that idiotic car, how in the hell are we supposed to learn anything?"

Frannie gaped at Robin. "What's so hard about reading a book and taking a test?"

Leslie said, "I was hoping there might be a paper or two instead of just exams. Like I said, I don't do well on tests. If you don't count English, all our courses have final exams, which makes it tough for me. At least English will be a Blue Book essay and I'll have a fighting chance."

"I don't see a single open table," Robin scowled.

Frannie pointed at Missy ahead of them in the line. "I'll go sit with Missy. That will make it easier for you guys to find seats. We need to be at Simpson by 2:30 to pick up our pledge cards and visit the sororities that chose us."

Frannie dropped into the chair Missy had saved for her. "Well, it seems that most of my classmates haven't declared a major either, so we talked a lot about options," Missy began. "Tell me about your classes."

"Not bad so far, Stephen's in my chem class. That's a plus, and I'm hoping we can be lab partners. Chemistry was interesting. Stephen and his friends asked the professor about the Jag he's restored, then kept him talking for an hour out of the two-hour lecture. I hardly had to pay attention or take notes."

"WOW! Missy said. Wish my teachers would talk about their cars instead of the boring stuff they go on and on about."

Look, Stephen is over there," Frannie pointed to him sitting with his gang. "I thought he might have waited to have lunch with me, or at least saved me a seat at his table."

"Well, maybe he'll be your lab partner," Missy said with a wink.

"I've been wondering how to make that happen. We don't have our first lab until next week, so I'll keep you posted. Finish your lunch, I can't wait to see us on the list for Theta Rho Xi. It will be wonderful to pledge together."

"You got that right, Girlfriend," Missy said. "Let's go."

They gave their names to the girl at the sorority registration desk in Simpson Hall. "Here you go," she said and held out an envelope for each of them.

"My hands are shaking so much, I can't open the envelope," Frannie said.

"Mine, too," Missy laughed. "Let's do it together on the count of three. 1…, 2…"

On 3, they both tore open their envelopes. "Wow!" cried Missy, reading the card inside. "Theta's my first visit. When do you meet with the Theta's?"

Frannie stood silent, her shoulders slumped, staring at her card in dismay. "Theta Rho Xi isn't on my list at all. How can that be?"

Missy hesitated, then forced a smile. "We can be in different sororities and still spend lots of time together. Maybe one of the others is the best for a nursing major. Come on. Let's get a seat and hear what comes next."

Frannie, still despondent, followed Missy into the auditorium. She couldn't take her eyes off the list that should have made her whoop with joy. Missy tapped her arm. "You're not listening. They're explaining the process for today."

With little enthusiasm, Frannie joined the group led by "Cathy with a C" who said, "Good. We're all here. Today, you'll have an hour to spend with each sorority on your list. You'll visit with the sisters so you can ask all your questions. They will have lots of questions for you, too. Only one of your two choices can invite you to join, so make a good impression."

Frannie lagged behind her group.

"Our first sorority, Phi Zeta Alpha, is my sorority," Cathy announced. "I'm glad that it was the first choice for some of you."

"*Yeah, great,*" grumbled Frannie. "*My last choice is somehow first on my list. Go figure. I guess the good part is that it's Cathy's*

The Wake-Up Call

sorority and she seems OK. She's in nursing, too. That's probably why they picked me."

Cathy continued, "Phi Zeta is considered an academic sorority, but that doesn't mean we don't have lots of fun. After all, a sorority is a sisterhood, and if we can't enjoy our sisters, what would *that* say about a sorority.

When they reached the Phi Zeta wing on the second floor, Cathy introduced an upperclassman. "Girls, I'd like you to meet Suzy. She's our House Guide for your tour today. Suzy's a junior and our RA on the Phi Zeta Alpha wing."

"Thanks, Cathy. You all know this is Cathy "Cathy with a C, right? We have four Cathys in our sorority, so that's important information." Suzy continued. "Phi Zeta emphasizes academic excellence, and we help each other as much as possible. We welcome all majors, but most of us are in nursing, science, or math. We've been accused of being the sorority for geeks, but we don't see ourselves that way. Our mission is to become wholesome, capable, independent women."

"What do you guys do for fun?" asked one of the pledges.

"We host parties throughout the year, sometimes with Zeta Xi Tau, our brother fraternity. You can invite your boyfriends, even if they don't belong to Zeta Xi. Guests are welcome as long as they are invited by a sister or brother. Last year, the float we built with Zeta Xi for the Homecoming parade took second place. Our floats have won a prize for the last ten years, at least." She paused. "You must have questions for me?"

"How much does it cost to join this sorority?"

"It doesn't cost any extra to live on the Phi Zeta wing, but our sorority dues are $100 a year. Spending money on Phi Zeta paraphernalia is up to you. It's hard to resist buying things with the sorority logo."

Another hand went up. "What about everyday stuff, like, do you sit together in the cafeteria?"

"We have different schedules, but we do tend to hang together when we can. That doesn't mean that your friends who aren't Phi Zeta's aren't welcome. We're not snobs."

"Who makes the decisions about what the sorority does?"

"A sorority is an organization, much like a business. We have officers, committees, and meetings. We even have bylaws. Every sister must attend at least 75 percent of our weekly meetings. We vary the day and time so that sisters who work or have evening commitments can meet the requirement."

"How do you get to be an officer?"

"In the spring, we have a call for nominations. You can nominate yourself or someone else, but every nominee must meet the criteria before she can be on the slate. Voting is by secret ballot. The winners are announced on June 1. The new officers appoint committee chairs and the chairs select their committee members, and by the time the Fall semester begins, everything is in order."

"Can anyone run for office?" the same girl asked.

"Every candidate must have at least a 2.5-grade point average and have must have attended no less than the required number of meetings. A candidate for President must have held at least one other office for a full term. The secretary must have good English skills and produce the meeting minutes in a timely fashion. Our treasurer needs to be able to balance a checkbook," Suzy grinned. "That's always a good skill for a treasurer to have, don't you think? Each sister is expected to serve on a committee and to participate in our community activities. My favorite is the Halloween party that we host for two local orphanages."

Cathy stood. "Suzy, let's give the girls a chance to wander around and talk to the sisters. Girls, meet back here in 30 minutes. Please don't be tardy. We want to have as much time for you to visit with Zeta Sigma Upsilon as you had here at Phi Zeta."

At 3:00, Cathy led the girls up the center stairwell to the Zeta Sigma Upsilon wing on the third floor. *"I'm glad our suite in Hadley is on the first floor,"* Frannie thought. *"Trudging up and down these stairs is a drag. The elevators in both dorms are no bigger than a broom closet and move like a slug on a hot summer day."*

Sandy, the Zeta Sigma Upsilon House Guide, handed each of the girls a huge round sucker with ZSU in bold letters. "Welcome to Zeta Sigma Upsilon. We call ourselves the Zeta Ups because

The Wake-Up Call

we're always upbeat about what's happening on the Crestmont campus. We host a social event every two weeks with Zeta Delta Zeta, our brother fraternity."

Frannie perked up a bit. *"Good and more like it. This will be my first choice since I can't be a Theta Rho with Missy."*

"The Christmas Gala is held each year in December and everyone gets to dress up in their finest, with girls in long formal dresses and oh so handsome boys wear tuxes. Zeta Ups are the best and I hope you get to be with us."

Thirty minutes later, the group returned their preference cards to Cathy. Frannie had no problem recording her choice.

※

Dr. Bennett returned each student's essay at the beginning of English class on Friday as she took attendance. Frannie unfolded hers and stared at the red *C* in disbelief, then noticed writing in red at the bottom of the page.

Ms. Braun,

While you have a good command of grammar and an adequate vocabulary, your essay fell short of my expectations. First, it is reminiscent of high school prose and does not rise to the level of maturity expected of college students. You convey the "what" quite well; however, notable in its absence is the "so what" that would explain why it matters. At this level, the effect of events is more important than a mere description of the events.

Frannie read the note twice. Her look of consternation caught Robin's attention and she whispered. "What's the matter?"

"This makes no sense," she insisted, shoving the paper toward Robin. "How can she say I write well, then give me a *C*? She says right here that my grammar and vocabulary are good. That's what an essay is all about, right?"

"Not really. In college, they expect that we've mastered the English language. College essays are about how we think and interpret the world around us. You need to explore what things mean, not just describe them. If you ask yourself *why* or *so what* when you're thinking about what to write, you'll be on the right track."

"Thanks, Robin," said Frannie, pleased that Robin hadn't brushed her off with a snarky comment. "Why didn't she just say that?"

※

That afternoon, Frannie waited on the steps of Simpson Hall for Missy, purposefully avoiding eye contact with an upperclassman who was making a student recite the school chant. Frannie held up her crossed fingers when Missy arrived. They hurried inside and retrieved their envelopes from the registration table.

"Okay. On the count of three like yesterday," Missy said. *"1… 2… 3…."* and they ripped open their envelopes. Missy whooped, "I'm IN! I'm a Theta Rho! I can't wait to call Mom." Her smile faded when she looked up at the silent Frannie. "What's wrong?"

"Nothing." Frannie sighed. "Not one sorority invited me to join." She looked up at Missy. "This letter says that if I'm still interested in joining a sorority, I'm welcome to participate in Rush Week next year. That's it."

Missy opened her mouth, then closed it. She could think of nothing to say to make Frannie feel better.

With a forced smile for Missy, Frannie said, "You call your Mom with the good news. She'll be proud of you."

Missy watched Frannie make her way slowly down the steps.

On the verge of tears, Frannie almost missed the voice from behind her. "Hey Coyote Baby, recite the school song."

Frannie stopped, took a shaky breath, and started to recite the first stanza. When her voice cracked, she nearly burst into tears. She turned toward the upperclassman and began again.

The Wake-Up Call

"Wait. It's Frannie, isn't it? You look like someone died. What happened?"

Frannie recognized Sam, Tess's friend from the cafeteria. Her voice faltered and a tear trickled down her cheek. "I - I didn't get picked for a sorority. Not a single one invited me."

"Oh Sweetie," Sam said with a sigh, "Is that all? You're in the majority. Only 25% of those who rush get an invitation. The 75% who don't are still pretty darn good folks. Dry your eyes. Believe me, this is nothing to cry about."

"Come sit with me a minute," Sam said, shepherding Frannie to a bench beside the path. "There's nothing wrong with sororities. They do lots of good work, and sorority sisters often become lifetime friends, but sororities aren't for everyone. A better bet might be the CU-SNA that we talked about at dinner. That's a fantastic organization that participates in some of the same community activities that the sororities do, and you'll have lots more in common with those women. Besides, once you get to your junior year, the nursing program will leave you precious little free time for sorority activities. By then, you'll be thankful that you didn't join one."

"Thanks, Sam. You made me feel better," Frannie admitted. "I wanted Theta Rho Xi. My friend Missy was sure to get in since her mother is an alum. They didn't invite me back. Then neither of the two I *did* visit wanted me either."

"When you put it that way, you just make yourself feel awful. The reality is that sororities only have a few slots to fill, and they choose candidates like Missy who have connections."

"That makes sense. Thanks, Sam." Frannie leaned forward. "Tell me about the nursing program. You like it, don't you?"

"Yes, absolutely! But, I have to admit that I had a rocky start. I was a great student in high school and it was a big surprise to find that the college math and science courses were harder than I expected. I couldn't believe it when I got *C's* my first semester. My grades got better when I buckled down and learned to study. I'm pleased to tell you that I've been on the honor roll since the second semester of my freshman year. The studying was worth it.

Upper-level courses are easier when you have a good foundation and good study skills. I hope you're taking your classes seriously and studying hard."

"I got all *A's* in high school, too. How different can college be?"

Sam sat up a bit straighter. "Frannie, college is nothing like high school. If you wait too long to figure that out, it'll be too late."

Frannie started to ask another question, but Sam said, "Frannie, I am going to be late if I don't move along. Just remember, sororities aren't all there is to campus life and don't forget what I said about studying. I promise you it's worth it."

Frannie gave Sam a little finger wave, "Thanks, Sam," she murmured as she watched her walk away.

"So, now what?" thought Frannie. *"Even if Sam was right about sororities, where do I go to make friends? Missy will be tied up with her new sorority sisters, and I don't know anyone else who's fun to be with. Robin is mean; Leslie is all about sports, and Katie is all about studying."*

Frannie walked the length of the oval to a shaded bench and stared at the oversized Coyote perched permanently in the center of the fountain, then continued to the dorm.

"Frannie?" Robin said, without looking up. "How'd the sorority thingy go?"

When Frannie didn't answer, Robin looked up. "Frannie?"

"Well…" she began, not as certain of her feelings as when she'd left Sam. "Well… it was pretty awful." Frannie collapsed onto her bed.

"Awful? What the hell happened?" Robin crossed the room to sit next to Frannie. "You look like you're about to cry."

Frannie took a deep breath, resolute. "I'm not going to cry. I didn't get into *any* sorority. Not one of them invited me."

"Those shitheads!" Robin declared. "That is so totally wrong, they think they're better than anyone!" Hearing Katie and Leslie return, she raised her voice. "Guys, do you know what those sorority shits did? They dissed Frannie! They didn't invite her to join any of their friggin' little cliques. What a bunch of turds!"

The Wake-Up Call

Robin's defense both delighted and surprised Frannie.

"Oh, my word Frannie," Katie said. "I know how important it was to you."

"To hell with them!" Robin continued. "We'll make our own sorority. We'll be the Nurseketeers …just us four."

All three girls gaped at Robin.

Leslie found her voice first. "Robin, what a fantastic idea. We are the four Nurseketeers. I love it." She pumped her fist into the air. "One for all and all for one!"

Katie gave Leslie a high five. "Right on!"

"You are all wonderful," Frannie said, standing to join them. "I love the idea of us being the Nurseketeers. Thank you. I met Tess's friend, Samantha, on the way back and she explained that it's hard to get into a sorority if you don't have a personal connection like Missy does."

"They should make that clear from the beginning," Robin said, "so you know what to expect. Those bitches don't care how they make other people feel."

"Sam also said that nursing students don't have time for sororities, and the CU-SNA is a better fit."

"Wise woman, this Sam," Robin said.

"She said she was an *A* student in high school, and when she got to Crestmont, her first semester grades weren't very good. She learned how to study and made the honor roll the next semester. I can do that!"

Katie's look quelled Robin's comment.

"Missy won't have time for me anymore since she's a Theta Ro. She'll be all involved with her new sisters, and we were just getting to know each other."

"That's not fair, Frannie," Katie admonished. "Missy was always going to be a sorority girl. There was never any doubt about that."

Leslie added, "Sororities are a social system, Frannie. The counselor at my high school told me I shouldn't even think about joining one, especially if I had other commitments like athletics and nursing."

"Sam said that, too," Frannie replied.

"Frannie, if you actually heard Sam say that you should study if you don't want to flunk out of school, then she's your new guru," Robin pointed out.

Leslie and Katie burst out laughing. "Robin, one way or another, you definitely get your point across. But, since it's a good point, we should all listen." Katie said.

"I get it," Frannie acknowledged. I'll study with you, but I am still going to date Stephen when he asks me out. Good students can have a social life, too."

"You idiot!" Robin stood, marched into the bathroom, and slammed the door.

Frannie stared after her, speechless, then stammered, "W-What…."

"She's disappointed," Katie said, taking a seat next to Frannie. "When you were talking about Sam and about studying, it sounded like you understood that we all have to take college seriously if we're going to succeed.

"But I do…" Frannie protested.

"We'll see. Talking about it is only the first step. What you *do* about it is the important part. Insisting that your social life comes first didn't give the impression that you understand."

Chapter 8

After dinner, Frannie and Missy went to the Game Room together for Frannie's game night date. "I hope Stephen will ask me out for a real date, like to the movies, or bowling, or anything where we'd be alone. I don't like hanging out with his friends. Besides, his hands belong on me, not on all those other girls."

"I get that girlfriend. I wouldn't mind getting J.R. alone for a bit."

"Wouldn't it be cool to double date?"

"Right on!" said Missy and high-fived Frannie.

Stephen stood by the pool table laughing with James and Greg. They stopped abruptly as the girls approached.

"They act like they were laughing at us," Missy commented, then pointed. "There's J.R. by the foosball table. I'll see you later."

By the time Frannie reached Stephen, James and Greg were engrossed in a game of pool. "Hey Frannie, how ya doing?" Stephen said, taking her hand, and pulling her close. "Let's get a *Coke*?"

They walked out of the Game Room, Frannie unaware of Greg and James' laughter that followed them. Stephen slid coins into the machine and pulled out two *Cokes*. Frannie hesitated but decided not to mention that she preferred *Dr. Pepper*. She was alone with him and that was enough. They sat on a couch nearby and Stephen draped his arm around her shoulders.

"You know Frannie, I like being with you," Stephen said and nuzzled her ear.

"Me, too," she replied, nestling into his arm. "Me, too. I saw you in my Chemistry class today."

"Oh, didn't see you. I needed to pick up a science course," Stephen explained. "A guy in pre-med told me how easy it is to get Phelps side-tracked by asking him about his Jag. Once he gets started, he forgets about the lecture. That sounded like just the course for me"

"Won't it make the course harder if he doesn't cover the material that's on his tests. That's what my roommates are worried about."

"Ah, that's just a load of bull shit. How hard can a freshman Chem course be, right?"

"I'm just as glad not to have to take notes for two hours. We can be lab partners. Wouldn't that be fun?"

"Well…" He hesitated "Sure. I am good with that." He stood, pulling Frannie up with him, and turned in the direction of the bookstore. "I need a new t-shirt. The one I wore at the Tug of War got ripped."

"Wonderful. I love shopping!"

Stephen picked up a shirt at random. "This one will do," He announced. "We're outa here."

"Oh, no! Not that one. It's all wrong for your skin tone and eye color."

Stephen stared as if she'd dropped in from Mars. "What?" he stammered. "What does *that* have to do with anything?"

She prowled through the bins, then held up a light blue shirt with a purple and yellow coyote on the front. "This one is perfect!" Holding it up to his chest confirmed her decision. "Yes. This one was made for you."

He rolled his eyes, then laughed, "OK, OK. Let's get out of here."

They left the bookstore holding hands and Frannie said, "It's nice to be alone with you."

"Hmmm..." Stephen looked around, then kissed her quickly on the lips. "Come on," he said. "I need to get back to play the winner of the next round."

Disappointed, she clutched his hand and followed. She watched him win game after game of pool, touching her lips and smiling at the memory of the kiss.

Missy tapped her shoulder. "J.R. is going to walk me back to Hadley. I'll see you tomorrow."

Frannie nodded. "Have fun," and waved as they left.

Before Stephen could start a new game, Frannie grasped his arm. "Stephen, it's getting late," she said and motioned to the clock.

Stephen hesitated, then caught Greg's eye. "Be my guest," he said handing Greg his cue stick. His arm encircled Frannie's shoulders and he pulled her close. Leaning down he whispered, "How about I walk you back to the dorm... the long way?"

A smile lit Frannie's face. "OK."

"Later, guys," he called over his shoulder, winking at Greg. James gave him a thumbs-up and a Cheshire cat smirk.

Stephen stopped at the fountain at the end of the oval and pulled Frannie into an embrace. His sensual kiss left her breathless and she nearly missed Stephen's question.

"How about a movie tomorrow night? The new flick *Patton* is showing, and I wanna see it."

"Uh...movies?" She stammered, "tomorrow night?". "I'd love to," she blurted. "I'd love to go with you."

"Super. Meet me in front of Hadley at 6:30. That'll give us time to get good seats."

They walked back to the dorm holding hands. Frannie thinking about what to wear on her first real date with Stephen. There was time to sit on the porch and visit, but when they reached the top step, Stephen pulled Frannie into an embrace and kissed her again, a kiss as intense as the one by the fountain. Without another word, he turned and hustled down the steps.

❦

Barb pulled up to the curb in front of Hadley Hall at nine o'clock on Saturday morning. The four girls piled into her car, Frannie, Robin, and Katie in the back seat, and Leslie in the front.

"We'll get to see a lot before it gets too hot," Barb suggested. "By the time we get to Neiman's, we'll appreciate the air conditioning."

Robin said, "I hope it doesn't mess up your plans, but I need to get back to the dorm by 2:30 so I can change and make it to work by 3:00."

"And I have a date tonight with Stephen," Frannie reminded everyone.

"No problem, Guys. I'll show you around, then we'll get a bite to eat. It would be neat to have lunch at the Neiman Marcus restaurant, but that costs about as much as a semester's tuition. There's a good sandwich shop near where we'll park the car. Their sandwiches are big enough that three of them will feed all five of us."

"I'm looking forward to today's adventure," said Katie. I grew up not too far from here, but I've only been to Dallas to visit relatives. I've never been downtown."

"I'm going to park behind the School Book Depository. That's where Lee Harvey Oswald was when he shot President Kennedy. We can see the window where a reporter saw Oswald's rifle from Dealey Plaza across the street. The grassy knoll is right beside the building. Dealey Plaza is called the birthplace of Dallas because the first house in town was built there. Now it's a gorgeous city park in the middle of the hustle and bustle of downtown."

They were downtown and parked in less than 20 minutes. They crossed Elm Street to stand in Dealey Plaza and gaze solemnly

The Wake-Up Call

at the infamous window on the sixth floor of the famous Book Depository. Even though they'd been young, each girl remembered exactly where she was when she heard the news of President Kennedy's assassination.

They moved on to the charming Old Red Court House. "The actual Court moved into a new building just a few years ago," Barb commented. "Right now, it's standing empty. Isn't it a gorgeous building."

"It looks like the Enchanted Castle from Disneyland," exclaimed Frannie, "except it's red. Philadelphia has lots of historical buildings. My favorite is Independence Hall where the Liberty Bell lives."

Behind the courthouse, they entered the 30-foot high walls of the Kennedy Memorial that seemed to float above the ground. Inside, the sounds of downtown faded away. The golden letters of the name *John Fitzgerald Kennedy* glowed with captured sunlight. "It's gorgeous," whispered Frannie, and everyone agreed. Circles decorated the walls. "It makes me feel like the room is round instead of square," mused Frannie. "What an interesting monument."

Walking down Commerce Street, Frannie pointed toward the sky. "Look, up there" and they marveled at the famous flying red neon horse sitting atop the 29-story Magnolia Hotel.

"That horse has been a Dallas landmark since 1934," Barb told them. "I've heard that, when you fly into Dallas at night, the pilot always points it out to the passengers. In the dark, the horse actually looks like it's flying." Then Barb pointed to a seven-story white building that took up the whole block between Commerce and Main. "That's Neiman Marcus."

"It's HUGE," Frannie said, amazed. "It's bigger than Wanamaker's, and I thought *that* was the biggest department store in the world. When I was about six, I got lost in there. My mother didn't notice when I stopped to look at a lady in a beautiful dress. I thought she was real. I pulled on her dress to get her attention, and she almost fell over. That scared me to death! I jumped back and reached for my mother, but she wasn't there. I started running around in circles, screaming. It was quite a show. For a while, I wouldn't let go of Mom's hand any time we went into a store." Frannie laughed, "Fortunately, I got over that since I spend a lot of time in stores now."

The girls walked through Neiman's, enjoying the air-conditioning, and marveling at the upscale merchandise. "I have to try on something special for my date with Stephen tonight."

"Rich bitch," Robin muttered under her breath. "The prices here are out of sight. Someday shopping will be more than a spectator sport for me."

"I'll be right beside you," Leslie murmured, and Katie nodded her agreement. "It's quite an experience. Barb, thanks so much for sharing Dallas with us. We've had a wonderful time. Where did you say we're going for lunch?"

"After I try something on," Frannie insisted. "Look at this darling dress. The color goes with the shirt that Stephen just bought. It would be perfect for tonight. I hope it fits."

"Even if it doesn't, your sales lady will find something just right for you," Barb explained. "That's what I meant about the service here. It's unbelievable."

The girls followed Frannie to the dressing room. A sale woman took the dress and ushered Frannie inside, saying, "I believe that this might be a bit too large for you, Dear. Perhaps I can find your size or something else that would be perfect. Did you say this was for a special occasion?"

"You weren't kidding about service." Katie marveled. Leslie nodded and Robin shook her head, disgusted at Frannie's obvious inability to set priorities.

After the saleswoman had carried several different garments into the dressing room, Frannie emerged. "This will be perfect for tonight. I'm glad I thought to bring my checkbook with me. I'll be ready in a sec and we can go to lunch."

They walked back to the car, Frannie skipping, and going on and on about her new dress. "Enough already!" Robin said. "Not all of us have unlimited free time and a bottomless bank account. Have you ever considered penciling *studying* into your

The Wake-Up Call

busy social calendar? And, while we're on the subject, a new shirt isn't going to turn a loser into Prince Charming. You're an airhead who's head over heels in love with a bad actor."

Deflated, Frannie pouted in silence.

"Here's the sandwich shop I mentioned," Barb announced. "Shall we have lunch?"

Robin looked to Katie and Leslie for confirmation. "Sounds like a plan."

"Do you think they have a Philly cheesesteak?" Frannie asked.

"No clue," answered Barb, "but we can ask."

There was no Philly cheesesteak. Barb ordered three different sandwiches and had them cut into fourths. "So," Barb said while they waited. "I know that Leslie grew up helping in her folks' grocery store like I did. What about you, Katie? What did you do growing up?"

Katie hesitated, not sure where to start or how much to share. "My folks have a farm in Atoka, Oklahoma. My older brothers and my dad do most of the farm work, but I had chores like gathering eggs, milking the cows, and tending our garden. I knew from the time I was little that I'd be going to college, so chores and homework always came before play. Farming's hard and my folks wanted me to have other choices." Katie decided that was enough. They'd learn more about one another as their relationships developed.

Barb turned to Frannie. "So, how about you?"

Frannie opened her mouth, then realized she didn't have anything specific to tell. "Well..." she hesitated. "When I was little, my Nana came to live with us because she has multiple sclerosis and it was hard for her to live alone. I spent time with her every day. And my brother Petey is the best brother in the world. He's five years older than me and he always took me everywhere with him. His friends never minded. I've never had a babysitter in my life."

The girls waited expectantly, but Frannie didn't know what else to say. "What about high school?" Barb asked. "Did you have a boyfriend?"

Frannie brightened. "Not a special boyfriend. My friends and I did things together, like going to the movies and dances at school. Nearly every weekend someone would have a party with music and dancing. I had a date for the prom every year, but he wasn't really a boyfriend."

"So, you've never had a job and you didn't do chores at home," Robin summarized with disappointment. "That explains a lot. Maybe it's time to grow up, huh, Roomie?"

Before Frannie could formulate a reply, Katie exclaimed, "Look at the time. We've got to get moving if Robin's going to make it to work. Barb, thanks so much for today."

Frannie had been primping for her Saturday night date with Stephen ever since they'd gotten back from their excursion. She made time for dinner with Leslie and Katie to be sure that her stomach didn't rumble during the movie. She was waiting on the porch when Stephen pulled up to Hadley Hall in his roommate's 1968 red Mustang. He waved to her. She waved back, and when he didn't open his door, she started down the steps. She stopped at the curb, expecting him to get out and open the car door for her. He didn't, so she walked around and opened the door herself.

She wore her new outfit and was disappointed that he wasn't wearing his new shirt. She'd brought a light sweater because she always got chilly in air-conditioned movies and restaurants

"Your car is super!"

"Well, it isn't mine, but I can get it any time I want."

"I feel like royalty in this car."

"You are. You're my princess." Then he pulled away from the curb and peeled out of the oval.

They didn't have far to go, but she liked riding in the red mustang. When Stephen pulled into a parking space behind the movie, Frannie waited to see if he would come around to open her door. He didn't.

The Wake-Up Call

Stephen announced, "C'mon Frannie, the ticket line is longer than I expected. Hurry up," he called over his shoulder as he walked ahead of her toward the end of the line.

She grabbed her small purse and threw the strap over her shoulder, then hurried to catch up to him. He grabbed her hand and pulled her along until they reached the end of the line.

Suddenly she remembered, *"My sweater! Oh well. Maybe I won't need it if Stephen puts his arm around me."* The line, though long, moved quickly and soon they were inside, tickets in hand. Stephen bought a *Coke* for each of them, and one large popcorn to share.

"I prefer Dr. Pepper *to Coke. I wish he'd ask me."* Frannie picked up a stack of napkins and her *Coke* and hurried to keep up with Stephen who was marching down the corridor.

Frannie liked sitting towards the middle of the theater. However, Stephen went no further than the back row where, he climbed over one couple and settled into a middle seat. Frannie shrugged, excused herself, and followed. By the time the preview of coming attractions had ended, their popcorn was nearly gone. Frannie had helped herself to two handfuls.

Stephen wadded up the empty popcorn sack and threw it on the floor. *"That's rude,"* thought Frannie. *"Well, maybe here in Texas the ushers take care of the trash between shows."*

The cold drink made Frannie shiver. Stephen didn't notice. She inched a little closer to him. What's wrong?" he asked.

"I left my sweater in the car and I'm cold."

"Hmmm, I can fix that." With a wolfish grin, he put his arm around her and pulled her toward him. He rested his hand lightly on her chest and moved his fingers slowly back and forth along the top of her breast. Frannie leaned into him, no longer shivering, mesmerized by his touch. Frannie lost interest in the movie. She breathed rapidly, aware only of how Stephen's caresses made her feel.

Stephen leaned in to kiss her, shifting his position to place his other hand on her leg just above her knee. *"He tastes like popcorn and Coke,"* she thought, as he parted her lips with his tongue. His right hand inched a bit higher on her thigh, his fingers caressing the skin under her short skirt. The delightful sensations sparked by Stephen's touch were new to Frannie. In the crowded theater, she was alone with her Prince Charming.

A series of artillery blasts boomed from the screen, startling them both. Frannie bolted upright and tugged her skirt into place. Stephen returned his hand to her shoulder and settled the other onto the armrest. They watched the screen until the credits begin to roll.

Stephen pulled her close and whispered, "I know a place we can sit and talk without the gunfire to interrupt us."

With a glance at her watch, Frannie said, "We don't have much time left. It's getting close to curfew."

"We have time," Stephen insisted.

Frannie nodded, remembering his touch. He pulled her to her feet and hurried her out to the car. He unlocked her door, then let himself in, leaving Frannie to fend for herself. He drove to a cemetery not far from the school.

"I don't think I am supposed to feel this good when a guy touches me. My parents would be upset if they knew where Stephen put his hand. I should be ashamed, but it felt marvelous."

After hiding the bright red car in a stand of trees, Stephen reached across the console to pull Frannie into an embrace. "Let's sit in the back seat so there's no stick shift between us."

"Stephen. There's barely 15-minutes left to curfew. I can't be late."

Stephen sighed and reached across the console to pull her close. Frannie leaned into his kiss and put both arms around his neck. He stroked her back and eased her blouse from her skirt. His tongue parted her lips and with one practiced pinch, he unclasped her bra and caressed the softness of her breast. Frannie was lost in glorious, unfamiliar sensations as her entire body responded to his touch.

For a moment she opened her eyes and the clock on the dashboard filled her vision: 10:55. She bolted upright, dread crowding out pleasure. "Stephen, the time! We have five minutes to get me back to the dorm! Hurry. I can't be late!"

Disgruntled, Stephen settled back into his seat, leaving Frannie to deal with her disheveled condition. "You'll be on time. That clock is a few minutes fast."

Stephen slowed to a stop in front of Hadley Hall just moments before 11. Frannie didn't wait for him to open her door. She grabbed her sweater and purse, then adjusted her skirt. Stephen pulled her into an embrace and kissed her as urgently as he had in the car. He whispered, "Next time, Frannie."

Frannie floated through the door to the suite to find Katie and Leslie laughing so hard they were holding their sides and crying. A huge bowl of popcorn sat between them, untouched, steam rising from the kernels. "What's so funny?" Frannie asked. "You two are a riot."

Between bouts of laughter, Leslie told the story. "You know the popcorn popper I brought from home? Katie and I got the brilliant idea we could use the heating element to melt marshmallows for s'mores, so, we walked to Barb's dad's Market and got all the stuff we needed. We put the marshmallows on the forks Mama packed and heated up the popper."

Leslie dissolved into giggles, so Katie picked up the story. "The idea was pretty good and we started toasting. Both marshmallows caught on fire at the same time, and when we tried to blow them out, the melting goo dripped on the burner and caught fire. The flames were shooting up and it smelled awful. We got the fire out and opened the windows in both bedrooms Then we tried to fan the smoke and the smell outside. You wouldn't believe the mess we had to clean up, and we never did eat a single s'more."

Leslie added, "We decided that popcorn was the best use for a popcorn popper."

"Want some popcorn?" Katie asked, "And you should tell us about your date."

Frannie grabbed a handful of popcorn and plopped into her chair. "He took me to see *Patton,* the show everyone was talking about it. It was almost three hours long, but it was marvelous. Stephen put his arm around me to keep me warm because I left my sweater in the car." She decided to keep the rest of the details of the evening to herself. She needed time to remember each moment and think about the feelings she had never felt before.

Robin came in from work just in time to hear Frannie's report. "Frannie, listen to me," she insisted. "I have something important to tell you and when you hear it, you'll believe me when I say that Stephen is a jerk-wad."

Frannie stared at Robin, not knowing what to expect.

"Stephen had a date with another girl before he picked you up this evening. He brought some blonde to dinner at Rob Rory's. That is so unacceptable. You need to think twice about giving that two-timing dick head the time of day."

Frannie knew there had to be a reasonable explanation. "It couldn't have been a date, Robin. It just isn't right to jump to conclusions. We had such a wonderful evening. I just know he's not interested in anyone else."

"Don't you get it, Frannie? That friggin' turd only has one thing on his mind and that is to get into your panties. Once he gets what he wants, he'll have nothing to do with you. You've heard of *love 'em and leave 'em*, right?" Robin took a deep breath and shook her head when she saw how hard Frannie was trying *not* to believe her. She shrugged her shoulders, then slammed the bedroom door behind her.

Frannie remembered that Tess had said the same thing. Then she burst into tears. "She is *wrong*. Stephen isn't like that. He cares about me. Robin says things like that just to upset me. Why does she say things that aren't true? Maybe she is jealous because I have a boyfriend."

"Frannie," Leslie offered, "I doubt Robin is jealous. Perhaps she is a bit harsh, but she is trying to protect you. She did see him with another girl just minutes before his date with you. That's significant to me. I'm surprised you don't think so. I can't imagine my thinking it's OK if Paul did something like that, and I know Paul a lot better than you know Stephen"

Katie squeezed Frannie's shoulders, "Why don't you wash your face and we'll call it a night. You can take time to think this through."

"Katie, she's wrong. Stephen must have had a good reason for being with that girl at the restaurant." Still sniffling, Frannie went into the bathroom. When she came out, she was grateful to have the sitting area to herself. She replayed the conversation, still wanting to believe that she was right about Stephen. The things she couldn't ignore were the similar words that Tess had used, and how Katie and Leslie kept defending Robin. "*They're all wrong.* "*They don't know him so they couldn't possibly know what he's like.*"

When Frannie pushed open her bedroom door, Robin was in bed, facing the wall. Frannie changed into pajamas and got in bed without a word, thinking about her wonderful evening, the way Stephen kissed her, and how his touch sent delightful sensations throughout her whole body.

Chapter 9

"Frannie, hurry up! If you're not ready when we leave for breakfast, you can meet us there," Robin called loud enough for Frannie to hear over the shower. "We're leaving in 30 minutes."

"I'm almost done. Don't leave without me." Frannie turned off the water. "My outfit is laid out, so it won't take me long to get ready."

"I hope we don't spend two hours listening to *jag talk* in Chem today," Leslie said. "I read the assignment through twice and I'm still not sure I get it. Phelps needs to explain that stuff in class or I'll be in big trouble."

"One thing's for sure," replied Katie. "We need to study together as much as possible. It helps that we're good at different subjects. I have to get good grades. My folks worked hard to get me here and I intend to make them proud of me. A good study routine is important."

"I've got to maintain a 2.5 to keep my scholarship," added Leslie. "I've always had to work hard for my grades so I'm on board with a study routine."

The Wake-Up Call

"A college degree is my ticket out," exclaimed Robin. "Nothing is going to get in the way of good grades for me, even if it means that all I ever get to do is work and study."

"Ticket out of where?" asked Leslie.

"My old life. I grew up in the dumps in Chicago," Robin explained. "Before I left, I realized what a bunch of losers my friends at home are... *were*. I went to say goodbye to them and ended up walking away for good. They couldn't have cared less that I was leaving. Gram put all she had into making sure I understood how important education is. There's no way I'll disappoint her."

"So, exclaimed Katie, "the Nurseketeers are committed to success at Crestmont."

"Yeah, if we can get the airhead to quit mooning over that loser long enough to pay attention," Robin added. "Stephen is a carbon copy of Jake, the dead-end guy I left behind... and he's only got one thing on his mind. Have you noticed the winks and evil grins he shoots back at his friends every time he leaves with Frannie? He's up to no good."

"I hope he's not as bad as you think," Katie said, "but he kinda creeps me out too."

"Maybe he'll do something so obvious that Frannie will see him for what he is. She isn't up for listening to anything I have to say about him, but I was hoping she'd listen to you two. After hearing her excuses for Stephen's dinner with another girl, I'm about to chalk her up to a lost cause."

"He gives me the willies," Leslie added. "He's the most selfish guy I've ever seen, and I thought Paul held that title. Paul doesn't want me at Crestmont because it's inconvenient for him. The real problem is that I got a scholarship and he didn't. We were great in high school and I thought we were *forever*. I never realized I'd look at things so differently. Compared to him and his whining, I feel like an adult."

"Compared to Stephen and Jake the Jerk, I'd consider Paul a real catch." Robin laughed.

"We can't let boyfriends be a priority right now. College is too important for all of us. Now is definitely not the time for romantic relationships." Katie said.

"Frannie sure doesn't get it, but I get the feeling that inside that space cadet, there's a sharp kid. She reads a lot and has a good vocabulary," Robin mused, and she has nothing but nice things to say about her family. Then she turns around and does something totally brainless. That just frustrates the hell out of me. I know something bad is going to happen to her and it doesn't look like there's a thing we can do about it. Sooner or later, she's going to get a wake-up call."

"Robin," Frannie called from their room, "do you know where my black platform sandals went? I put them under my chair, but they're not here."

"Frannie, for God's sake!" Robin retorted. "If you put them there, they'd be there. Obviously, you put them somewhere else. Look in the closet."

"Found them. I forgot I put them under the bed."

Robin rolled her eyes.

"Phelps *has* to review the reading assignment," Leslie whispered as they took their seats in the back. Unfortunately, the lecture was no improvement over last Thursday's fiasco. Stephen and his cronies continued to hijack Phelps' time with questions about his Jag.

Frannie whispered to Katie, "this is soooo boring," and spent the class alternating between the novel she'd tucked inside her open textbook, and ogling Stephen who lounged between two girls and periodically waved his hand to capture Dr. Phelps' attention.

Leslie fidgeted in her seat. Several times she raised her hand to ask a question, then lowered it in disgust when Dr. Phelps ignored her.

After an eternity Dr. Phelps dismissed the class. The four girls gathered their belongings and made their way toward the

The Wake-Up Call

door. Frannie craned her neck, looking for Stephen. "I thought he would wait for me, but I don't see him anywhere," she whined. "He had to walk mighty fast to be out of sight already." Then she brightened. "Maybe he went to save us two seats in the cafeteria."

"Or not" Robin retorted.

"Well, at least we'll be together this afternoon. I know that he was excited when I asked him to be my lab partner."

"I hope you pay more attention in lab than you did in the lecture," Robin interrupted. "I don't think Chem is as easy as you think, and reading a novel isn't going to help you with the exams."

Frannie retorted, "Science was one of my best subjects in high school, and I hardly ever studied. Besides, I already read a little of the Chem assignment."

As Robin had predicted, Stephen had not saved Frannie a seat. He sat with his buddies and the two girls from chem class. Frannie forced a smile to hide her disappointment.

Missy joined them in line. "It's getting crowded in there," Missy commented. "I doubt we'll find five seats together. Is it OK with you guys if we split up and Frannie and I sit together?"

"No problem," Robin answered.

They left the line with full trays and split up to find empty seats. Twice, Robin saw Stephen glance at Frannie, then turn to his friends with an expression that made her blood boil. She gestured toward Stephen with her chin. "He's doing it again. Watch Stephen's face every time he glances over at Frannie. Whatever he's saying to his buddies is no compliment. That guy is a real turd."

The girls watched Stephen while they ate. "I see what you mean," Leslie commented. I can't imagine what he's saying, but it's pretty obvious he's talking about her, and it's clear he's not saying anything nice." The three turned their attention to lunch. "I wonder if they'll let the three of us be lab partners," Leslie mused. "I feel like I need the Nurseketeers in this class."

When Frannie entered Chem lab after lunch, Stephen stood with his hand on the shoulder of a girl she didn't recognize, leaning toward her as she talked. Frannie, first abashed, then determined, strode toward Stephen, and challenged him. "You haven't forgotten that we're lab partners, have you?"

He looked confused but recovered quickly. "Of course not." He turned toward the girl, shrugged, and said, "Sorry." She seemed miffed but walked away. "See? I've already gotten us a lab table and it's kinda off by ourselves," he added with a sly smile.

Tess Aikens, their lab assistant, allowed Katie, Leslie, and Robin to work as lab partners. When she asked why Frannie wasn't with them, Robin gestured over her shoulder. Tess frowned. "I need to keep my eye on them," she murmured. "He's not the partner I would have chosen for Frannie." Before Robin could ask her for more information, Tess turned to answer another student's question.

"I wonder what she knows about Stephen." Katie pondered.

"Me, too," added Robin. "If I get a chance, I'll ask her."

Frannie noticed Tess glance her way while she was visiting with Robin, Katie, and Leslie. She wondered if they had been talking about her.

Frannie's focus on Tess made Stephen uncomfortable. He clasped her shoulder and turned her toward him. "You're more interested in what's going on up there than you are in me." he pouted.

"Silly! I just noticed that my roommates all got to be lab partners and that Tess is our Lab Instructor. She was nice at the Tug of War. I liked her. Besides, I thought you and Tess were friends."

"Yeah, we're friends," Stephen shrugged. As much as Stephen liked girls, Frannie thought his reaction was odd. She brightened when she remembered Tess had said that she wasn't interested in Stephen.

Tess called for everyone's attention. Dr. Phelps sat on a stool in the back of the room reading a vintage auto magazine. "Even though you and your partner will be working together, each of you must describe the process and the results of your experiments independently and document your own conclusions. Your lab journals will count for 40% of your lab grade. Lab quizzes will also count for 40%. Some of them will be pop quizzes, so you will need to stay current with your reading and your lab work.

"For the remainder of today's lab, use your checklist of supplies to be sure that your station is fully stocked. If you are missing something that you need for an experiment, it will cost you valuable time to replace it and your grade will suffer if you can't complete your experiment.

The remaining 20% of your grade is all about you… your organization, cooperation, responsibility, communication, and punctuality. Accountability is important in college. Only you are responsible for you. So, inventory your materials, and we'll review the first assignment when you're done." Tess walked among the tables, answering questions, and offering help.

Leslie caught Tess's attention. "If Dr. Phelps doesn't cover the text in lecture, Tess, would you help us understand it? Can we consider you our assistant Chem teacher as well as our student lab assistant?"

"I'll be happy to do what I can," Tess replied, with an expression that made it clear she understood what Leslie meant.

"That's a relief." Leslie sighed. "We'll be studying together, but it's nice to know we have somewhere to turn when we need help."

Stephen and Frannie were engrossed in conversation while the itemized resource list lay untouched on the table. Tess noticed but decided not to intervene. She'd meant it when she'd said that no one was responsible for your success in college but you."

***

At lunch after Math on Friday, Frannie commented to no one in particular, "Mr. Elwood is so cute."

Robin retorted, "I'm more impressed that he makes Math relevant and interesting."

Leslie added, "He teaches like Math is his favorite thing in the world. He explains things so well that doing the homework problems is fun."

"There's nothing fun about Math homework," Frannie insisted. "The problems make no sense at all. I don't know how you guys can call that *easy*."

"I thought you'd have caught on by now," Robin said. "You solve the problems by choosing the right formula. If you can't put what you know to good use, then it's hardly worth knowing anything."

"But how do you know which one to use?"

"Why am I surprised? You know good from bad and right from wrong, but you can't seem to use what you know to see what a conniving bastard Stephen is."

"English, on the other hand," Katie interrupted, "is a different story. "It's not that I don't enjoy it. Mrs. Bennett gives an interesting lecture. But… her *learning by doing* philosophy is killing me. She assigns reading and papers as if English were the only class we're taking. Thank heavens gym class doesn't have homework."

"Old Testament is my favorite," Leslie volunteered. "Dr. Creighton treats the Old Testament like an adventure story, with lessons to be learned."

"I like writing the essays he assigns," said Frannie. "It's fun to figure out how lessons from the Bible are still relevant today. I don't much care for the textbook, but I agree that he makes it come alive."

"Frannie, that's just what Dr. Bennett's wants you to do with *her* assignments. She's looking for your interpretation of the relevance of the topic when she assigns an essay." Katie suggested.

"Dr. Bennett would be pleased that Dr. Creighton grades on grammar and spelling, too. He sounds like my parents when he says *A college graduate has learned nothing if he can't communicate effectively*," Frannie giggled. "My grandmother taught me to read before I started school, and she still corrects me just like an English teacher." Then a serious expression crossed her face. "Sometimes, I miss home," she whispered.

The Wake-Up Call

"Chem is going to be the death of me," Leslie announced. "We pretty much have to teach it to ourselves, and I'm just not getting it. Dr. Phelps never reviews the assignment, and he doesn't spend much time answering our questions either. Every time I raise my hand, he ignores it. He hasn't called on me once. I know more about his Jag than I know about compounds and mixtures. He spent less than 40 minutes on chemistry in our last two-hour class."

"Don't worry, Leslie. In my experience," Frannie explained, "it all somehow comes together. If Dr. Phelps doesn't explain things, we'll just figure it out when the time comes."

"Well," Robin jumped in. "I, for one, am *not* clairvoyant, and when something doesn't make sense, I need someone to explain it to me. I'm grateful that we'll be studying together. Frannie, you need to join us. You should be planning your social life around studying, not the other way 'round."

"But..." Frannie began.

"No *buts*..." Robin interrupted. "Oh, never mind. It's not worth arguing with you. We'll just let the real world teach you what you need to know."

"We can reserve one of the little conference rooms on the fourth floor," Katie suggested. "We won't have to whisper and all the resources we need are nearby."

"Great idea," added Leslie. "The library is opened every day until curfew, and we can make it back to the dorm in five minutes."

"Leslie and I will have to schedule library time around athletics and work," Robin said. "Frannie will have to squeeze in her studying around Stephen and Missy,"

"I'll study with you," Frannie insisted. "I just don't see why I can't have fun, too."

"We'll see," Robin shrugged.

"I'm anxious to get started," Leslie said. "Our first Chem test is a week from Thursday, and I'm determined not to flunk it."

"You'll be fine," Frannie assured her. "You know more than you think you do. Whenever I thought I wouldn't do well on a test in high school, it always turned out better than I expected."

Stephen and Frannie reached Hadley Hall at the same time the girls returned from the library. Frannie turned to Stephen for a goodnight kiss but, he was already halfway down the porch steps. Disappointed at his abrupt departure, Frannie, followed her suitemates inside.

"I almost feel ready for the Chem test tomorrow," Leslie said. "Katie, I'm going to try your suggestion to answer the questions before I look at the answers. If I know the answer, I should spot it right away. I'll mark it and move on. I promise to resist the urge to change an answer unless I'm positive I made a mistake. Did I get it right?"

"Perfect," Katie said.

"Won't it be great if it works, said Leslie. Then, being a lousy test-taker will be ancient history."

"Count on it," Robin assured her. Being a lousy test-taker isn't a disease. It's a state of mind, and you just changed your mind. You go, Girl!"

Leslie smiled. "From your mouth to God's ears."

"If you have a good memory, the right answer usually just pops out," Frannie announced.

"Frannie," Robin said, "That might have worked in high school. Now, you actually have to think. You need to apply the material, not just remember it. Smart as you are, I expect this test will be a wake-up call."

"Robin's got a point," Katie said. "You can't just memorize chemistry equations. You have to know when to use which one. You keep thinking that Robin is picking on you, but down the road, you're going to appreciate what she says. I just hope it's sooner rather than later."

The Wake-Up Call

Robin and Katie each managed a *B* on the first chemistry test. Leslie was pleased with her *C*. The *F* on Frannie's paper blared like a neon sign. "I couldn't have failed that test." Frannie wailed. "I *never* fail tests. I read most of the material and it didn't seem all that hard. It's the way Dr. Phelps wrote the questions. He's a horrible teacher."

"Frannie, wake up!" Robin glared at her roommate. "WE managed to understand the questions. It's not the damned test or the horrible teacher. Before you say I'm picking on you because I hate you, THINK. You didn't complete the reading assignments; you read some trashy romance novel or mooned over Stephen during every lecture, and you spent precious little time studying with us."

"But... I always got good grades in high school. I..."

"COLLEGE ISN'T FRIGGIN' HIGH SCHOOL! Crestmont is full of students who *want* to be here. We passed entrance exams to get in. Every one of us is smarter than the average high school student. So, for you, my favorite airhead, college will be challenging, even though high school wasn't. College doesn't just *happen!*

"But..."

"Frannie," Katie interrupted. "You *have* to listen. Robin isn't picking on you. She just told you the facts before Leslie or I could. We all know you're a smart person. You're probably smarter than we are, but it's more important to be a *quality* student than a *smart* student!"

"But I understood what I read, Frannie insisted.

"Obviously not well enough to answer the test questions," Robin snarled.

"Frannie, if you fail freshman courses, you don't get to stay with us in the nursing program," Leslie said. "You *do* want to be a nurse, don't you?"

Frannie shook her head. "I don't know." She paused. "Look, this is *one test*. I've passed all the quizzes and papers so far, and

Stephen and I are doing OK in lab. One test isn't that big a deal. You'll see how much better the next one will be."

Robin took a deep breath, ready to try again, but Katie caught her eye and shook her head. "Not now," she mouthed, and continued, "So, let's give ourselves something to look forward to. My folks wanted to drive down for a weekend, but wouldn't it be super if we could all drive up to the farm instead? If there's a weekend when you and Leslie can both get time off, we could drive Nellie to Atoka. Is that okay with you, Leslie? It's less than a three-hour drive and we can split the gas."

"A trip to Atoka would recharge Nellie's battery," Leslie said. "I'll check with Coach Thomas. He tries to look tough, but he cares about us. He gave Barb a second shot at the basketball team because he knew we wanted to play the same sport."

"If I give plenty of notice," Robin added, "the Davises will give me the weekend off."

"My parents will be thrilled not to make the two round-trips. We have room for all of us. Frannie, you'll be coming, too. No excuses. Stephen can manage one weekend without you. "

"I doubt that will be a problem," Robin added. "I've never seen him without his arms draped over at least one girl."

Frannie realized that Robin was right and felt a pang of unease, imagining what Stephen might do while she was gone. With exaggerated cheerfulness, she turned to Katie. "Of course, I want to go."

⌘

In Thursday's Chem class, Dr. Phelps reviewed the test and answered questions. *"I guess I didn't understand the material as well as I thought I did. I'll just read the homework assignments more carefully."* Frannie pondered briefly, then returned to *Love Story*, the novel hiding behind her text. *"I might as well find out what happens to Jennifer and Oliver. Listening to Phelps's ramble about his jag won't help."*

The Wake-Up Call

In the suite before dinner, Leslie reminded the others, "Our first home game is in just two weeks. The bonfire the night before is a big event. All the sororities and fraternities have booths in the stadium parking lot to sell stuff. Tess mentioned that the CU-NSA is going to sell baked goods. Wouldn't it be fun to bake something to contribute?" Too bad we don't have a real kitchen."

"That *would* be fun," Katie replied. "Do you think Barb and her Dad would let us bake in her kitchen if we brought all the ingredients and promised to leave the kitchen clean?"

"That's a super idea," Leslie replied. "It's not too late to call Barb and ask."

"That would be fun," Frannie mused. "When I was little, my mother made cupcakes a lot, and she let me and Petey lick the beaters and the bowl. Petey's favorite was yellow cupcakes with chocolate icing, so they were my favorite, too."

Leslie called to share their plan with Barb and waited while Barb got her dad's approval. "Mr. Philips said it would be fine," she announced. "I told Barb that we'd like to come on Wednesday and assured her that we'll leave the kitchen spotless."

"What fun!" Frannie exclaimed. "I'm glad he said *yes*."

Robin chimed in with "Good job, Leslie. We can work out the details about shopping and baking."

Leslie smiled. "Oh, and one more thing. The basketball team has a bye week, so there's no game on November 7th. Katie, do you think that can be our Atoka weekend? Robin will have plenty of time to arrange for the weekend off, and we could leave after lunch on Friday. We'd get to Atoka at a reasonable hour, and we wouldn't have to be back until Sunday evening."

"I'll phone Mom and be back in a sec," Katie grinned.

Moments later, Katie pumped her fist in the air. "We're ON! The Nurseketeers get to spend the weekend in Atoka!"

"So, what's with the *C* on your English assignment?" Robin asked as they walked toward the chapel for Old Testament. "I thought you said English was an easy essay."

"Beats me," Frannie shrugged. "Dr. Bennett asked about the last chapter she assigned, and I described everything that was in it. She just doesn't like me."

"Come off it, Frannie. She didn't ask us what was covered in the chapter. The assignment was to describe how what happened changed the family's perspective. We keep telling you to *use* what you read, not just show that you read it. College professors *expect* us to do our homework. They give tests to see what we *learned* from it."

"But I *did* show her that I learned what happened in Chapter Seven. Why didn't I get an *A*?"

Robin screeched, "Because all you did was prove you *read* it. So what? She assumed that you'd read it. Dr. Bennett asked what difference it made. Did it change anything?"

"Then why didn't she just ask that?"

"She *did*." Robin pulled Frannie to a stop. "Look at me. If you don't quit believing you're still in high school, there will be three Nurseketeers next semester, not four." Then she marched on, leaving Frannie staring, open-mouthed.

※

In chem lab on Tuesday, Frannie asked, "Stephen, where's the calcium chloride we need for this experiment?"

"Beats me," he replied. "Should be in the cabinet. Didn't you inventory that stuff the first day like Tess said?"

"Me? I thought you checked the supplies. You told me you were a chem whiz in high school, and I thought that meant you were in charge. I thought you'd know what stuff we'd need."

"Of course, I'm in charge, but it was your job to do the shopping list." Before Frannie could protest, Stephen continued. "Never mind. One bad lab grade won't make a difference. Look busy or Tess will be over here chewing us out. I've got connections so I know how the experiment is supposed to turn out."

"Well, I don't. You need to come to the library with me tonight and help me get my summary done."

"No way..." Stephen began to protest, then changed his mind. "Sure. That won't take long. Then maybe we'll take a drive in the Mustang."

Chapter 10

"This is going to be a super weekend," Leslie exclaimed to her suitemates. "It's our first home game and we stand a good chance of winning. The Ravens are good, but Coach is sure that our Coyote teams are better. We're roasting three huge papier-mâché Ravens over the bonfire to cheer the Coyotes on to victory."

"Let's splurge a little and skip dinner in the cafeteria so we can enjoy the food at the fundraising booths. There will be hamburgers and hot dogs, for sure, and we can count on our cupcakes for dessert."

"Let's get going. We need to stop at the Market and get to Barb's," Katie said.

"Can I lick the beaters?" Frannie asked. "It's the best part of baking anything."

Robin grinned. "Sometimes you're refreshing, you little Twit. You can lick *one* beater. I get the other one. Since we're making two batches, we might have to share with the others."

"It's a deal!" A huge smile spread across Frannie's face. "*She called me a Twit, and it didn't hurt my feelings.*"

"I have my mom's recipe and we can split the cost four ways," Leslie said.

At the Market, Barb showed them where to find everything. "Dad said I could take off. I think he knew how much I wanted to join your party."

Arms full, the girls walked to the house and followed Barb into the kitchen. "We're glad your Dad's a mind-reader," Katie grinned. "We were talking about how nice it would be to have you here."

Leslie took charge. "Barb, since you know where everything's hidden, can you get the mixer and stuff? I'll preheat the oven and stick the recipe on the fridge so we can all see it. Robin, measure the ingredients. Katie, manage the mixer. Frannie put the cupcake papers in the tins and pour the batter into them when we're ready. We'll clean up and start over with the second batch while the first batch is baking. I'll dry dishes if one of you will wash, drying is always my job at home. Frannie, don't fill the cups too full so we'll have some extra cupcakes, just in case. We can work on the icing while the cupcakes cool. Hopefully, we'll be able to get the purple right. Does that cover it all?"

Four pairs of hands gave Leslie a round of applause. "Girlfriend, a master chef couldn't organize a kitchen better than you just did," Robin exclaimed. "Bravo! Our cupcakes are going to be nothing short of amazing."

"Barb, who are the boys with you and your dad in those photos in the living room? Frannie asked.

"My brothers. They're all married and not one of them lives in Dallas. It's just Dad and me in the house now." Barb said.

"Where's your mother?"

Leslie gasped at the insensitivity of Frannie's question, but Barb continued without hesitation. "My mom died right after I was born, so I never really knew her."

"That sounds like quite a story. Four brothers! The no mother part sounds like a bummer." Leslie said.

"I suppose it is, but when you grow up with four older brothers they either treat you like one of them or like a china doll.

Speaking of dolls, I'm not sure there was ever one in the house. I'm a bit of a tomboy so, I was just one of the boys and the baby of the bunch. I did wonder sometimes what it might be like with a mom around, but June our next-door neighbor, let me hide from the testosterone periodically. She was a major help when I first got my period. I can talk to Dad about a lot of things, but *that* needed a woman."

"That certainly accounts for why you and your dad are so close," Katie said. "I guess we'd better get to it."

They cranked up the radio and began their assigned tasks. While they were drying their utensils after the first batch, Frannie asked. "Leslie, did you invite Paul for the weekend?"

"I did. He'll be driving up on Friday. I hope he gets here in time for the bonfire. He loves basketball, so I know he'll enjoy the games. Afterward, I'll show him around campus and maybe we'll drive around the city a bit. We haven't seen each other since I got here. Maybe when he sees how happy I am, he'll quit complaining. At least I hope that's how it's going to be. Will you be going to the bonfire with Stephen?

"Oh yes. He invited me the other night. I'm going to meet him at his dorm, then we'll walk to the bonfire from there."

"He's not picking you up at Hadley?" Robin frowned.

"No, he said I should pick him up since his dorm is on my way to the bonfire. He'd have to go out of his way to come back to Hadley to get me," Frannie explained with enough conviction that Robin thought she might actually believe his excuse.

Leslie and Barb looked at Frannie, both deciding not to comment.

"Look here!" exclaimed Robin, giving Katie a high five. "Perfect purple icing! We couldn't have gotten a better Crestmont purple if we'd commissioned it from a bakery."

When the cupcakes were cool, the girls iced the chocolate ones with yellow frosting and the yellow ones with purple. Does anyone else want to lick a beater?" Frannie held one out.

"Go ahead, from the looks of the first one no one will have to wash them…" Robin chuckled.

The Wake-Up Call

"We need to thank your dad for giving us these boxes, Barb," Katie said. "They're perfect for keeping the cupcakes safe until Friday. Do you think he'd like a few cupcakes since we made extra?"

"His sweet tooth would love that, and he'll appreciate the gesture."

"Barb, how about you keep the ingredients that we didn't use," suggested Robin.

"Thanks," Barb said. "I'll help you carry the cupcake boxes out to the car. This was fun. We'll have to find an excuse to do it again."

The night of the bonfire, the girls sat in the lobby, each holding a box with a dozen cupcakes. Missy joined them and they waited for J.R. and Paul.

"J.R. is so considerate, and he's always on time," Missy said.

"If Paul doesn't get here soon, you guys head for the bonfire and we'll catch up with you there," Leslie said.

"It would have been nice of Stephen to pick you up here," Robin said. "J.R. didn't think it was out of his way to come for Missy. But, of course, we wouldn't want to inconvenience Stephen, would we?"

Before Frannie could think of a response, J.R. arrived and gave Missy a hug. "Hey y'all. It's a great night for the bonfire. Leslie, if Paul's on his way, let's wait a bit. We have plenty of time." J.R. took a seat and pulled Missy down beside him.

In just a few minutes, Leslie jumped up and waved. "Paul," she called, running toward him. Paul scooped her into a bear hug and gave her a quick kiss. He took her hand and turned towards the door. "Let's go, Les. Can't wait to spend time with you. Seems like a coon's age."

"Wait!" said Leslie, pulling him back toward the group. "Meet my friends. We're all walking over to the bonfire together."

Disappointment flitted across Paul's face, replaced quickly by a forced smile. "Paul," he said, reaching to shake J.R.'s hand.

"J.R., and this here's Missy."

"Nice to meet you, Paul," Missy said.

Leslie made the rest of the introductions. "It's great that you made it in time for the bonfire," Robin said.

"I hope you're not dead tired from that long drive," Katie added. "It's going to be a fun evening."

"I'm looking forward to roasted raven," Leslie said with a smile. "Paul you're gonna love the games tomorrow. The Ravens are good, but the Coach is sure we're gonna take 'em! - both the men's *and* women's teams."

Paul shrugged his shoulders and took Leslie's hand.

"Let's walk Frannie to Mitchell Hall to pick up Stephen," J.R. suggested. "Then we can all go to the bonfire together."

"That's sweet of you," Frannie said. "I hope we can hang with you guys tonight. Sometimes Greg and James give me the creeps."

At Mitchell Hall, Stephen was nowhere to be seen. "He'll be out in a minute," Frannie said. You can go ahead if you want."

"We'll wait," Robin insisted.

It was another ten minutes before Stephen emerged, talking with Greg, James, and several other guys. Without a glance around, they walked down the steps and onto the path to the Sports Center.

"Stephen," Frannie called. "Stephen!"

He turned, startled. His companions turned with him. Greg grinned and patted Stephen on the back. James said, "You go man!" Then each gave him a thumbs *up,* and walked on, laughing and glancing back over their shoulders.

Stephen stood where he was, waiting for Frannie and her friends to reach him.

"You told me to meet you here," Frannie said, puzzled.

"Nah, we were going to hookup at the bonfire."

"Oh well, we are together now." He reached for her hand, and pulled her along toward the stadium, ignoring her friends.

The Wake-Up Call

"Wait, Stephen. I want you to meet Paul, Leslie's boyfriend from home."

Stephen stopped, his irritation evident. He thrust out his hand. "Stephen," he said.

"Paul Saunders," Paul shook hands.

"Leslie," Frannie said, "Maybe we could double date when Paul comes for a weekend."

"Yeah," Stephen cut in, grabbing Frannie's hand. "Let's get going." He pulled her down the path, leaving the group behind.

"That guy just rubs me the wrong way," J.R. commented.

"You can say that again," Robin agreed. "He's rude, inconsiderate, and I think Frannie actually believes the excuses she makes for his behavior."

❈

"We don't need them tagging along," Stephen growled as pulled ahead of Frannie's friends.

"It's sweet that you want to be alone with me, but I wish you hadn't been rude to my friends."

"I'm hungry. How 'bout you?" Stephen asked, ignoring her comment. "How 'bout one of those cupcakes for me, Cupcake?"

Frannie clutched the box protectively. "No, Silly, they are for the CU-SNA booth. Let's drop them off and get something to eat."

"Last year, the Zeta Sigs had the best food station, and the Zeta Delts will be set up right next to them with drinks."

Zeta Sig did, in fact, have a good-looking menu. "We'll get chopped Bar-B-Q sandwiches." Stephen decided.

"And coleslaw to go with it," Frannie said.

"I don't like coleslaw," Stephen announced and purchased two plates without slaw.

At the adjacent booth, Stephen called, "Hey Bob, two *Cokes* here, unless you have some beer stashed somewhere."

Frannie was surprised to see Stephen shove two beer cans into his pockets. Then he handed Frannie two cups of *Coke* and picked up their plates.

"There's not supposed to be any alcohol at this event."

Stephen gave her a sidelong glance, shrugged, and said, "If you have the inside scoop, you can get what you want. Besides, I couldn't survive this bonfire hoopla without a beer. There is a cool place on top of Simpson Hall where we can eat and be alone."

"Oh, Stephen, I've been up there. The Gazebo is so romantic." Frannie cooed. "Let's go. We have plenty of time before they light the bonfire."

They climbed the stairs to the roof and settled into the Gazebo. Stephen handed her a plate then wolfed down half of his sandwich. "You want a beer?"

Frannie hesitated. "I've never had a beer."

"Are you shittin' me?"

Frannie reached tentatively for the can. She took a deep breath, then a small sip, and wrinkled her nose. "Hmmm… interesting. Different, but interesting."

"You *are* a baby, aren't you?" He grinned. "Drink up," he ordered, then polished off his sandwich and emptied his beer can. He dropped his plate and empty can on the gazebo floor and sidled up to her. "We could stay here all evening, alone, together."

Frannie took another sip of her beer. "I'd love to be alone with you, but I don't want to miss the bonfire."

"We should be able to see it from here. Besides, the fire lasts a long time."

Stephen put his arm around her and pulled her closer. "So, tell me about Frannie. Where did you grow up? What's your family like? What pets do you have? I want to know all about you."

Frannie began her story, pleased that he was interested. "I grew up in Philadelphia. I don't have any pets and my brother, Petey, is in the Army. Nana lives…"

Stephen interrupted, "You have a brother in this crappy Vietnam war? We shouldn't even be over there. Those guys are baby killers."

"Stephen! How can you say that? Our soldiers are protecting America from Communism, and Petey is NOT a baby killer! That was a terrible thing to say. Besides Petey isn't even over there;

he's stationed in Maryland." Frannie pulled away from him, her expression fierce. "Tell me you didn't mean that?"

He pulled her back to him. "Ah, Frannie, I was just pulling your chain. Go on, tell me what you do for fun?"

Frannie paused a moment, her cheeks still pink. She began, a bit unsteadily, "Well, …I like movies and bowling. I-I play tennis, but I'm not very good." She giggled. "I like playing darts with you, and foosball. Growing up, Petey and I played cards and board games, sometimes just us, but lots of times the whole family would spend an evening playing games."

"Great," Stephen said, already bored with the conversation.

"What about you Stephen?" Frannie asked, looking at him dreamily. She felt a bit unsettled; not dizzy, but not normal.

Stephen surprised her with a slow, lingering kiss. She gasped with pleasure and he pulled her into an embrace. He kissed her again, investigating her lips with his tongue.

Frannie drew back in surprise, but Stephen pulled her into another kiss sending bolts of lightning coursing through her body. Cupping her head with one hand, he reached under her peasant blouse and explored her back, heightening the delightful sensations, and short-circuiting her brain.

Stephen unhooked her bra, deepening his kiss when he felt her tense. When she relaxed into him, he moved his hand to her breast, tracing arcs with his thumb. When he touched her sensitive nipple, Frannie jumped as if she'd been shocked, suddenly conscious of where she was and what she was doing.

"No, Stephen. Stop! We can't do this. It isn't right." Frannie looked around, grateful that they were alone. "What if someone came up here? Let's go to the bonfire. They'll be lighting it soon."

Stephen tried to move in again, but Frannie was firm. He backed off, disgusted.

Frannie reached up and touched the side of his face. "I love being with you, Stephen, but we can't do this." She fastened her bra and Stephen guzzled the remainder of her warm beer, crushed first one can, then the other, and stuffed both into a pocket. Frannie collected their trash.

Grudgingly, Stephen took her hand and they walked back to the bonfire in silence. Frannie played tug of war with her delight at the sensations that Stephen had evoked and self-reproach for participating in something so wrong. *What if someone had come along?* She imagined her shame if her parents knew.

Stephen and Frannie watched the bonfire, his arm draped across her shoulders. The crowd roared when the flames reached the Ravens on the spit. "Stephen isn't this fun!"

Ignoring her question, Stephen searched the crowd, oblivious to the frenzy that surrounded them. "There they are," he pointed. "Over there." He pulled Frannie through the crowd.

"Checked Zeta Delt recently?" Stephen asked Greg and James.

"Dry as a bone," Greg replied. Stephen muttered a curse. "We'll hang with the guys a bit, and then I'll take you back to the dorm."

Disappointed, Frannie listened half-heartedly. No one attempted to include her in the conversation and eventually, she interrupted, "Stephen, let's walk by the fountain."

James leered. "Stephen, take the loooooong way around the oval."

Greg winked, "And don't forget to smoooochie by the fountain," making wet kissing noises.

"What's with those guys," Frannie asked as she and Stephen walked away. "They act like little kids."

"They're just jealous. They think you're cute, but I got you first." Frannie's heart sang a chorus of *Hallelujah*.

Stephen steered Frannie off the crowded path and onto the grass. "Can't be alone in a crowd, can we. We can walk toward the oval this way." He gave her a half-hearted kiss at the fountain, but it still sent a shiver through Frannie.

"I love when you kiss me," she murmured. Stephen grinned and pulled her close, then kissed her with a bit more enthusiasm. Hand in hand, they walked to her dorm, climbed the steps, and stood among the crowd of students on the porch. "I enjoyed tonight," Frannie said.

"In a couple of weeks, there is a big Halloween bash. Wanna go?"

"A Halloween party!" she said. "What fun. Is it a costume party? We can wear matching outfits."

"Whoa! Yes, it's a costume party. If you're not in costume, you can't get in. I'm going as a Texas Ranger."

Frannie thought a moment. "I have a better idea. How 'bout you be Marshall Dillon from *Gun Smoke*, and I'll be Miss Kitty. We'll be a couple. Your Ranger outfit will do just fine, but you need a red shirt to match my dress. We'll look fantastic together."

"Whatever. The dance is in the Practice Gym, come by Mitchell and pick me up. It's on your way."

Frannie hesitated. "All the other guys come to Hadley to pick up their dates."

"C'mon, Frannie. Mitchell is a lot closer to the Sports Field than Hadley. If you want, I'll walk you back to Hadley after the party."

He left without another word or goodnight kiss.

"Frannie," Missy called from the porch swing where she sat with J.R., who pulled her closer to make room.

"Hey, you two. Great evening, wasn't it?"

Missy smiled up at J.R. "We had a great time. We all hung together until Leslie took Paul to show him around campus and have a little alone time. Mike walked Katie back to Hadley."

"Frannie," J.R. said, sounding serious. "I owe you a bit of an apology for not being very hospitable to Stephen, but I'm concerned."

"Why..." Frannie began, but J.R. interrupted.

"I'm concerned that you don't know Stephen as well as you think you do," he continued. "This afternoon in the dorm, I overheard him saying some uncomplimentary things about a girl. He was bragging to his friends about her being *easy* and how it hadn't taken him long to *get to first base*. No decent guy trashes a girl like that. You're spending a good deal of time with him, Frannie, and he could have been talking about you."

Frannie said, relieved. "J.R. you are such a gentleman. It's so sweet of you to care about me. I can't imagine who Stephen was talking about, but I'm certain that it wasn't me. I don't know what "easy" means, but we've never been anywhere near a baseball field together. You didn't hear my name, did you?"

"No, but talking about *any* girl that way should let you know that he's not someone you can trust. He doesn't respect girls, and you deserve better than the likes of him."

"J.R., I love that you care about me, but I am sure Stephen didn't mean to be rude. I know that he likes me."

Frannie nearly added "*He's a perfect gentleman,*" but realized how often his ungentlemanly behavior disappointed her. She'd *have* to convince him to pick her up at Hadley in the future, ask her what she wanted before ordering for her.

She stood. "I'll leave you two to enjoy the last few minutes before curfew. See you tomorrow, Missy. We're still going shopping, aren't we?"

"You bet, girlfriend."

On the way to the suite, she recalled how wonderful Stephen had made her feel, and the shame when Stephen had unsnapped her bra again, without so much as asking.

Robin came in from work at 10:15 and joined the girls in the sitting area. "Leslie, what did Paul think of Crestmont?"

"To be honest, I'm disappointed. It was such a great evening, and he couldn't bring himself to enjoy it. I finally told him that I am happy with my decision to come here and I have no intention of changing my mind. If he can't enjoy it with me, then I'm prepared to enjoy it without him."

"Did you really say that?" Katie asked.

"Maybe not in those exact words, but I was pretty clear about being tired of his complaining. I assured him that I care about him, and our relationship needs to follow us into the future. I left it up to him."

"Well, for his sake, I hope he comes through for you," said Robin, "cuz if he doesn't, it's his loss, not yours."

"Robin's right, Leslie," Katie agreed. "You're the one making good decisions."

"Thanks, Guys. That makes me feel better. I was a little sad to see him leave because I'm not sure he can pull it off. He feels sorry for himself and nothing he said gave me confidence that's going to change."

"I had a great time," Frannie chirped.

Robin turned to her, ready to remark on her insensitivity, when Katie said, "What did you and Stephen do?"

"Remember the gazebo on the Simpson roof? We took our food up there to eat. The sky is gorgeous with nothing to block the stars. Stephen is so romantic." She stopped short, remembering how the evening had ended. "Then he walked me home," she concluded.

On Saturday mid-morning, Frannie grabbed her purse. "Ready," she said to Missy. "Later, Everyone. I'll be back for dinner. Don't go without me."

"So… shall we wander around nearby or take the bus downtown?" Missy asked.

"Let's check out the stores around here. I don't think I'm ready to explore Dallas without Barb to keep us from getting lost. I want to see if they have a cool dress shop, and we might find something perfect for Halloween while we're at it."

"We could grab lunch at Rob Rory's or at that cute sandwich shop. I have a date with J.R. tonight. He's coming at six. If we're back by three, I can spend a couple of hours in the library studying for my English exam and still have time to get ready. So, let's hoof it."

"Missy, it's Saturday your test isn't 'til Monday. Skip the library so we can have all afternoon. You can always study tomorrow. How hard could an English test be? Just read the assignment and it will be a piece of cake."

"It doesn't work that way for me, Frannie. I need good grades to stay in Theta Rho and that won't happen if I don't study. You should come with me."

"Nah, you can go back if you want. I'll just shop a while longer and get back in time for dinner. Stephen will probably be in the Game Room, and I can spend the evening with him."

"Suit yourself, Girlfriend. Let's go do some shopping."

Chapter 11

The four girls settled into seats in the Freshman Nursing Seminar. Mrs. Reynolds announced, "On the same day as the campus Halloween party, CU-SNA and our campus sororities host a Halloween party for two local children's homes. Your participation is requested, though not required. Bringing joy to underprivileged children is an engaging and exciting experience. We'll finish in plenty of time for you to prepare for the campus party.

"That sounds like fun," Frannie whispered. "I love children."

"CU-SNA and sorority members will join us during our Seminar prior to the party to help us fill sacks with candy. These children miss out on the traditional trick-or-treat experience, so the party is special. They love costumes, so please dress for the event, but remember that there are small children, so take care not to frighten them.

Frannie raised her hand and asked, "What costumes would be too scary for the children?"

"Well, I'd avoid goblins, ogres, and the devil. Witches are so much a part of Halloween that the children are used to them, but please stay away from green makeup and bloody appendages. We are nurses, of course, so we'll have plenty of other opportunities to deal with blood and gore."

The laughter was hesitant until the class realized that Ms. Reynolds had a good sense of humor. "Keep it light and simple. Create fantasy for these children and have some fun yourselves. These flyers will answer all your questions. We'll organize transportation. If you have a car with room for additional passengers, please stay for a moment after the seminar."

"Our question for today's discussion is: *What safety precautions are appropriate for children ages 4-16?* Patient safety is a primary concern in every healthcare environment. Creating a treatment area for children is similar to preparing your home to accommodate a child. Think about mishaps you or your siblings have experienced and ways they could have been prevented.

"Prevention isn't limited to a safe physical environment. Educating children to behave safely is equally important. Patient education is a nursing responsibility. In this case, consider what children might need to learn to protect themselves? Who would like to start the discussion?"

※

"Ride with us, J.R.," Leslie said as they left Montgomery Hall. "I'm sure Missy's sorority will be participating, so she could ride with us as well. She'll have to sit on your lap," Leslie winked.

"That'd be super," J.R. replied with a mile-wide smile. "Missy and I are gonna be a caveman and cavewoman… the happy kind, not the beat-her-over-the-head-and-drag-her-around by-the-hair kind. You don't think a big ugly guy carrying a club will be too scary for the kids, do ya?"

"Not with *your* smile. Think Teddy Bear with a fat baseball bat," Robin teased.

"The kids will be all over you," Frannie assured him.

A flush crawled across J.R.'s cheeks. "Alright, giant cave teddy bear it is." He waved, then turned onto the path to Mitchell Hall.

The Wake-Up Call

"I hadn't intended to go to the campus party," Robin said, "so I didn't ask for that day off. I do want to participate in the kids' event."

Katie said, "Do you think you can switch with someone?"

"Maaaaybe. I'm sure no student would be willing to give up Halloween, but there's a young woman who might. I'll ask her tomorrow. Keep your fingers crossed."

"Super. So, what are we doing for costumes?" Katie said.

"Stephen and I will be Marshall Dillon and Miss Kitty from *Gunsmoke*," Frannie announced. "I'm going to look for some black crinoline material for my red dress. If one of you knows how to sew, we could put it under the skirt to make it look old-fashioned. If we put some around the neck and the sleeves, it would look just like the dresses saloon ladies wore." Frannie looked expectantly at the others. No one volunteered.

"I can draw a mole on my cheek with eyeliner and I'll wear bright red lipstick. I'll try to find a big feather for my hair, and I'll wear black high heels. Then all I need is fishnet hose. What about you, Katie?"

"Hmmm… I hadn't thought about a costume. I wasn't planning to go to the campus party, but I wouldn't miss the children's party for anything. I don't want to be the only one not in costume."

"You look like an Indian Princess," Frannie said. "That would be a great costume."

"Katie, I think you'd make a statement, a good one," said Robin. "You'd be gorgeous, and so authentic."

"Thanks, guys," Katie said. No one noticed how tense she'd become. "That's sweet of you, but I didn't bring anything authentic, and I won't be going home before the event. I was thinking of being a Roman citizen. I could fashion a toga from a bed sheet with some help from my creative roommates."

"Great idea," squealed Frannie. I can pile your hair up high and do your makeup.

"Thank you, Frannie. That will be half the costume. I'll go with the off-the-shoulder look and sandals. That should do it, don't you think?"

"I can already picture you as a regal Roman beauty. What about you Robin?" Leslie asked.

"No clue. I didn't need a costume until a few minutes ago."

"We'll come up with a great costume for you," Frannie chimed in.

Robin suggested, "I could be a waitress. That would be a *no-brainer*, and it wouldn't cost anything. Or… or I could be Charlie Chaplain. I could pull that off."

"Definitely not a waitress," Frannie said, "but Charlie Chaplain gave me an idea. What about a mime? You have black slacks and I have a black and white striped scooped neck t-shirt you can wear."

"Hmmm. A mime. That's an interesting idea, Frannie," Robin nodded. "You're on to something."

Leslie snapped her fingers, "Sally had on a pair of red suspenders the other day. They would look great. I'll go ask her if we can borrow them. Be right back."

Frannie raised her index finger. "I have a little black tam in the storage unit downstairs, and I'm sure there's a pair of white gloves somewhere, the perfect finishing touch."

"Sounds good. It really does. Thanks."

Frannie basked in the warmth of Robin's smile.

Leslie hurried back in the room, suspenders in hand.

"Suspenders were a great idea, Leslie. Thanks," said Robin.

Frannie said, "White pancake make-up is the one thing we need to buy. I have mascara to make your lashes long, and we can use lipstick to put red spots on your cheeks."

"Whoa. I hadn't thought of make-up. I guess a mime wouldn't be a mime without a white face. My face will be your blank slate, Frannie. It doesn't hurt to have a fashion genius for a roommate."

Frannie grinned, thinking it would be great if she and Robin could get along this well all the time.

"How 'bout you, Leslie? Robin asked. "You haven't said what your costume will be."

"I was going to take a page from your playbook, Robin, and go as something I do all the time. I'd thought about wearing my basketball uniform, but I changed my mind when Frannie came up with that great idea of your being a mime. What do you think about *Wonder Woman,* from the comic books? We'd have to tone down her outfit a little. It's way too sexy for me."

"Ohhhh," Frannie cried. "That would be *such* fun to put together."

Leslie continued, "I think people would recognize *Wonder Woman* if I wore blue shorts and a red top. I could pull my red knee highs over my shoes to look like tall red boots."

"She wears a wristband and crown," Frannie added. "We could make them from yellow construction paper. Then we could cut out a *W* to pin on your shirt." She thought for a moment. "What can we use for a cape? A cape would look so cool."

"My red towel pinned around your neck," offered Katie. "Frannie's right. A cape would complete your outfit."

"You need big, sexy eyes," Frannie instructed, "and I can take care of that!"

Laughing, Robin said, "Of *course,* you can,"

※

They filled bags with candy during Freshman Nursing Seminar. Within the hour, there were enough bags organized into transport boxes for each child to have two, with plenty of extras for guests. "We'll give one bag to each child when they arrive," explained Ms. Reynolds, "and the second bag will be their Halloween gift to take home. Whatever bags left after the party will go to the local children's hospital. You've done an excellent job today. I appreciate your enthusiasm and energy. Those are valuable characteristics for a nurse."

"I want to thank our sorority guests and CU-SNA for organizing this project. Now, let's distribute the boxes among your cars. Hold up your fingers to indicate how many boxes you can take."

Leslie held up four fingers. "We can get three boxes into the trunk, and one on someone's lap. Is that OK?" she whispered to Katie, standing next to her.

"No problem," Katie whispered back.

"You must have a big car," Mrs. Reynolds said. We appreciate your taking four boxes.

Leslie smiled. "Yes, Nellie's big. Sometimes driving her is like driving a tank, but she's comfortable and dependable."

Robin called to J.R., "Hey, big guy."

J.R. turned. "At your service, M'Lady."

"Would you mind carrying my box back to Hadley for me? I need to rush straight off to work. A colleague at Rob Rory's traded shifts with me so I could go the party on Saturday. I don't want to be late."

"My pleasure. I'll take two boxes, and you three ladies can take turns with the other two. If Missy's in the dorm, we might go to the Game Room for a bit before dinner. Y'all can join us if you'd like.

※

"I'm so glad you invited me to the children's party," Missy said as J.R. and the girls loaded boxes into Nellie's trunk. "I love kids. I just might have to transfer into the nursing program," she said with a sly look at J.R.

"I love all of our costumes," Frannie announced surveying *Wonder Woman*, the mime, the stately Roman woman, and the cave couple. "Thank you for adding the crinoline to my dress, Katie. It *made* the costume."

"If you only knew how hard it was to get out of Mitchell Hall in this get-up. The guys were giving me fits!" J.R. wore a ragged, furry top that nearly hid his shorts, tire tread sandals, and carried a baseball bat, huge with lumpy papier-mâché, to complete the costume. Missy wore a bright red wig with her slinky cave women outfit.

The Wake-Up Call

Leslie announced, "Consider it worth it. WOW! You two look like *Fred and Wilma Flintstone*. Missy, that red wig just *makes* your outfit."

With the last box of candy settled in Robin's lap and Missy in J.R.'s, Leslie pulled away from the curb. "I sure don't mind *this* kind of crowded," J.R. said, wrapping his arms around Missy. "Too bad it's such a short drive to the party."

Missy giggled, "I love being with all of you. Do you believe this big hunk of a guy wants to be a nurse? I shouldn't be surprised, though. He's the gentlest, most caring person I know."

The group entered a large room, still empty of children. Frannie squealed, "This is a Halloween paradise!" Scattered around the room were corn stalks and pumpkins, and hay bales for seating. "Can you imagine the work that went into carving all of those jack o' lanterns? I love the way they flicker with the candles inside. And the music just makes it perfect"

"Carry your boxes to the tables over there," instructed a CU-SNA volunteer.

"Frannie, look at these." Robin pointed to several impressive scarecrows. Behind them, the noise level suddenly increased.

Children streamed into the hall in an orderly fashion, wide-eyed and pointing, already enjoying themselves. Staff members shepherded groups of younger children, allowing the older ones to wander the room and talk to the human scarecrows.

The Director's amplified voice silenced the room. "Welcome everyone, and thank you, Sponsors." Volunteers handed each child a bag of candy. "There is punch for everyone. When you unwrap your candy, put the wrapper back in your bag so the room will stay nice and clean for our party. Enjoy yourselves, Children."

"Look," said Missy, pointing to a gaggle of children of all ages surrounding the caveman. "The children love J.R." They watched him lift children onto his knee, swing them in the air, tell stories, and lead marches around the hay bales.

Frannie noticed a little girl perched on a hale bale, watching J.R. from a distance. She grabbed two cups of punch and sat beside her. "Hi. I'm Frannie. You're very quiet." The child looked up, a bit fearful. "Here's punch to drink with your candy."

The little girl reached for the cup with her right hand. Frannie pretended not to notice that the left hand that she tried to keep hidden was missing two fingers. "What's your name?"

"Kawen," the little girl replied, gazing shyly through her lashes.

"I'm happy to meet you, Karen. I'm Frannie. How old are you?"

"Almost six," she replied, "Next week on my buffday I'll be six yeeuhs old."

"That is fantastic. Your birthday is in November, so you're a Scorpio. That's a wonderful sign. It means you have great passion."

Karen stared wide-eyed.

Frannie realized that Karen had no clue what she meant. "Karen, a November birthday means you are *very* special."

Understanding *special*, and beaming, Karen said, "I'm special!"

They talked until the music stopped. Karen jumped down, then turned to give Frannie a big 6-year old girl hug before running to stand with her group.

Frannie was watching Karen cross the room when Robin sat down beside her and handed her a fresh cup of punch. "That looked like a pretty neat conversation."

"She's a cool little girl."

Robin hugged Frannie's shoulders briefly, then got up, leaving Frannie bewildered and elated at Robin's unexpected gesture, and near tears thinking of Karen.

The music stopped for the last time. "Boys and girls," instructed the Director, "Let's thank our guests for the wonderful party." She led the children in an enthusiastic round of applause. "Staff, please be sure that each child gets a second bag of goodies."

Frannie rose from the hay bale. A smiling Karen ran up and hugged her, then turned and scurried away. Frannie wiped tears from her cheeks.

Missy was the first to spot Frannie. With J.R. close behind, she went to investigate. "What's wrong, Frannie? Are you okay?"

Robin, Katie, and Leslie joined the huddle. "I'm fine," Frannie assured them. "It's not me. I met this darling little girl named

Karen, and I have no idea why I'm crying. She came all the way back to give me a hug before she left. She's nearly six, and shy, and she's missing two fingers. The thing is, she seemed so happy to be with me. She made me happy and sad at the same time."

Katie said, "I heard a number of sad stories about these children. I'm glad we got to participate in this event. The children appreciated it so much."

"There's no way our campus party can top this one." Leslie said.

"Let's help clean up and get back for dinner," Katie suggested.

"What an experience!" Robin exclaimed. "Frannie, you need to consider pediatrics. I think you're a natural. That little Karen recognized it right away."

※

"Coming, Frannie?" Katie called. Frannie appeared, twirling her red skirt to show the crinoline, and she, Miss Kitty, *Wonder Woman*, and the Roman stateswoman left for the lobby.

When J.R. and Missy joined them, Frannie said, "You two look even more amazing tonight than you did this afternoon."

When they reached the path to Mitchell Hall, Frannie said, "You guys go on. There's, no need to come with me. Stephen and I will catch up with you."

J.R. hesitated, then said, "OK, see you there."

Stephen was not on the porch. With a sigh, Frannie climbed the steps and settled into a chair, stifling her disappointment.

Stephen emerged ten minutes later with Greg, James, and three other boys. They were teasing Stephen about something. Stephen punched Greg on the shoulder, hooked his thumbs in his belt and sauntered over, John Wayne style. "Howdy little lady. My name is Matt Dillon... Marshall Dillon. And what might be your name?"

Giggling, she responded, "Well, Marshall Dillon, you can call me Miss Kitty. I run the saloon here in Dodge."

He forced a laugh and leaned in to give her a light kiss on the lips, checking out the cleavage framed by the bodice of her dress. She kissed him back, pleased that he felt so comfortable kissing her in front of his friends.

Stephen grinned wolfishly at Greg and James. "You guys get going. I want to be alone with my lady." They left, laughing, and making hand gestures that puzzled Frannie.

"I love your get-up, Marshall Dillon. Where did you get the guns?"

"I've had 'em forever. I must be a tad bigger around the waist than when I was six. Go figure," he explained with a grin. I had to swap for a bigger belt." A cowboy hat, boots, and a tinfoil star with *Marshall* written in black marker topped off his outfit.

"We make a fantastic couple," Frannie exclaimed, as they walked down the steps hand in hand. "Wait 'til you hear about the party we hosted at the children's home today. It was fabulous!"

"I'm sure it was," Stephen replied dismissively. "Let's hustle. We don't want to miss anything. This shindig starts with a big show, like a pep rally. Then there's live music, but I'm not much for dancing. I could use something to drink."

Frannie hurried to keep up. She was disappointed that Stephen wasn't interested in hearing about the party.

"Quite a show, like I said," Stephen announced as they entered the huge space decorated with Halloween paraphernalia and ghostly lighting. Stephen ordered them each a *Coke*.

Frannie still hadn't thought of a tactful way to tell him that she preferred *Dr. Pepper*.

The skit began with spooky music and a Coyote sheriff on a broomstick galloping in pursuit of the rival Cowboys. The party-goers clapped their appreciation of the clever combination of team spirit and Halloween celebration.

Following the skit, dance music replaced the spooky Halloween sounds and the lights dimmed. "Are we going to dance?" Frannie asked, "We make a good-looking couple in our matching costumes."

"Later. I told you I'm not much for dancing," Stephen said grabbing her hand and pulling her toward a distant booth where Greg and James stood in line.

"You have to see this," Stephen said over his shoulder. "They've set up a dunking booth and I heard the Dean of Students volunteered for the plank. I can't wait for a shot at him." Stephen purchased a ticket for three throws. "Stand here," he told Frannie. "You'll have a perfect view when I topple that asshole into the drink." Stephen handed her his drink and got in line, itching to demonstrate his pitching prowess.

The Dean of Students was perched on the platform, his smug expression indicating he'd survived a volley of misplaced pitches. The smug expression disappeared when Stephen's first throw hit the mark and he plunged into the water. The crowd cheered.

"Gotcha!" yelled Stephen as he jumped into the air, pumping his fist.

The Dean emerged from the water, sputtering, and climbed back onto the platform. His expression said, *Lucky shot, Punk. You won't do that again.*

Stephen glared at his target, took aim, and let the ball fly. The crowd roared again as the Dean plunged into the water.

This time, when the Dean emerged his expression was hostile. As soon as he was seated, Stephen fired the last ball and the Dean disappeared into the tank for the third time. The crowd filled the air with "Way to go! Good eye! Great job!" The booth captain handed Stephen a small, stuffed Coyote, then, hollered, "Next."

"What was that all about?" Frannie asked as she handed Stephen his drink.

He shrugged, "That guy had it coming. He has been on my case since I came to CU."

"How come?"

"Ahhhh, last year in English, Dr. Benton got a burr up her butt about my plagiarizing something, and that asswipe Dean of Students believed her. I owed that guy and you gotta admit, I showed him a thing or two. Let's have some fun," Stephen said, putting their drinks on a table and pulling her close for a slow dance.

"But I thought…" Stephen's "shhhh" cut her off as he positioned her arms around his neck and pulled her into him. Frannie's breath quickened. A fast dance followed and they left the floor. The loud music made conversation difficult and Stephen whispered in her ear, "You smell great tonight. What is that you are wearing?"

Enchanted by his interest, she replied, "It's Revlon's *Jean Naté*. My brother first bought it for me on my sixteenth birthday and it's my favorite."

"Cool. You should wear it every time we are together."

They settled at the table where Stephen had left their drinks. "Wait here while I go to the men's room," Stephen instructed. When he returned, his jeans' pockets bulged noticeably. "Let's go to the gazebo. It will be lots cooler and quieter."

Pleased at the thought of being alone with him, she rose without a word. "The Gazebo will be our own private place." At the same time, she remembered their last encounter in the gazebo, the magnificent new sensations and the confusion and guilt that had overwhelmed her. She didn't resist as he pulled her along, but she determined to keep the situation under control.

Frannie looked through the gazebo's glass walls across the campus. "This is such a Cinderella place."

Stephen gently pulled her down onto a bench and withdrew a beer from his pocket. "You just have to know the right people," he said, popping the top and handing her the can. He opened a second for himself.

He pulled her close. "You were going to tell me about some kids' party."

Elated that he'd remembered, she described her encounter with Karen and explained what an emotional experience it had been. She sipped her beer as she spoke, Stephen listened without comment. "It was an amazing event," she concluded.

"Hmmm, sounds interesting. Glad you had fun." He took Frannie's nearly empty beer and placed both cans on the ground. He leaned in and kissed her, then nibbled her ear. She snuggled closer as he trailed kisses down her neck and gently stroked her back. Frannie was lost in the waves of delightful sensation that coursed through her body with each touch and each kiss.

The tug of conscience she felt as he inched her zipper from neck to waist and unhooked her bra faded with the pleasure from the warmth of his hand on her bare back. When Stephen cupped her breast and teased her nipple, she recognized the spasm of passion that arced through her body, the memory making it all the more delicious.

Her mind was lulled into submission; she took cues only from her body. She basked in the thrill of his touch, the sound of his whispered endearments, and the newness of the experience. It wasn't until he parted her legs and stroked her inner thigh over the fishnet hose that her mind engaged and apprehension penetrated her delicious trance.

"Stephen," she murmured, "No, don't"

He made no comment as he probed gently.

"Stephen," she said as she struggled to overcome her mental paralysis. "We have to stop this now. We can't do this. It's wrong."

"There's no one around," he whispered into her ear.

She hesitated, but pushed him away, her mind winning the war. "No. Not here, not like this. I love the way you make me feel, but… I know this isn't right. This is for married people."

He realized she was serious and the moment lost. "Okay, fine…" his voice chilly. "I'll take you back to the dorm."

His abruptness confused her. "Stephen, I want to be with you. I like it when you hold me and kiss me, but we can't do more than that. It's wrong."

"Okay," he sighed, accepting the temporary defeat.

She fastened her bra. "Will you zip my dress, please?

When the zipper reached the top, he leaned in and kissed her neck. She stiffened momentarily, then leaned into him. "Do we have time to take a walk and still be at the dorm before curfew?" she asked.

"Sure, why not?" Stephen answered in an icy tone. He collapsed the beer cans and pocketed them. They sauntered, holding hands, saying little. On the Hadley Hall porch, Stephen kissed her goodnight and left without a word. Frannie stood and watched until he was out of sight, smiling as her body remembered how he had made her feel. Then she frowned as her conscience reminded her that good girls shouldn't do what she had been doing.

Chapter 12

Stephen dropped his backpack on the lab table and pulled Frannie to him for a hug. Frannie snuggled into his arms, then pulled away, embarrassed by the snickering from the next table. "It's so much more romantic when we're alone," she whispered.

"Then let's do something romantic on Friday night. I can borrow the Mustang," Stephen announced with a satisfied expression.

"I'd love…" she began, then realized that she would be leaving on Friday for the weekend at Katie's. "I… I can't," she continued, her disappointment obvious. "I'm going to Atoka with my suitemates this weekend. I would have declined if I'd known you were going to ask me out, but I can't back out now."

With a look of disgust, he said, "Have a good time."

The remark took Frannie aback. *"What is wrong with him? That's selfish! I hope he's just disappointed, not angry."*

"It's only one weekend, Stephen. I'll be back on Sunday, maybe even early enough for us to spend some time together."

Stephen shrugged. "Sure. If I'm not busy, maybe we'll do something."

The Wake-Up Call

The sitting room was empty when Frannie entered the suite. She opened the bedroom door. Robin dressed in pajamas, sat cross-legged on her bed, and looked up, startled. A ring sat on her left palm; on her lap was a letter. She swiped tears from her face. "Oh, hi," she said, forcing a smile. Did you have a good evening?"

Frannie gazed at Robin, concerned. "R-r-robin, are you OK? What's wrong?"

"Oh, it's nothing. I started to pack for the weekend since I'm working tomorrow, and I discovered this in my drawer. My grandmother gave me a package the day I left for Crestmont. Our first day was so hectic that I put it away to open later, and then it slipped my mind."

"Well, what is it? Why did it make you cry?"

"It's Gram's wedding ring. I had no idea that it was in the package. It's her most valuable possession. Gram's family comes from Ireland. She is a descendant of the only three that made it to America during the potato famine. This was her great-great grandmother's wedding ring, and it's been passed to the oldest girl in each generation since then. I knew it would be mine someday, but something made her give it to me early. That's what made me cry. I'm worried about Gram…"

"Look. I have something like that," Frannie interrupted, lifting the locket she wore around her neck. "My brother, Petey, gave this to me on my sixteenth birthday, and I never take it off. He's the most wonderful brother. He's smart and handsome. He was in ROTC in college and then went into the Army. Now he's a Second Lieutenant. He's stationed at Fort Meade in Maryland. We're lucky because he's not too far from home and can come over to visit often. He's in Intelligence so he doesn't think he'll have to go to Vietnam."

Robin sighed, slid the ring onto her old gold chain, and clasped it around her neck. "Let me see the locket, Frannie."

Frannie opened the locket. Robin leaned forward to see the picture. "Is that Petey? He's a cool-lookin' dude."

"He's gorgeous. He's five years older than me, and he's always looked out for me. I can't understand how some brothers and sisters just *hate* each other. Petey loves me. When I was little, he was my babysitter and he didn't mind at all. Then when I was old enough, he would take me with him wherever he went… except on dates, of course. But he always made sure I liked the girls he was dating."

"You are a piece of work, Roomie… sweet, but so naïve."

Frannie continued to gush. "I know Petey would just *love* Stephen. Petey likes when I'm happy, and Stephen makes me happy."

Robin decided that Frannie needed a reality check. Without a doubt, if someone didn't wake *Sleeping Beauty*, she was going to get herself in deep shit. "Frannie," Robin began. "If Petey is a fine man, he wouldn't like Stephen at all. He'd see him immediately for the conniving, arrogant, selfish, rude creep that he is. He'd notice right away how Stephen treats you compared to how J.R. treats Missy."

Frannie's face fell. "But…," she began, and Robin interrupted.

"Listen to me, you're on your own now. Your folks might still be paying the bills, but they're not here to take care of you. When you make bad decisions, your folks and Petey won't be able to pick up the pieces when things turn to shit. It's a shame that Petey's not here to remind you how a gentleman behaves."

"But…"

"Listen up! Stop saying *but*. We're your friends. We're trying hard to protect you, and you're not helping at all. Making excuses for that badass instead of listening to us isn't your best option. I'm sorry, but I think you're going to wish you had."

※

Convincing Frannie she only needed one suitcase for the weekend had been a challenge. After stowing the suitcases, Leslie shut

Nellie's trunk. "Does anyone get carsick?" she asked. All three girls shook their heads. "Then it makes sense for Katie to sit up front to navigate."

"We're off on an adventure," Frannie giggled. "If Stephen were coming, it would be perfect." Robin groaned. Leslie's and Katie's sighs acknowledged the futility of any effort to enlighten Frannie.

"We'll get to the farm before dinner," said Katie. I asked Mom to invite my best friend, John, and his dad so he can meet all of you. I'm excited to be going home. Can you believe that this is the first time I've ever been away?"

"I think Crestmont is a first for all of us," Robin said.

"I've never been on a farm before," Frannie exclaimed. "You have cows and horses, don't you? I love animals. I've never ridden a horse or touched a cow."

"Yes, we have horses and cows… and pigs, chickens, and a goat," Katie laughed. "Our animals are for working the farm and food. We raise crops to sell. I'll introduce you to the livestock when we get there, Frannie."

"I've never been on a farm, either," Robin mused. "I've lived in a noisy, crowded city my whole life. This weekend is going to be a breath of fresh air."

Frannie, her nose plastered to the window, pointed out every cow and horse they passed.

"What a great drive this is," Leslie said, sweeping eyes over fields and trees. "The countryside is different from Abita Springs, but it's just as peaceful. Paul was so disappointed that I wanted to spend the weekend on your farm instead of coming home. He accused me of liking my girlfriends more than him. I thought that was funny but as unhappy as he's been with every decision I've made since high school, he might just be right."

It was 4:00 when they turned into the drive and rolled to a stop in front of the house. Katie's parents and John rushed down the porch steps to greet them.

"Give me a big hug." Katie's mom stretched her arms wide and Katie ran into them.

"Hey there, girls," said Katie's Dad. "It's nice to see you again, Leslie. Move-in day seems like a long time ago. John and I will take your suitcases inside, and you can pull the car around."

"You can't imagine how we've missed you. We're so proud, Katie Girl." Katie hugged her mother again, realizing that she'd missed her more than she'd admitted to herself.

Releasing Katie, Mrs. Grayfox turned to Leslie. "Leslie, Katie tells me that you're on the basketball team and that the Coyotes are doing well this season. Your parents must be proud of you."

"Thank you," replied Leslie. "The team *is* doing well. Katie chose this weekend for us to come because we don't have a game and I wouldn't have to miss the trip. It's nice of you to have us."

"Robin extended her hand. "I'm Robin, and that's Frannie." Frannie stood gazing wide-eyed at the chicken coop and the goat eyeing them from her pen by the barn.

"I'm John," said the tall, handsome young man coming back down the steps. "Nice to meet all of you. I live next door. The Grayfoxes are my second family and Katie's been my best friend as long as I can remember. Welcome home, Princess."

"How's your Dad?" asked Katie, concern evident in her voice. "Is he doing as well as you've written?"

"He definitely is," John assured her. "He's certain that he'll be right as rain by spring and will be able to manage the farm so that I can head off to college."

"Fantastic!" Katie said, relieved. "I wasn't sure if you were just trying to keep me from worrying."

Katie's mother interrupted, "Katie's brothers should be in shortly to clean up. Then we'll have dinner. First, you four settle in. Katie, I put you in Naomi's room." Turning to the others, she explained, "I made up a cot in Katie's room for one of you and the other two can share her queen bed."

"That sounds wonderful, Mrs. Grayfox," said Robin. "C'mon, Frannie."

Frannie pulled her eyes away from the goat. "Isn't that the cutest goat you ever saw?"

The Wake-Up Call

"I think he's the ONLY goat I've ever seen," Robin laughed, pulling Frannie up the steps into the house.

"Katie, I love your room," Robin said. "Mine at home is half this size."

"Well, girls," said Mrs. Grayfox when they all came down for dinner, this is Mr. Brown, John's father. Amos, meet Leslie, Katie's roommate, and Robin, and Frannie. These two strapping fellows are Sam and Joe, Katie's brothers."

Mr. Grayfox walked to one end of the table and John pulled out the chair at the other end for Mrs. Grayfox. Mrs. Grayfox reached out a hand to Katie on her left and Sam on her right. Everyone followed her lead, holding hands around the table while Mr. Grayfox gave thanks to the Creator for the company gathered in their home, for the food they would eat, and for the health and well-being of the family and their guests.

Katie explained, "Everything on the dinner table comes from the farm. We grow crops to sell, but we keep a garden and a small orchard just for us."

"Seems like forever since I've had a real home cooked meal," said Leslie.

"I hope you enjoy it." Mrs. Grayfox acknowledged the compliment.

After dinner, the girls helped Mrs. Grayfox with the dishes, then left with John for a walk in the fresh evening air. Frannie asked, "What time do the animals go to sleep at night? Will any of them still be up?"

"You can meet Daisy. I don't think she ever sleeps, and you two seemed to be making friends when you first arrived," laughed John.

"Is Daisy that adorable goat?" Frannie exclaimed. "Can I pet her?"

"Let's find out." He and Katie walked side by side, leading the three girls toward the barn.

"Daisy, I'd like you to meet Frannie," John said as they approached the small white goat. John opened Daisy's gate and ushered them into her pen.

Daisy stared at Robin. "I think she likes your red hair," Katie giggled. Robin scratched the goat's neck. Just think, 18 and I've never touched a goat before."

"Can I pet her, too?" asked Frannie, moving closer. Daisy leaned toward Frannie, took a mouthful of her peasant blouse, and pulled her close. Frannie, speechless and a little frightened, stared while the hem of her blouse slowly disappeared as the goat chewed. "What do I do?" she cried.

The others couldn't stop laughing. John reached a finger into the side of Daisy's mouth, making her release the wrinkled, wet material. "She likes you." John laughed. "She wouldn't eat just *anyone's* blouse."

Frannie couldn't tell if John was serious or teasing. With one hand holding her blouse tight to her body, she reached with the other to Daisy, who leaned into her hand. "Her ears are so soft," Frannie said, "and I think she *does* like me. Next time could I bring her something to eat besides my clothes?"

"Sure," smiled Katie, knowing that Daisy would eat anything. "If you're up early tomorrow morning, we can feed the chickens and gather the eggs."

"Not gonna happen," said Robin. "Frannie never gets up early."

Frannie's eyes were wide. "Can I do that? When I was little, my parents took me to the petting zoo near Hershey Park, but it was *nothing* like this."

"So, girls," said John. "Tell me about college. I need to know what to look forward to. It seems like I'll be starting next year."

"What's wrong with your dad?" Frannie blurted out while the others were thinking of a polite way to ask.

"He had an accident a year ago. The tractor rolled over and crushed his pelvis. It's a miracle that he's able to walk. I've never seen anyone so determined to recover. I was supposed to start college this year, but I stayed home to keep the farm going. He's determined that I'm not going to miss another year. He's an amazing dad."

"Where's your Mom?" Frannie asked. The girls cringed.

The Wake-Up Call

John replied without hesitation. "Mom's been gone about ten years. She died right before my ninth birthday. I was lost, but dad stepped up and did a terrific job of being both parents for me. We grew close and it made mom's passing less devastating. I'm sure he feels that his commitment to my mother will be fulfilled if he can send me off to college to seek my fortune."

"I remember when John's mom died," Katie said. "I thought that John and Mr. Brown were going to die, too, they were so sad." She gave John a shy smile. "She would be so proud of both of you."

The group walked on, enjoying the quiet evening and the clean, earthy smell of growing things. "Katie," Robin said, reaching out to squeeze her hand. "Thanks for inviting us. This is going to be a glorious weekend. I could spend it just walking around enjoying the peace and quiet, not to mention not having to work."

"Tomorrow can I see the rest of the animals? Do all of them show how much they love you by eating your clothes?" They all laughed, though Frannie really wanted to know.

※

The next morning, Katie awoke at six. She lay in bed, thinking *"How nice to be home."* Naomi was still asleep at 6:30, so Katie dressed and joined her mother in the kitchen. "Let your friends sleep as late as they'd like," Mrs. Grayfox said. "When you live with a schedule, it's a treat to sleep in. Do you girls have plans for today?"

"No, nothing special," Katie replied, "unless there's something going on in town. I haven't talked much with them about living in a Choctaw community, but if there's something interesting to share, I wouldn't mind bringing up the subject."

Mrs. Grayfox poured Katie a cup of coffee. "There's nothing like cream from a cow," Katie mused, pulling the cream pitcher from the refrigerator. "I think they make what we have at school out of chalk dust and dishwater."

"There's a lot to be said for growing up on a farm. Katie, I have hesitated to ask, but have you had to deal with anything like the "Squaw Girl" situation in high school?"

Katie looked up at her mother. "Not at all so far. I think the problem in Atoka is that there are lots of Choctaw in town and that gives the immature Whites a big choice of targets. Most of the kids at college are white, but we have some Negroes… Blacks, I should say, and Latinos, and I haven't seen evidence of prejudice against anyone. Sometimes I think that my Indian heritage could be an asset with the current emphasis on equality and equal opportunity."

"That's good to hear, Sweetheart." Mrs. Grayfox reached across to squeeze her hand. "It made me so sad and angry to see how unhappy those White girls made you in High School. I am positive it was jealousy. None of those girls were good students, and you were. The White kids who were bright didn't behave that way."

"I feel more grown up for having experienced that," Katie confided. "It's interesting how different one freshman can be from another. Take the four of us. We couldn't *be* more different. Robin comes from a broken home in what sounds like a seedy part of Chicago. Her grandmother took her away from abusive parents and, according to Robin, her Gram did a fantastic job of raising her. Robin's a bit rough and she cusses a lot, but I don't think she even realizes it."

"I hope Dad doesn't hear her. He's not tolerant of disrespectful language."

"She's pretty sharp. I think the language she uses depends upon the situation and who's involved. She's toned down in the couple of months we've been in school. You can bet she'll cuss when she talks about Frannie, though. They're such opposites. Robin is street smart. Frannie is clueless and comes straight out of a Beaver Cleaver family where Daddy provides and Mommy takes care of everything. She's never had to take responsibility for anything. If we didn't help, she'd never get her laundry done, her bed made, or her clothes put away."

"That's hard to imagine. What child doesn't have chores when they're little and odd jobs to earn spending money later?"

"That's easy," Katie smiled. *Frannie!* What's worse is that she's bright and didn't have to study in high school, so she's convinced that it will be the same in college, even after failing the first chemistry test and getting a *C* on an essay she was positive was *A* material. She's in college because that's what you do after high school. She chose nursing because her grandmother lives with them and has multiple sclerosis.

"The sad part is that she's never had to face challenges nor make decisions on her own. Worse, she knows nothing about boys, and she's head over heels in love with a real dud. It's so obvious to everyone but Frannie what he's after. We're all concerned for her, but she's determined not to listen. Robin's the toughest on her, but it's because the friends Robin left behind in Chicago were losers, and she says that Frannie's heartthrob is just like her ex-boyfriend. Robin's positive that Frannie's going to get hurt."

Mrs. Grayfox shook her head. "I do hope that things will work out for her."

"Leslie is more like me than Robin or Frannie. She grew up in a big family and has always worked in her parents' grocery store. She has to study for her grades, and to make it harder, her athletic commitment takes a lot of time that she would otherwise spend studying."

"I'm sure you study together when you can. That should help both of you." Mrs. Grayfox put her finger to her lips to warn Katie that someone was coming down the stairs. She was sure it was one of the girls because Naomi would sleep until ten, and Mr. Grayfox, Sam, and Joe had been out in the fields since six.

Robin and Leslie came into the kitchen together. "Good morning, Mrs. Grayfox," said Robin. "Thank you for having us here. It's such a treat to be away from campus and not have to work even one shift all weekend."

Leslie said, "Frannie's still asleep. We decided not to wake her unless you have plans that she won't want to miss."

"Shall we wait for breakfast until she comes down?" asked Mrs. Grayfox.

"I'll go wake her," said Robin. "She won't want to miss breakfast, and we'll be ready for dinner if we let her wake up on her own. Come to think of it, she'll be upset if she misses anything this weekend. She's like a kid at… what did she call that park with the animals?"

"Hershey Park, I think… like the chocolate," Leslie volunteered.

"Right, she's like a kid at a petting zoo." Robin left to wake Frannie.

"So… what would you like for breakfast?" Mrs. Grayfox asked no one in particular.

"I would love a glass of juice." Leslie smiled. "We might not want to wait on Frannie to get breakfast started. She can take forever to get ready for the day, no matter what's on the agenda."

They sat around the table enjoying coffee and juice. "Leslie, tell me more about the basketball team."

"It's exciting when we win. But, it puts a lot of pressure on the team to stay on top. The girls are good and we've been practicing hard." Leslie took a breath. "Coach Thomas is a big teddy bear. He talks loud and acts gruff, but he's not." She took a deep breath. "It's such a treat to be here. No practice and no games for three whole days."

Everyone was surprised when Robin came down the steps leading Frannie by the hand. "I told her we were waiting on her for breakfast so she can primp on her own time."

"You look so fresh and pretty, Frannie," said Mrs. Grayfox. Frannie smiled through sleepy eyes.

"Now that we're all present and accounted for," Mrs. Grayfox said, "what shall we fix for breakfast? Robin? Frannie? Coffee is right there if you would like some, and there is juice in the refrigerator."

Breakfast was a feast… omelets with bacon, sausage, and cheese, homemade biscuits with fresh butter and homemade jam, orange juice, and milk. "I missed gathering eggs this morning, didn't I?" Frannie asked, lifting a forkful of omelet to her mouth.

"Would someone get me up early enough tomorrow so I don't miss the eggs again?"

"We all missed that this morning. By the time I got downstairs, Mom had fed the men, the chickens, and everything else," Katie said.

"Oh!" Frannie exclaimed, disappointment clear on her face, " I guess I won't get to feed chickens after all." She brightened, "So, what are we doing today? John said we can walk around the farm and see the animals. Is John coming over?"

"He certainly is," came a voice from the back porch. "Morning, everyone. Are you ladies up for a trip to town? There's a fair in Atoka this weekend. It would be a great opportunity for Katie and me to show off a bit. Indian handcrafts are quite impressive, and this fair will have the best of them on display. Anyone interested?" John asked the girls.

Mrs. Grayfox interrupted, "Day plans can wait until after breakfast. Join us, John. I'm sure that you and your dad didn't take the time for more than a slice of toast and coffee." To the girls, she said, "Men will eat like breakfast is their only meal of the day *if* it's waiting for them, but they can barely manage coffee and toast if they have to fix it for themselves." She turned to John with a no-nonsense look, "You be sure your dad understands that we expect him here for breakfast when you're away at school. You tell him that it's *not* a bother and I won't accept any excuses."

John said. "He'll appreciate that, though I know you'll have to reassure him that he's not putting you out."

John swept his gaze around the table. "So, girls, how about the Fair?"

Robin, Leslie, and Frannie all spoke at once, then stopped and giggled. "I'm in," said Robin.

"Me, too," chorused Leslie and Frannie

John said, "Katie, I hope that artist from Sulphur is there. Remember how impressive his beadwork was? And those magnificent paintings by the artist from Hugo. His subjects were so real they could have walked right off the canvas."

"I remember," Katie replied. "There were other artists I would love to see again, too. It makes me proud to see the beautiful things that our people produce. I'm glad that we'll get to share a bit of our culture."

"Oh, and there's something else I'm sure you've never seen before," John said, pleased that he'd thought of it. "Stickball. It's a wild game that Choctaw men have been playing for centuries. Stickball was how men used to get into good physical condition… call it the *Gold's Gym* of the Choctaw nation. It was also an official way to settle disputes. It is a rough and tumble game, but it's a lot less deadly than dueling.

"So, picture thirty strong men on each team," John continued, "each one wielding two hickory sticks with a small cup at the end to capture and throw a small, hard ball called a *towa*. Oh, and no protective gear. The only rules are no touching the towa with your hands, and no head-butting. They score by throwing the ball against the opponent's goal post or touching the goalpost with the stick when the ball is in the cup. Thirty guys want that to happen, and the other thirty are determined that it won't. Trust me, watching a match is an experience."

You all hurry along and have fun. This will be your last vacation until Thanksgiving. I expect that you'll all be going home for that long weekend."

"I will," chirped Frannie, "and Petey is supposed to get leave and spend the whole weekend with us, too. I can't wait."

"Me, too," replied Leslie. "Thanksgiving has always been a big event in our household. It's a busy time at the store, so we're either at the store helping Daddy or at home helping Mama with Thanksgiving dinner. Somehow it all comes together. It's one of my favorite holidays."

When Robin didn't volunteer any information, Mrs. Grayfox said, "Robin, is Thanksgiving a big event in your family?"

"I'll be staying in Dallas to work that weekend, then I'll fly home for Christmas vacation in less than a month."

"Hmmm," murmured Mrs. Grayfox then decided not to pursue the matter. Shooing them out, she said, "You'll want plenty of time at the Fair. John, take our pickup. The girls might enjoy riding in the back, letting their hair blow."

"Really?" said Frannie "I've never ridden in a pickup before."

"I was going to suggest that Naomi go with you, but she's still sleeping. I think this is a case of *you snooze, you lose*. Katie, take a couple of quilts. It will be cold in the back when you come home. If you won't be home in time for dinner, please call and let me know."

The four girls' grabbed handbags and sweaters, then settled onto feed bags in the pickup bed.

"Don't stand up until we get there," John cautioned. "It's hard to keep your balance when the pickup is moving."

The ride into town took less time than it took to find a place to park. The town was bustling and the fairgrounds teemed with people.

"Are we going on the rides?" Frannie asked.

"With the other six-year old's?" Robin retorted.

"Okay, then. Where *are* we going?" Frannie turned to John, trying not to look hurt.

"I suggest starting with the Arts and Crafts tent over there," John said. "When we get hungry, food is in that red and white striped tent next to it. You'll be impressed at the variety of dishes people bring. I think Mrs. Grayfox mentioned not coming home for dinner because she knows how much amazing food there is. Frannie, that smaller blue and white striped tent over there is the petting zoo. We can stop there to make up for missing the chickens this morning if you want."

"Oh yes," crooned Frannie. "That's a must!"

As John had predicted, the arts and crafts were impressive, with bright colors and intricate designs. "Katie!" Robin exclaimed, "With outfits like these, you would have made a spectacular Indian Princess at the Halloween party."

Katie was pleased that Robin was open and enthusiastic about her Indian heritage. From behind them, a voice called out, "Well, lookee here. Squaw Girl showed up!" Katie tensed, her face reddening. She turned her back to the voice. "Hey, Squaw Girl, how's *kahhhhledge?*"

Robin turned and saw a tall, rough-looking White girl flanked by two others, snickering and pointing at Katie. She balled her fists and moved menacingly in their direction. The girls towered over her 5'5" frame, but Robin's flashing green eyes forced them back. She growled, "Who the hell do you think you're talking to, Bitch? Do you have a problem with my friend? Or do you have a problem with education? Or am I missing something?"

The girl stood dumbfounded.

"You deaf?" Robin challenged. Fists on her hips, Robin closed in on the girls. "I asked, what's your problem, Punks?" The three girls backed slowly away from Robin. "Actually, *I* have a problem… with *YOU!*" Robin pointed at the leader. "A lowlife like you can't talk to your betters like that. Get it? I think an apology is in order, Bitch." The girls turned and ran.

Robin watched them retreat, then turned back to her friends. Frannie opened her mouth to speak, but Leslie squeezed her arm. Robin grinned and a smile crept across Katie's face. John watched the entire incident with obvious satisfaction. He put his arm around Katie's shoulders and broke the silence. "Shall we move on?" With no further discussion, they continued to enjoy the artwork, marveling at the quality and complexity of the items in the craft tent.

"I love these moccasins," cooed Frannie. "They'd go great with my pedal pushers. Will you all wait while I buy them? Every time I wear them, they'll remember what a great weekend we had.

While Frannie was writing a check, Leslie leaned toward the others, "How much do you want to bet that she's going to buy something for Stephen?"

"Disaster in the making," Robin responded. "She'll be disappointed because he couldn't care less, and he won't even have the smarts to pretend that he does. I can read that asshole like a book."

"I wonder what I should buy for Stephen," Frannie chirped as she rejoined her friends. She looked bewildered when Katie, Leslie, and Robin burst out laughing.

"Nothing. You should buy him nothing." Robin stated. "Guys give girls gifts. It's not his birthday or Christmas… Move on!"

Frannie thought for a minute, *"Robin has a point. How nice that she didn't just say something snarky."*

"Thanks, Robin. That makes sense."

John and Katie walked together, watching Frannie, Leslie, and Robin as they examined the arts and crafts. "Katie, it's good to see you happy. I can't get over how different you four girls are, and yet you get along just fine."

Katie replied, "It's worked out well. Frannie is a bit of a challenge. She grew up so sheltered that she's hardly ready to be on her own. But worse, she has terrible taste in boys. She's gaga over a guy named Stephen whom Robin has pegged as a bad actor."

"I like Robin," John said. "She has a strong personality, and she likes you. You two seem like opposites, but you have the same values. You're both wise but in different ways. I hope she comes back to visit."

Katie smiled. "I can tell that Mom is determined to get her here for Thanksgiving. She almost invited her this morning."

"That would be great. Thanksgiving is just weeks away, and I've missed you a lot."

"Missed you, too. I'm glad that you thought of the Fair. We're all having a great time."

As John had promised, the stickball tournament was an amazing experience. The sixty men on the field were of every height and build, but they were all in excellent shape. The girls were caught up in the excitement, screaming for whichever team was close to scoring a goal.

Frannie commented, "The entire town participated in *Running of the Bulls* in Pamplona, Spain, so why shouldn't all of Atoka play today."

"Well, maybe you do get something from all those love stories you read," Robin said.

While they were watching the game, and cheering for both sides, a child's wail caught Frannie's attention. She turned to see a little boy about five holding a cone and staring at a scoop of ice cream on the ground at his feet. A girl a few years older was trying to soothe him. "She didn't mean to bump you. It was an accident. You can share my cone. Mommy didn't give me enough money to buy you another one." The little boy continued to wail, staring at his lost treat.

Frannie knelt by the child. "My goodness," she said with a smile. "What happened here?"

The little girl looked surprised but smiled at the pretty blonde who had gotten her little brother to stop crying. "A lady knocked Jimmy's ice cream on the ground. She didn't mean it."

"Well," Frannie said, reaching into her bag. "I just happen to have an extra twenty cents. Can you get Jimmy another one?"

"Really?" The little girl beamed. "Thank you, Lady. Jimmy, say *thank you* to the nice lady."

Jimmy sniffled and said "Fank you, Lady" and looked at his sister. "Can I have my ice cream now?" he insisted. Frannie winked at the little boy and went back to watch stickball.

Robin watched the interchange, then turned back to the game before Frannie realized that she'd been observed.

The group made their way back to the red and white striped tent to sample the array of homemade foods. Two favorite Choctaw recipes were Banaha cornbread cooked in corn shucks like a tamale, and Nipi Shila, deer jerky smoked over an open fire right at the fair. "Watching them fix that food is fascinating but the taste is even better," said Frannie.

"Let me call Mom and tell her that we won't make it home for dinner, I'll be right back," Katie said, running off to find a payphone.

"I hate to miss one of Katie's mother's fantastic meals, but I don't know where I'd put another mouthful," Leslie said. "I'll have to run extra laps all week to lose the pounds I've put on this weekend"

"What a day this has been," Robin said. "Thanks for thinking of the Fair, John. You were right about the amazing art and the crafts. I've never seen anything genuinely Indian-made before, and I am impressed. You and Katie have good reason to be proud of your heritage."

Chapter 13

"Katie, what a weekend!" Frannie exclaimed. "I'm going to write a thank you note to your mother and I need your address."

"She'll appreciate that. I'll write the address down for you."

"That's thoughtful," said Robin. "There *are* things we can learn from you." Frannie's smile faded when Robin continued, "and there are things you can learn from *us*, like putting studying ON and taking Stephen OFF your *to-do* list!"

Robin caught Katie's eye. "I had an awesome time, too. Your mother is super cool, and John was such wonderful company. It was a great weekend."

"That goes for me, too," added Leslie. "Frannie, can we all sign your thank you note?"

Frannie brightened. "Sure, I'll write it from all of us."

"This season is the best part of the whole school year," Leslie commented. Homecoming is in two weeks, then Thanksgiving, and before you know it, Christmas vacation.

The Wake-Up Call

"Speaking of Thanksgiving, Robin," Katie smiled, "my mother wants you to spend it with us, and she insisted she'd accept no excuses."

"That's kind of her, but I'm scheduled to work over the holiday weekend."

"You have plenty of time to negotiate with Mr. Davis for the time off. Thanksgiving is such a long weekend to be here all alone. Please think about it."

"It *would* be nice. I could offer to work Homecoming weekend to get Thanksgiving off and maybe pick up a few extra hours in January Interim session. I'm sure Mr. Davis would be happy with that because no one wants to miss Homecoming."

"Sounds like a plan," said Katie, relieved that she hadn't had to argue her point. "It's a good thing Mom doesn't have to twist your arm," Katie smiled. "You have no idea how persuasive she can be."

"Oh!" Leslie exclaimed. "Katie, you and Robin can have Nellie that weekend and save your folks two round trips. Mama and Daddy bought me a ticket to fly home 'cuz they didn't want me to make the ten-hour drive to Abita Springs alone."

"Wow, that's an amazing offer," exclaimed Katie. "Robin, now it's even more important for you to come. You don't want me to have to make the drive by myself, do ya?"

"You've convinced me, but don't tell your mother until I check with Mr. Davis."

Frannie chimed in, "I can't wait for Thanksgiving. Petey is coming home for the whole weekend. We're so lucky that he's stationed close to home. He might come home for Christmas, too."

"It's nice that you and Petey are so close," Katie commented. "My brothers are more like uncles to me because they're so much older. John and I have been best friends as long as I can remember. I didn't realize how much I missed him until I saw him this weekend, so I can imagine how much you miss Petey. You'll have the whole Thanksgiving weekend to catch up."

"Katie, I just thought of something," Frannie said. "Does your family celebrate Thanksgiving the same way we do? It seems to me that American Indians might have a different perspective."

"Thanksgiving is one of my favorite holidays because, in our house, there's always been a feeling of joy and appreciation. Indians and White settlers shared that first Thanksgiving, so it just makes sense to take the word literally and give thanks."

"Your Thanksgiving dinner must be a feast since your mom is a great cook and you grow all that food," Frannie said. "Robin, you definitely have to go home with Katie."

"Our holiday will be a lot like yours, Katie," Leslie added. "It's one of my favorites, too, because it's always a happy time with loads of guests. Mama invites anyone who doesn't have a place to celebrate. One year she invited a whole family who'd just moved to town. Mama figured they wouldn't be settled in time for Thanksgiving, so there were seven of us Bleus, that family with four kids, my three cousins who were visiting, and two more people who showed up at the last minute. That year we had 18 for Thanksgiving dinner."

"WOW, that's more like a neighborhood bar-b-que than a sit-down dinner," Frannie proclaimed, "So… Robin, if you go home with Katie, we'll all have a fantastic Thanksgiving. Then Christmas is one month after that. I love this time of year."

<hr />

"Homecoming is just two weeks away," Leslie reminded her roommates. Paul is coming in and I hope he's more excited about Homecoming than he was over the bonfire weekend. He complained from the time he got here to the time he left."

"Guys can be dumb butts," commented Robin. "They think the world is all about them."

Leslie considered. "I shouldn't ruin Homecoming by expecting the worst."

"Good plan," Robin agreed. "If he acts like a dipshit, you'll know you've outgrown him."

Leslie sighed. "I hope it doesn't turn out that way. We were a great couple in high school. He knew my scholarship would determine where I'd go to school, so it's nonsense to think I picked Crestmont to get away from him."

"He should be proud of you for getting that scholarship," Frannie said.

"Thanks. I think part of the problem is that he didn't get one. He assumed that he would, but he didn't, and he never thought to have a plan B. I'll just have to wait and see how it goes."

"Homecoming is going to be the best weekend Stephen and I have had yet. We're going to the game on Friday and the dance on Saturday."

Robin asked, "Katie, do you think that John might come for Homecoming? You'll be alone for the game with these others paired up and me working. "I know you'd have more fun if he were here."

Katie smiled, "John's my soul mate, not my boyfriend, so I didn't think to ask. Anyhow, now's not the best time for him to be away. It's harvest, and his dad needs the help. John hasn't left the farm for more than a day since his Dad's accident."

"With his dad doing so well, John might consider a couple of days away. If this isn't the best time, then you need to ask him to come to the next campus shindig. Your folks are right next door if Mr. Brown needs help."

Leslie added, "If Paul and John came for a weekend, they could share a room. That would save them both money and I know they'd like each other. It wouldn't hurt for John's supportive attitude to rub off on Paul."

"John could meet Stephen, too," Frannie added. "I know Stephen would like him, and I'd much rather Stephen and I spent our time with you than with Greg and James."

"We'll see," Katie replied. "John will be pleased to know that all of you want him to come for the weekend.

"I'm going to the Game Room to see if Stephen's there," Frannie announced. "I haven't seen him all weekend, and Missy and J.R. might be there, too. Anyone want to come with me?"

Certain that she was speaking for all of them, Katie replied, "No, thanks, Frannie. You go have fun. We're going to get ready for classes tomorrow."

◆

Frannie panned the Game Room and spotted Stephen in the far corner, his arm around a girl as usual. As she approached, Frannie caught snatches of their conversation: "*Free for the weekend… great time, wasn't it?… again sometime…*" The girl looked up, then touched Stephen's lips to shush him.

"Stephen, I'm back." Startled, he turned toward her, then gave the girl's shoulders a squeeze and said, "Another time." The girl shrugged and left to watch the foosball game.

"Stephen, I had such a good time at Katie's, but I missed you. You would have loved it! Katie's mother is a great cook, and her friend John took us to the Fair on Saturday. I bought the most gorgeous pair of moccasins to go with the pedal pushers I'm wearing when we go out this weekend. What did you do this weekend?"

"Nothing," Stephen replied. "Hung out with the guys. Made my own fun."

"Who was that girl? I didn't recognize her."

"Oh, no one… a friend from home. She was in Dallas this weekend and stopped by to say *hi*. So, do you want to play a game of darts?"

"Uh… sure…" Frannie said, but…"

Stephen walked quickly to the dart board and had thrown two red darts by the time Frannie caught up.

Frannie picked up the blue darts. "You know," she pondered, "Homecoming is only two weeks away. I told the girls how great we'll look together. We have to go shopping for a tie and handkerchief for your suit jacket…"

"Suit? What do you mean? No one gets dressed up for Homecoming. Most folks just wear jeans and a nice shirt."

"But, Stephen, my new dress is glorious. The blue matches my eyes and it has an empire waist with a white ribbon. You *have* to wear a suit so the tie and handkerchief match my dress."

Stephen started to object, hesitated, then conceded with a sly smile. "Wanna grab my roommate's car and take a drive? We have plenty of time before the dorm closes. After all, you've been gone all weekend."

Frannie brightened. "I was hoping you missed me. I'd love to go for a ride with you."

Stephen put his arm around her shoulders and led her to the foosball table. Greg raised his eyebrows and tossed him the Mustang keys.

Frannie snuggled closer as they walked across the campus to the car. He unlocked Frannie's door, then walked around to unlock his. "We'll get something to drink," Stephen said as he settled into the car, "then park in the graveyard where we can be alone to talk?"

Frannie nodded. "I can't wait to tell you all about the weekend."

"Whatever," Stephen replied, and pulled in to the 7-11. "I'll be right back."

Frannie thought of all the details of the weekend. She didn't want to leave anything out.

Stephen dropped a sack behind his seat and drove to the cemetery. He backed the car into the stand of trees and shut the engine off. "C'mon Frannie," he said, opening his door. "The back seat is more comfortable."

"OK." She opened her door and they folded the front seats forward to give themselves added room. Frannie snuggled close to Stephen, and he reached to pull two beers from the sack. She wished he'd bought *Cokes,* or better still, a *Dr. Pepper* for her. Stephen opened both cans and emptied half his in one long swallow.

Frannie took a sip, then another. She glanced at the clock. They had just over an hour before curfew.

"Stephen put his arm around Frannie and pulled her close. "So, what did you do out there in the sticks?"

"Oh, we had a wonderful time. Katie's family has animals and a goat nearly ate my blouse. Her name is Daisy and she's the cutest thing you've ever seen. Katie's mother is a great cook and Katie's friend, John, took us to the fair. They had all kinds of wonderful things to buy. We ate so much we had to call Katie's mom and tell her not to fix dinner." She took a deep breath, then a gulp of her beer, and continued her story.

Stephen silenced her with a kiss, and Frannie melted into his arms. Stephen held her close, tracing gentle circles on her back as they finished their beers. Light-headed, Frannie cuddled deeper in the warmth of Stephen's body.

Stephen worked her blouse from the waistband of her slacks and continued tracing circles on her back. He unsnapped her bra and eased her back to lie on the seat. When he cupped her breast, she sighed, then, gasped when he gently pinched her nipple. He anchored her to the seat with kisses, his tongue teasing her lips apart. He stroked her tight abdomen with one hand and caressed her breast with the other. Detached from conscious thought, Frannie floated in a sea of pleasure.

"You're beautiful," he whispered in her ear as he lifted her shirt. Her breathing quickened when he encircled her breasts and nibbled at her nipples. She moaned and arched her chest to meet him.

When he unfastened her slacks, she stiffened reflexively. When Stephen ran his fingers just inside the waistband of her panties, she pushed him back and struggled to sit up. "Stephen, we can't do this. It's too far."

"Frannie, relax. We can't stop now. I need you."

Frannie stammered, "No Stephen, we can't do this." She pushed with both hands on his chest.

He took her wrists. "Frannie, trust me. It's alright. It's fine." He kissed her and tried to ease her back.

She shook her head as if to clear it. "No Stephen." she struggled to sit up, covering herself with her arms. "We can't do this now… not until we're married."

Stephen groaned and turned away from her. He sucked in a breath and repositioned his now uncomfortable erection. In a huff he climbed out of the car, leaving Frannie to manage for herself.

Frannie called to him. "I do love you Stephen, but we can't do that now. It just isn't right." Frannie refastened her bra, tucked in her shirt, zipped her pants, then climbed out of the car. Stephen was walking around, obviously uncomfortable.

"Frannie," Stephen said, taking a deep breath, "I care about you, but you can't just push me away like that. It hurts when you make me stop."

"I know," she replied, misinterpreting *hurts*. "I love you and I know that you love me, but we are moving way to fast."

"Frannie, I need you now. You can't just stop me like that."

"I know, Stephen," she said, missing the point. "We need to take our time. Think about what a wonderful evening Homecoming will be. You'll see how much fun we can have together doing other things"

"Right!" he snorted and climbed into the car. "Get in or you'll be late for curfew."

They drove to Hadley Hall in silence. Stephen pulled up to the curb and waited for her to get out, then drove off without even a *goodbye*.

Frannie was grateful that everyone was asleep. She climbed into bed and turned off the light that Robin had left on for her. She lay in bed thinking about how the evening had ended, the delightful sensations a distant memory. *Why was Stephen so angry when I told him to stop. I explained that we can't do that yet. I don't know what I would do if we went further. Stephen would marry me, but my parents would never forgive me."* Frannie drifted off with those troubling thoughts clouding her dreams.

Frannie sat with her friends in the Hadley Hall lobby, waiting for Stephen. Everyone was dressed in their Sunday finest for

Homecoming. "Stephen promised he would pick me up here this time," Frannie assured them. "He must have lost track of time."

J.R. muttered, *"How gallant of the prick."*

"He'll be here soon," said Leslie. "Stephen doesn't seem to care much about being on time."

Several tense minutes passed before the door opened and Stephen, his dress shirt unbuttoned and a wad of blue fabric in his hand, sauntered in with Greg and James in tow. He stopped just inside the door and pointed at Frannie. "There she is, Guys. C'mon, Frannie," and turned back toward the door. Frannie followed Stephen out of the dorm.

"Did you see that?" J.R. said. "He just walked in, summoned her like a puppy, and she got up and followed without a word." He shook his head and frowned. "Someone has to make her listen to reason. That dude is a prick and that whole relationship is a disaster just waiting to happen."

❦

Stephen waited for Frannie to catch up, then thrust his tie into her hands. She knotted it for him, while Greg and James made lewd comments about a girl dressing a guy in public.

"Stephen, why don't they just shut up and leave us alone?" Frannie hissed. Behind Frannie's back, Stephen gave them a *thumbs up.*

Stephen had not made a single comment about her dress or her hair, swept high on her head. Katie had said that she looked *a* like a fairytale princess."

Frannie took in the ballroom, the lovely prom decorations, and the dance music. "Let's dance," she said, reaching for Stephen's hand.

Stephen shrugged from her grasp. "Guys, find out where the girls are saving us a table. Frannie, I need a drink You can come with me or go with the guys."

Disappointed, Frannie hurried after Stephen as he strode toward a drink table. He winked at a student and said, "I'll take a couple specials." The student nodded and poured drinks into two plastic glasses that Stephen passed to Frannie. "Thanks, Man. Got two more?" He walked off with a drink in each hand, leaving Frannie to follow.

He found Greg and James, set his glasses on the table and pointed, "Get your drinks at that table, Guys. If you both go, you can carry extras." He sat, leaving Frannie to pull out her own chair, and downed the contents of one glass.

Frannie picked up a glass, took a sip, and wrinkled her nose. "What IS this?"

"A *real* drink. Don't make a scene. I sure as hell don't want to get caught."

The boys returned with drinks and several girls whom they didn't bother to introduce. Frannie finished her drink, surprised that it wasn't as bad as she'd thought. The *Coke* softened the bite of the liquor. "Stephen, can we dance?"

"Not now. I'm too hot in this get-up." He lifted his second cup. "Maybe once I get a little more of this in me." Disappointed, she sipped her drink and wondered if there were a way to salvage the evening. She paid little attention to the raucous laughter and missed the point of the off-color jokes. After what seemed like an eternity, Stephen asked her to dance.

Frannie grabbed his hand. "Whoa, girl." He tossed his jacket onto a chair. She pulled him to the dance floor and he scooped her into his arms.

"This is what I've been waiting for, slow dancing is so romantic." With her arms around his neck and his hands on her waist, they swayed to the music.

Two dances later, the music picked up and they separated, adjusting to the tempo. Before the end of the dance, Stephen announced, "I need a break," and turned toward their table. Frannie hustled after him. Stephen stuffed his tie in his jacket pocket and unbuttoned his top three shirt buttons. He flapped his collar to cool off, then said. "Be right back," and he took off before Frannie could ask him to bring her a *Dr. Pepper*. She sat back, fanned herself with a napkin, and finished her second drink.

Stephen set three drinks on the table. He leaned toward Greg and the red mustang keys changed hands. While Frannie sipped her fresh drink, Stephen guzzled one of his, then pulled her to the dance floor for a slow number. She was dizzy and held him tight. "It's hot in here," he said when the music stopped, propelling her toward their table. "Grab your drink and we'll get a little air. A spin in the Mustang will cool us off a bit."

Hot, dizzy, and anxious to have Stephen to herself, Frannie agreed without hesitation.

Stephen grabbed his jacket and his fresh drink. He steadied Frannie as they walked. "Let me carry that," he said after she'd sloshed some of her drink onto the floor.

"You're suuuch a gentleman."

The cool air felt good and Frannie walked to the car without stumbling. Stephen set the drinks on the hood, opened Frannie's door, then handed her the cups once she'd settled herself inside.

She sipped from her cup as he drove, finishing the drink as he backed the car into the trees at the cemetery. He polished off his drink, then walked around to open her door. She tottered slightly as he tilted the seat forward, then tumbled into the back seat. Stephen climbed in and settled himself beside her.

"I love dancing with you," Frannie gushed. "You said you didn't dance, but you are a marvelous dancer. It was such fun." Her words tumbled over one another.

"You are something, Frannie. I don't dance with just anybody. I get way too hot, but dancing with you makes me a special kind of hot." Frannie giggled at the comment, appreciating his enthusiasm but having no clue what he meant.

Stephen wasted no more time in conversation. He held her close and Frannie settled into his embrace, losing herself in the sensations his kisses and caresses evoked in her. Her inner voice was silent.

Stephen slowly unzipped her dress, then unclasped her bra, exposing erect nipples. Frannie marveled at how her body responded to him. Pleasure came in waves and an unfamiliar moist warmth spread throughout her lower body. When his hand stroked her thigh, she ignored the warning that niggled at the edges of her conscious mind. Soon, Frannie's panties lay somewhere on the floorboard, her delight in her body's responses to Stephen's touch overshadowing the vague awareness that she shouldn't be doing this.

His fingers traced the crease between her thigh and her torso, nearing but not quite touching the moist center of her being. Her breath came in ragged pants and her body seemed to know exactly what to do. She pushed against him, heightening her pleasure.

A blinding light pierced the car, and two blips of a siren brought them both upright. A policeman climbed slowly out of his cruiser. The delightful sensations that had engulfed Frannie were replaced by the fear that her heart might fail at any moment.

"Shit!" Stephen fumbled with his clothing.

Frannie tugged her bra over her breasts but couldn't fasten it or zip her dress. She was both terrified and mortified with no idea of what to say if the policeman spoke to her. She sat straight and still, trying to be invisible. The policeman's flashlight lit Stephen's face, then her own. She began to tremble.

The cop motioned Stephen out of the car. He stood shirtless, exposed in the beam of the flashlight. "Son, this isn't the place for what was going on in that car."

Frannie kept her eyes down, pretending that if she couldn't see the policeman, hoping he wouldn't be able to see her either if she didn't look at him. She gulped when she spotted her new blue bikini panties on the floor at her feet. The policeman couldn't miss them if he looked into the car. She inched them out of site with her toe and prayed, *"Please Lord, oh Please Lord, don't let him look in the car. If he sees my panties or the drink, I will drop dead from embarrassment right here in this spot. There is no way I can ever face my parents if they find out."*

The flashlight beam blinded her. "Are you alright, Miss?"

Frannie could barely form words. "Y-yes, Sir," she managed. "I am fine, thank you."

"It's late, Son," the officer said, sure that the incident traumatized the two young people enough to make them think twice before doing it again. "You need to take this young lady home, NOW! She has a curfew, right?"

"Yes sir," Stephen said, swallowing hard. Stephen stood motionless while the policeman backed his cruiser onto the lane, turned off his spotlight, and pulled away. He gave two short blips on his siren as a reminder of his instructions.

Mortified, Frannie vowed never to tell a soul what had happened. It was the last thing her parents or Petey could *ever* know. *"What would my suitemates think? I can never let this happen again."*

She had never seen Stephen flustered. He grabbed his clothing and dressed in record time. She fastened her bra and he zipped her dress without a word, their earlier euphoria a distant memory. At Hadley Hall, he opened Frannie's door and walked her to the door, then he was gone.

Frannie's heart seized when she realized that her panties were still on the floor of the Mustang. She turned to call out to Stephen, but the Mustang had pulled away from the curb. Her shoulders slumped and she clutched her chest. She couldn't face anyone, not tonight.

Frannie tiptoed across the sitting area and silently pulled her bedroom door closed. She undressed and climbed into bed, hoping to fall asleep before Robin came in from work. She tried to reconstruct the evening but was able to remember only bits and pieces, until the policeman arrived. After that, she could remember every minute detail. She was mortified that her panties were still in Greg's car. She drifted off to sleep thinking she had let Stephen do something wrong and she couldn't remember even trying to stop him.

Chapter 14

Frannie's mood catapulted between the excitement of going home to the agony of keeping a terrible a secret. She got off the plane and ran straight into Petey's open arms. "You can't imagine how I've missed you. Mom, Dad, and Nana too, of course…" Her words tumbled over one another.

Petey hugged her close. "Let's get your bags. Dad carried Nana downstairs so she'll be right there when you come in.

The front door burst open as soon as Petey pulled to the curb. "You go ahead, Sis. I'll bring your bags."

"Can you believe it's been three months since I've seen my little girl?" Mrs. Braun said pulling Frannie into a hug.

The joy of the homecoming swept away Frannie's anxiety, and she hugged her grandmother and her father in turn. *"Oh, my… I don't remember Nana looking so frail."*

"I've missed you, Darling," Nana said. "I want to hear about all of your college adventures."

Frannie's chest tightened. She worked her mouth into an exaggerated smile and swept the living room with her eyes. "Nothing has changed."

Petey laughed. "Things don't change much around here in three months. You shouldn't have any trouble finding your way around." The day passed in a flurry of preparation for the grand Thanksgiving meal with all the traditional dishes. At 10, Frannie fell into bed, exhausted from the effort of deferring talk about school by asking question after question about family and friends.

On Thursday, seated in their routine places, the family held hands around the table for the blessing. As they passed plates and platters around the table, Petey said, "So, Sis, tell us about college."

Frannie nearly choked. "Uh… well… my suitemates are great. Robin still gets on my case. She's pretty regimented, so she gets impatient with me when I forget to do something."

"Like what?" Mrs. Braun asked, surprised.

"Oh, like doing laundry, putting my clothes away, making my bed, getting myself up in the morning…"

Mrs. Braun interrupted, "Getting yourself up in the morning?"

"Yeah…, "Frannie explained, "I guess I was used to your letting me sleep until I *had* to get up or miss the bus. The first couple of days, I slept through my alarm. I couldn't understand why it was such a big deal for Robin to wake me, but Katie said it wasn't fair to make her get up an hour early so I could use the shower first. That made sense, so I took the alarm clock to bed with me. Eventually, that did the trick."

"My Princess is learning to take care of herself," Mr. Braun grinned, "just like we planned."

"Well, she certainly didn't need to go thousands of miles from home just to learn how to turn off an alarm clock."

"I suppose your classes are just fine," Nana interjected to forestall the impending argument. "You've always been such a good student."

"Yeah, they're fine," said Frannie.

"So, which are your favorite subjects?" her father prompted.

"I like English and Old Testament best. Math is okay. I like the professor, and his lectures are fine, but my test grades haven't been all that good. I know the formulas, but he never asks about them on the test."

"Math was my best subject," Petey said. "Maybe I can help you figure out the problem. What kind of questions does he ask?"

"All the questions are stories about how fast people run and how long it takes for trains to get places. I guess the formulas are supposed to help, but I can't ever figure out, which ones to use."

"Frannie," her father said, "that's just a matter of common sense. The stories provide the variables and you solve for the missing information. If you can identify the variables in a story, the formula you need is obvious."

"I guess," Frannie murmured. "It just didn't seem that obvious to me."

"Try to think about *why* you've learned something," her father suggested. "Ask yourself what you might be able to *do* with new information. That's adult learning."

"Yeah. I think I get it," Frannie said. "But, Dad, chemistry is a drag. Our professor talks about his Jaguar and never gets around to teaching. If it weren't for lab, I'd hate that course." She stopped abruptly, realizing that any questions about lab would involve Stephen.

"Well, sweetheart," said her mother, "I know you'll do just fine."

"So, Sis, tell us about the guy who's smitten with you," Petey coaxed.

Frannie took a cautious breath. "Well, you know his name is Stephen Barton and he's a sophomore. He's tall, good-looking, has long brown hair, and he likes me a lot. We mostly hang out in the Game Room with his friends. We went to the Halloween party and the Homecoming dance," she added, "For Halloween, we were Marshall Dillon and Miss Kitty. We made a super cool couple, and his outfit matched mine at Homecoming, too. He's getting us tickets for the Christmas Gala. "

"Well, sweetheart, it sounds like you're having a good time," her mother said. She looked pointedly at Gerhart and added, "I still don't see why you couldn't be doing all that, right here in Philly."

"What's been happening here?" Frannie jumped on the opportunity to steer the conversation to safer ground. The neighborhood news, their extended family, current affairs, and the Vietnam war occupied their conversation for the rest of the meal. According to Petey, the biggest news was the Philadelphia Eagles finally winning their second football game of the season, beating the Giants, of all teams, 23 to 20.

After pie and ice cream, Mrs. Braun cleared the table and Mr. Braun carried Nana to her room. Frannie followed and curled up with her grandmother. "Nana, have you been reading my letters?"

"Of course, Sweetheart. Your mother shares every one of them. Tell me more about Robin and your other friends."

For the next hour, Frannie described each of the girls and regaled Nana with a detailed description of their trip to Atoka. "We have one guy in the nursing program. His name is J.R. and he is a big teddy bear of a guy. I know he's going to make a wonderful nurse. He and Missy really like each other."

"He'll stand out, for sure," Nana observed. Such a big man in a class full of women. What about your Prince Charming? You haven't said much about him."

"Oh, he's fine. We mostly play darts, foosball, and ping pong, but he did take me to the movies to see *Patton*."

"Is he a good student?"

"Yeah, I guess. He's a sophomore, so we don't have any classes together except chemistry."

"Tell me more about him and his family. I'd like to know this boy since he's important to you."

Realizing how little she knew about Stephen made Frannie uncomfortable. She had no idea where to begin. "Well, he doesn't talk much about his family, but he's fun to be with."

When Frannie didn't continue, Nana prompted, "Isn't there more you'd like to tell me? There must be more to this young man."

"Well, he's handsome, and he's good at all the games in the Game Room. He's actually the best foosball player in the whole school."

"Hmmm…" Gram studied Frannie's face. "Alright, but you know that you can always talk to me about anything."

Frannie knew she wasn't off the hook but appreciated the reprieve. "I know, Nana. I've always been able to talk to you." She leaned in to give Nana a hug. "How have you been? You look wonderful!"

Nana frowned. "Hardly wonderful, Sweetie. Your mother takes good care of me. I'm waiting for you to become a nurse so I'll have two superb caregivers. Could you rearrange these pillows, please? I need to rest a bit."

Frannie helped her into a comfortable position and kissed her cheek. "I'll come back when you wake up. We can talk more about Robin, and you can help me figure out what to say when she gets cross with me."

Friday morning was cold as Frannie and her mother bundled up for a day of shopping. "Mom, do you realize that we've gone to Wanamaker's on Friday after Thanksgiving for as long as I can remember?"

"I have been doing it since before Petey was born." Mrs. Braun said. "I'm glad we can carry on the tradition… even though you've moved so far away."

Frannie winced but let the jibe pass. They shopped with determination in the festive, crowded store and by mid-afternoon they were both exhausted. "Let's see what the guys have been up to," Frannie said, climbing the porch steps, with a mound of gift bags in her arms.

Inside, the atmosphere was anything but festive. Mr. Braun and Petey sat in the living room, somber and silent. Mother and daughter dumped their bags onto the dining room table. "What on earth is the matter?" Mrs. Braun asked. "You two look like you've lost your best friend."

The men sat unmoving, each waiting for the other to speak. "Well?" prompted Mrs. Braun, concern evident in her voice.

Petey broke the silence. "Mom, I got orders today. Special Delivery, since it's a holiday."

"Orders?"

"I'm going to Vietnam after all."

"No! That can't be!" she exclaimed. "You can't be going. You're in intelligence. When do you leave? Where will you be? What will you be doing?" Mrs. Braun asked, not waiting for answers. "I thought you wouldn't have to go. What happened?"

"I don't know," replied Petey. "I wasn't expecting this either."

"But Petey," cried Frannie, "you *can't* go! What if something *happens* to you?"

Silence followed Frannie's outcry. No one had an answer. Frannie fingered her locket and burst into tears. "I'm sorry," she sobbed. "I just can't bear to think of you so far away."

"I'll be OK," he said. I'm not infantry."

"You won't be in danger?" Frannie asked, relieved.

"Probably not, and we still have the whole weekend. I don't leave until December 11th. Besides, he said giving Frannie a wink, you're my good luck charm."

"You'll be gone for Christmas," Mrs. Braun murmured.

"You won't be here when I come home for the holidays," Frannie echoed her mother. "You can't leave that soon. It isn't fair!"

The room was quiet except for Frannie's sob. There was nothing to say. Nana called from her room, "Frannie, come sit with me." Frannie got up slowly, sniffling, and walked to Petey. Without a word, she gave him a tight hug, kissed his cheek, and left for Nana's room.

Chapter 15

Stephen welcomed Frannie back from Thanksgiving with an invitation to see *On a Clear Day* the following Friday. He made no mention of the debacle with the policeman.

"Oh, Stephen, I'd love to," she cried. "I LOVE Barbara Streisand and the music is way cool. It's so romantic. I can't wait."

He shrugged. "I'll pick you up at 5:30. We can get a hamburger or something and make the 7:00 show." They met in the Game Room twice during the week, and both times he declined invitations from others and played darts and foosball with Frannie.

On Friday, he arrived on time, opened the car door for her, held her chair at the sandwich shop, and asked what she'd like to order. After the movie, he drove straight back to Hadley Hall and they cuddled in a porch swing while Frannie told him about her Thanksgiving and lamented Petey's deployment.

"That sucks," Stephen said, hugging her to his side. "You shouldn't worry, though. You said he's in intelligence, so he'll probably never get near the front. By the way, the Christmas Gala is next week. I bet you'll look gorgeous."

All Frannie could think about was the Christmas Gala and how Stephen turned out to be a gentleman after all. "He opened my door and pulled out my chair for me," she told Robin. "You were wrong. He *is* a gentleman, just like I've been telling you."

"We'll see," Robin cautioned. Leopards don't change their spots overnight. He's up to something, so *please* be careful."

She paid little attention in class all week. She and Missy had found the perfect dress for Frannie in a boutique shop near the campus. The deep blue, almost purple skirt flowed from an empire waist to the floor. Sashaying around the suite, she exclaimed, "Isn't this elegant? I love how the material shimmers when I move. Missy and I found a bow tie and cummerbund for Stephen that matches the color."

"Yes, your dress looks super." Robin said, "but…"

"You don't have to worry, Robin," Frannie interrupted.

Forestalling a confrontation, Leslie said. "I'm glad we got to the ticket line early. Our seats are close to the stage so we'll have a great view of the show. I've heard that some of the performers are Crestmont alumni. Pretty impressive if you ask me."

Robin added, "The Davises go every year. They told me Crestmont started the program to encourage an active connection with the community. It was initially called *Hanging of the Greens,* then it became a formal event and they changed the name to *Christmas Gala*. The concert has gotten so popular over the years that Blakemore Chapel is the only place large enough to hold it.

"I can't wait," Frannie said. "I wish we were sitting with you. As nice as Stephen has been since Thanksgiving, I still don't like being around his friends."

The night of the Gala the girls, dressed in their finery, waited in the decorated, music-filled lobby for the men to escort them. "This is so rad," Frannie gushed. "We look like Cinderellas."

Missy squealed with delight when J.R. and Mike arrived. "You look scrumptious. I could just eat you up," she cried. J.R. pulled a wrist corsage from behind his back and slid it onto Missy's wrist. He leaned down to kiss her on the lips. The hoots and snickers were good-natured; J.R. and Missy were a popular couple.

Mike said, bowing toward the girls, "Ladies, I have never seen anything more beautiful than you. He looked directly at Leslie, who blushed at the compliment.

Frannie kept glancing at the door, disappointed that Stephen was late. His tardiness surprised her since he'd been such a gentleman since Thanksgiving.

"We need to move on if we want to be in our seats before this shindig begins," J.R. said.

Missy pulled on his arm. "J.R., we can't leave Frannie. Stephen will be here soon."

J.R. sighed, then nodded.

Stephen hurried into the lobby carrying his tie and cummerbund and a small white cardboard box. Frannie forgot her disappointment and rushed to throw her arms around him. "You look so handsome, Stephen." He opened the box and Frannie gushed, "It is beautiful. The flowers are perfect for my dress." He slipped the corsage onto her wrist.

"Come on, everyone, we have to get going," J.R. said, putting his arm around Missy's shoulders, and escorting her to the door. Mike followed with an arm around Katie on one side and Leslie on the other. Frannie grabbed Stephen's hand and followed.

Greg and James were waiting outside and Stephen stopped when he reached them, letting Frannie's friends walk on ahead. "Frannie, will you help me with this tie and cummerbund?"

"Of course. My Dad taught me how to tie a bow tie." She looped the tie around his neck, completed the bow, and fastened his cummerbund in the back while Greg and James made lewd comments.

"Shut up, you Morons," Stephen hissed.

Frannie took a deep breath, grateful that Stephen found them as insufferable as she did.

"You are one foxy mama tonight," he said, shooting a warning glance and a wink at Greg and James who stifled their snickers and walked on ahead.

As they stepped into the Chapel vestibule, Frannie said, "I hope our seats are down front. This is going to be a great evening, and I don't want to miss anything."

"Well," he hemmed, "not exactly. Greg picked up our tickets and he didn't get there until late."

Frannie frowned as he ushered her to their seats in the back. They climbed over several girls, then Greg and James, to take seats in the middle of the row. *I wish I'd picked up our tickets. We could be down there with my friends where we'd actually be able to see the show.*

Stephen slipped his arm around her, pulling her in close, and Frannie forgot all about the seating arrangements. The show was wonderful, even from the back. Candlelight enhanced the atmosphere and a group of hand-bell ringers produced delightful Christmas music. The talent was impressive and most of the performers did, in fact, turn out to be Crestmont alumni.

Following the event, they walked to the Student Union Ballroom for the elegant reception. Stephen stopped at a drink station, picked up too small cups, and led Frannie toward the last two empty seats at a table crowded with his friends. Frannie sipped her drink, surprised to find it quite tasty. The punch masked the liquor and she emptied her cup.

"Let me get you another," Stephen said, pleased that she hadn't complained. He returned with two large cups.

Still thirsty, Frannie drank half of her drink, then looked around for her friends, but couldn't find them in the crowd. "Stephen, I feel a little dizzy. I think it's because I haven't eaten. Can we get something?"

"We'll go to Keller's. They have great burgers and we don't have to get out of the car." Stephen signaled Greg who tossed him the Mustang keys.

"Grooooovvvvy… I can diiiggg it." Frannie slurred. She stood unsteadily and, their drinks in one hand and his other at her waist, Stephen ushered Frannie outside. The cool air cleared her head a bit, but she leaned against Stephen to steady herself."

Stephen opened her door, set both drinks in the console's cup holders and settled her into the Mustang. He found some popular music on the car radio and they listened in companionable silence until they pulled into a slot at Keller's Drive-In. A few bites of hamburger and some fries calmed Frannie's stomach, though she still had difficulty keeping things in focus. Stephen hadn't ordered her a *Coke*, so she reached for her punch. Stephen's hamburger and fries were gone. "Do you want mine?" she offered. He finished her hamburger in three bites, then took a bit longer with the fries. Frannie finished her drink while he ate.

"We have hours before curfew. Let's go someplace where we can be together and chill."

"I like it when we're alone," she sighed, pleased that his annoying friends were nowhere around. "Be right back," he said and pushed open his door. Frannie dozed off, then startled awake when Stephen opened his door. He put a six-pack of *Coke* on the floor behind his seat, then climbed behind the wheel, leaned across the console, and kissed her gently. Frannie purred but said nothing.

Stephen drove to a secluded spot some distance from where they'd encountered the policeman. He helped Frannie into the back seat, threw his jacket, tie, and cummerbund onto the front seat, and climbed in after her. He pulled his shirt out of his pants and undid half the buttons. "Now I'm comfortable. I hate the whole suit and tie get-up." He encircled her with his arms and kissed her gently, whispering in her ear, "You look awesome tonight."

"And you're so handsome," she murmured back, returning his kisses with fervor.

"How about a toast to us?" Stephen leaned across Frannie and pulled two *Cokes* from the bag. They drank from their cans, then he reached into the glove compartment and pulled out a flask. He poured bourbon into their cans and toasted, "Here's to you, Frannie. You're the prettiest girl I know."

"Thaaaank you, kind siiirrr." She touched her can to his, then took a long swallow. They sat in companionable silence. Stephen held her close and kissed her gently while they sipped from the cans. He periodically topped off her can, and when the first two cans were empty, he opened two more, took one large swallow from each, and refilled both from his flask.

As Frannie sipped her drink, she reached tentatively to touch Stephen's bare chest. Briefly she relived the amazing sensations she'd experienced before the policeman had ruined their evening. It was like a dreaming with thoughts and images coming in and out of focus.

She was hardly aware that Stephen had unzipped her dress and unfastened her bra. He stroked her back, cupped her breast, and gently rubbed her nipple. The explosive sensations coursing through her body were familiar and delightful. He slipped the dress off her shoulders and pulled her to him, her chest against his. The feel of his skin against hers was heavenly, leaving her wanting to cuddle with him forever.

From a distance, she heard, "Finish this, Princess, and I'll get us another. We still have two cans left."

They were sipping from their third can when Stephen moved her hand to his fly and said softly, "Here, unfasten my pants," and helped her with the zipper. He kissed her deeply and maneuvered her hand into position. He writhed as she touched him and Frannie's breathing quickened as she explored the novel sensation of his hot, supple skin. Her brain was numb and no uneasy thoughts interrupted her pleasure.

Stephen bunched up the soft fabric of her long dress and caressed her thigh, whispering, "I need you so much," He kissed her again and again, inching his hand upward as she writhed with pleasure. She moaned when he kissed her breast and tightened her grip when he nibbled her erect nipple. Her breathing grew ragged and her entire being was enveloped in delightful sensations.

When Stephen slid a finger inside her panties and stroked her, she cried out in ecstasy. The sound seemed to come from

The Wake-Up Call

somewhere else. She leaned into his touch, unable to distinguish one ecstatic pulsing sensation from another.

He inched her panties gently over her hips. He'd worn no underwear and freed himself quickly from his trousers. She marveled at the hardness of him.

He moved up and down, sliding back and forth through her hand. She tightened her grip and he moaned. "Frannie, you have the touch of an angel," he whispered in her ear. "How good you make me feel." With supreme effort, Stephen slowed his rhythmic pace when he realized that if it were over too soon and he might never get another chance to accomplish his mission. He hovered above her, then lowered himself until they connected.

She cried out at the touch of his hot skin and lifted her hips to meet him. He searched for the warm wetness that would accept him. Wonderful sensations coursed through her each time they connected. She squirmed to engage with him and with both hands clutching his torso, she pulled him to her, her entire body taught, her eyes squeezed shut.

She arched toward him as he slid inside her, gently at first, then more forcefully. She felt the fullness of him, and her eyes widened at a sudden sharp pain. Then there were explosions of indescribable pleasure as he stroked her with each thrust. She wrapped him tightly with her legs and matched his pace as he moved in and out, faster and faster. When he thrust for the last time, she felt the pulsing of his climax and an explosion of her own. Then she moaned and he collapsed on top of her, breathless.

They lay for several moments silent and panting. Then Stephen murmured, "Frannie, that was fantastic. You were better than I imagined you'd be."

Frannie sated, dishrag limp, drunk, and disheveled, was only aware of the glorious sensations still pulsing throughout her body. She lay there, gazing up at Stephen. "You're amazing," she whispered. *"There is no one in the world who can make me feel like you do."* In a dreamy voice, she said, *"*I love you, Stephen, with all my heart."

It was Stephen who finally said, "We have to get you back to the dorm before curfew." He sat up, retrieved his clothing, and began to dress staring at her uncovered breasts. Frannie wriggled into a sitting position. "We need to get you dressed, too," he said.

He opened the door and helped her out, her chest still bare. She was shivering and unsteady and he pulled her close to him. He pulled her bra from the car and slipped the straps over one arm, then the other. He cupped her breasts and kissed each one before fastening her bra. With little help from Frannie, he worked her arms into her dress and zipped it up. He fluffed the long skirt and settled her into her seat, then knelt and slipped her shoes onto her feet. Her panties remained, unnoticed, on the floor of the Mustang.

The alcohol and her first sexual experience left Frannie euphoric and hardly aware of her surroundings. Then slowly, she began to feel the cold and an unusual dull pain between her legs. Confused and conflicted, she couldn't seem to organize her thoughts or her feelings.

Stephen rapped on the door to Hadley Hall at seven minutes after eleven. Sally opened the door and, wide-eyed, pulled Frannie inside. She glowered at Stephen, then closed the door without a word. Sally didn't report that Frannie had returned to the dorm drunk and late for curfew.

At 10:30 Robin returned from work. She found Frannie asleep, sprawled across the bed, still wearing her dress and shoes. Frannie slurred "Hi, Robs," and tried unsuccessfully to sit up. When she started to throw up, Robin rushed over with their trashcan. Frannie vomited and lay back, then vomited several more times. Robin contained the mess as best she could and emptied the one can of room deodorizer they had in the suite.

She went to empty the trashcan into the toilet and discovered that vomit soiled the toilet seat and the floor. "You've gotta be shittin' me!" Robin, exclaimed, pissed that Frannie couldn't hear her.

Robin worked Frannie out of her ruined dress and noted the missing panties. "What the hell have you been up to, Frannie?"

She cleaned her up as well as she could and got her into bed. Then she began the chore of cleaning up the bathroom. At least once an hour throughout the night, Robin got up to deal with Frannie's bouts of vomiting.

When Katie came in on Saturday morning to see if they were ready for breakfast, Robin told her they would sleep in. Robin woke at 10:30, showered, and while she was dressing, Frannie stirred.

"Ooohh," Frannie moaned when she tried to sit up. "I have an awful headache."

"Now THERE'S a surprise," Robin retorted. "What the hell did you expect?"

Frannie stared at Robin, surprised at the outburst. She knew there was something she should remember, but her memory of the night before was out of focus and disjointed. "I remember the Gala, then going to the reception," she murmured. "I drank punch…, punch with rum in it." The memory made her nauseous and she gagged.

"Don't even think about throwing up in bed!" Robin warned. "If you don't get to the damn bathroom, you're on your own to clean it up. I'm friggin' fed up with this whole ordeal. I spent all night holding your head while you puked and cleaning up afterward. I'll bet you don't remember a thing! I might have been better off letting you choke on your own vomit. And you owe me a new trashcan this one is beyond hope."

"Robin, I…"

"Forget it! I'm going to go get some breakfast and when I come back you better be in all kinds of states of remorse." The door slammed behind her.

"Frannie pressed her palms to her temples and tried to think, but the room spun. She tried but couldn't remember where she and Stephen had gone after they left the ballroom. She dozed and woke feeling less nauseous, but her head was still pounding. She tried to recapture the evening. Bits and pieces of memory peeked through the fog in her brain. As the sequence of events emerged, she fell back onto the pillow and groaned, *"oh no…"*

She lay there aghast, remembering what she and Stephen had done in the red Mustang.

"*Robin may have saved my life. She never asked me what happened. If she knew, she'd call me a slut. Well, I'm not. I'm sure Stephen loves me. What we did was only wrong because we're not married yet.*

"*What if I'm pregnant? Oh Lord, No, that can't be. I wouldn't know what to do. If Stephen used protection, I wouldn't have to worry at all. I need to ask him.*"

Frannie didn't see Stephen again until Thursday. He hadn't been in the Game Room all week. When she walked in, he was watching Greg and James play ping pong. She pulled on his shirt sleeve. "Stephen, I need to talk to you."

"Later, I play the winner and I need to show these turkeys how an expert plays this game."

Frannie couldn't believe her good fortune when Stephen lost the game to James. She wouldn't have to wait all evening. "Let's get a drink in the *SnakBaR*. I'd like a *Dr. Pepper*."

They sat at a small table in the corner. "About Friday night," Frannie began.

"Great evening," Stephen interrupted. "You had a good time, didn't you?"

"Yes, but, that's…."

"Then what's the problem? Guys and girls are supposed to have fun together, and we had fun."

"Stephen, there are things about the evening I can't remember. I think it's because I drank too much of the *Coke* with whatever you put in it."

"You're a baby, Frannie," he cut in. "You have to learn to handle your liquor. You can't do that if you don't practice. Isn't that what college is for?"

"Yes, I guess, but…"

"See. I'm doing you a favor."

"I was sick as a dog and Robin is still upset with me. I thought I'd die the first time I saw Sally, but she never said a word. It was like she was telling me *it's our little secret. I'm giving you a second chance.*"

"Smart lady, that Sally. She understands that it's all part of growing up and Robin, well, she can just get over it; that is what roommates are for."

"Well, I don't want to drink like that again. It made me horribly sick and I felt awful for two whole days. Besides that, Stephen, it was wrong to do what we did. We need to wait until we're married… or at least until we're engaged."

Stephen's eyes widened, and he bit back a retort.

"Did you use protection? I can't remember. It's important. What if I got pregnant? My parents would never forgive me. Did you?"

"Don't worry, Frannie. You'll be fine. Besides, you liked it well enough at the time."

"I tried to remember, but I can't."

"You had fun and that's what counts. Besides, girls never get pregnant the first time they do it."

Frannie smiled at the memory. "I love how you make me feel, but we can't do that again, not until we're married. Promise me."

"Frannie…"

"Promise me," she insisted.

"Whatever," he said, standing, and pulling her up. He kissed her lightly. "I've got a game to play and I thought you wanted to get back to the dorm."

She walked back slowly, relief not quite overcoming guilt. "*I hope he's right that I can't be pregnant because it was my first time. But it was wrong to go all the way. My family would never forgive me. I think Nana can read my mind. What if I DID get pregnant? No, I can't think about that. He didn't say if he used protection.*"

A week later, Frannie sat on the plane, twisting the napkin that came with her *Dr. Pepper*, overwhelmed by guilt. The flight seemed interminable. At the same time, she didn't want it to end.

"So, my little girl is home for the holidays." Her father's voice startled Frannie as she entered the terminal. Lost in thought and consumed with worry, she'd almost walked right past him.

"Dad!" exclaimed Frannie, forcing a bright smile onto her face and she stepped into his embrace.

"Welcome home Sweetheart. Let's get your luggage. Your mother and Nana can't wait to see you. Mom has been in the kitchen all day. I don't think there is a single favorite dish of yours that will be missing this holiday season."

"It's wonderful to be home," said Frannie, her smile in place. *"I have GOT to get hold of myself."* Her face relaxed a bit.

Frannie opened the front door and breathed in the heavenly smells from the kitchen. "Frannie!" cried her mother, rushing to envelop her daughter in a hug. Frannie melted into the embrace, reminding herself to enjoy every moment of her parents' affection, while she still could.

"Mom, it smells wonderful in here," Frannie stood back. "Let me run up and give Nana a hug."

"She's right here. We've moved her into the spare room downstairs for the holiday so she'll be close to everything."

"Frannie, is that you?" came Nana's soft voice.

"I'm home, Nana," she said and rushed in to give her grandmother a hug. Frannie lingered in the embrace and bit back tears, overcome with feelings of love, appreciation, and regret. *"I will NOT ruin this moment."*

"How are you, Nana? I like your new room." The questions tumbled out. "I love that you're down here close to everything. I've missed you so much."

"I'm fine, Darling. Your mother is the best nurse in the world. That is, of course, until you graduate and take over. Now, come sit by me and tell me all about school, and that boy you were sweet on over Thanksgiving."

Frannie's breath caught in her throat. "Well…" Frannie hesitated, organizing her thoughts, and fighting to control her anxiety. *"Focus on the positive and ignore everything else,"* she commanded herself, though it was proving difficult to follow her own instructions.

"I love being at Crestmont, Nana. It's a beautiful school, and the weather in Dallas is amazing. Can you believe it was almost Thanksgiving before I needed a jacket during the day? I don't think it's ever going to get cold enough for my winter coat. I think you'd like it there. You get to be outside so much more of the year. Except in the summer, it's really, really hot."

"Slow down, Sweetheart. We talked about all of that at Thanksgiving. Tell me about your classes. It sounded as if you were struggling. The first semester is over now."

"The semester was harder than I expected and I'm surprised how different college is from high school. My grades aren't as good as I thought they would be, which I don't understand at all. I study just as much as I did in high school. I always read my assignments… well, most of them. It's the tests; the questions are never what I expect they should be. Either I didn't read the right material, or more likely, the test covered material that the professor didn't explain. But I passed everything."

"Perhaps you have to study differently from the way you did in high school? It's not surprising that college presents a challenge. Now you're not just learning facts. I presume your professors expect you to *use* what you've learned to address complex issues and to solve problems."

"I guess so. It's just confusing. I read the assignment and the test questions don't ask about what I read. What makes me mad is that teachers don't make a lot of sense. Like, for instance, my English teacher, Dr. Bennett, told me that she was impressed with my vocabulary and sentence structure, and then she gave me a *C* in the class. I'm so bummed."

"Did you ask her why you weren't getting *A's* on your papers?"

"Of course, I did. She told me that my command of the language is good, but my writing is immature. As if I'm supposed to know what THAT means.

"Perhaps she means that it's not enough to just know something. It's the ability to apply your knowledge that demonstrates maturity. Learning to recognize the difference is part of growing. You're a smart girl. You'll figure it out."

"I suppose," Frannie hesitated, unsure of how she was supposed to make that happen.

"Tell me about the classes you'll be taking after the holidays."

"January is called *interim semester*. We have just one course, so we get to relax a bit before the Spring semester starts with another full load. The interim semester course is *History and Philosophy of Science*. It sounds cool and I know I'll get a good grade."

"That might be a good opportunity to apply what your English teacher suggested. The value in history and philosophy is that you can learn from it. When you know how things turned out in the past, you can use that knowledge to make better decisions for the future. Otherwise, we'd learn everything by trial and error. Think of maturity as benefiting from past successes and failures."

"Nana, you're such a good teacher. I learn more from you than from all my classes combined."

"This should be a wonderful time for you, Sweetheart. It's your opportunity to figure out who you're going to be and how you're going to become that person. So, tell me about your friends? What do you do when you're not studying?"

Frannie realized that she'd talked little about her life and friends at Crestmont over Thanksgiving since they'd been focused on Petey's departure.

She took a deep breath, "My best friend, Missy, is from Baton Rouge. She's so *southern*. I just love her accent. She was taking general courses but is leaning to the Liberal Arts program 'cuz she doesn't want to be tied to a specific discipline. Her whole family went to Crestmont including her mother, her grandmother, and two of her aunts, and she got into the same sorority her mother was in. I went through Rush but none of the sororities had room for me. Sam, she's an upper-class nursing student, told me that you have to be *connected* to get in, like Missy. But it's no big deal because we made our own sorority, the Nurseketeers, just for the four of us in the suite."

"What a good idea," Nana said. "It sounds like you and your suitemates have become friends. Tell me about them."

"My suitemates are all nice. Except for classes and meals, I don't spend a lot of time with them because Leslie has an athletic scholarship and she's always busy with sports. Katie spends most of her free time in the library studying, and Robin works at Rob Rory's and studies with Katie, so she's hardly ever around. We go to breakfast together every morning because we have the same classes, but in the afternoon, we all do different things. Mostly we eat dinner together, too, but Robin gets to eat at the restaurant the days she works. She works a lot because she needs to buy her own ticket to go home for holidays."

"Robin sounds like a responsible young lady." Gram commented.

"Yeah, she is." Frannie sighed. "All of my suitemates act pretty grown up. Katie… Remember Katie? We all went to her farm for a weekend earlier in the semester?"

"Oh, of course… the lovely Indian girl."

"Katie is so mature. She always knows exactly what to say when Robin picks on me. Leslie has to work to get good grades because she's an athlete and could lose her scholarship. Robin is the smartest, I think. She gets the best grades of all of us. All Robin does is study and work. She didn't even go to Homecoming. She worked that whole weekend so that other students could have the time off."

"It sounds like you and Robin are getting along now."

"Well… every time I think she might like me, she yells at me about something. I just haven't figured her out yet."

"I want to hear all about Robin, but I need to rest a bit. I'll take a little nap and then you come right back and tell me more."

"I will, Nana." Frannie helped Nana get comfortable, kissed her cheek, and whispered, "Sleep well."

Frannie's mother was sitting at the kitchen table. She swiped a tear from her cheek as Frannie came in. "There you are, I know how happy Nana was to see you. Have a cookie, they're your favorite." Mrs. Braun pulled her daughter into a hug.

"Mom, why are you sad?"

"It's the first Christmas without both my children at home."

Frannie hugged her mother, then sat beside her. "Let's pretend that Petey's here in the States but just couldn't get home for Christmas. That way you won't worry so much. When I'm at school, I imagine that my family is exactly the way I want them to be and it makes being away from home so much easier."

"You've always managed to live your fantasies, Child," her mother said. You make me smile."

"I'll take one of those delicious-smelling cookies," said Frannie's father, pulling out a chair for himself. Let's not wait for Frannie's next vacation before you make these again, Ingrid. They're my favorite, too. Frannie, it's wonderful having you home, and not just because your mother makes these delicious cookies."

"So, what have you heard from Petey?" Frannie asked.

"He writes nearly every week," her mother answered. "He tells about how interesting intelligence work is, but of course, he doesn't say anything specific. If he's fortunate, he'll complete his tour without seeing any combat at all, and he'll come home safe and sound."

"Of course, he will. He has to!" Frannie exclaimed. "Nothing can happen to him! He should be home by summer, don't you think?"

"He told us it would be a six-month assignment. Let's hope that doesn't change," her father added. "He should be home by the time you're finished with your first year in college. And speaking of college, tell us about your classes. You must have gotten your grades before you came home."

"Well, I don't want you to be disappointed. I passed all of my classes, but my grades weren't as good as I thought they'd be. I don't understand why because I read the assignments, but the tests are always different from what I expected."

"I'm sure you'll do fine, Sweetie," her mother said. "It can take a while to get used to a new environment and all those new teachers."

"Perhaps," added her father, "but you should think about *why* things are different and adjust your expectations. That's part of the *growing up* we talked about."

"I *am* growing up," Frannie retorted.

"I'm sure that college professors expect more of their students than your high school teachers did. By the second year, only the students who take college seriously remain. If you're going to be a nurse, Frannie," he said, looking directly at his daughter, "you'll have to figure out what it takes to do well and adjust your behavior and study habits."

"You're right, Dad," Frannie agreed. "I do need to get better grades. I'm sure that next semester will be better, now that it's not all so new. When I get back to Crestmont, I have just one course for a month before the spring semester begins. It will be interesting, and I'm sure I can get an *A* in that class."

"Yes, you can," her mother said. "My daughter will do just fine."

"Frannie," came Nana's soft voice from the bedroom.

"Coming, Nana," Frannie called as she stood, smiled at her parents, and escaped to spend time with her grandmother.

※

"Did you sleep well, Nana?" Frannie said climbing onto her bed.

"Yes, thanks. Little naps during the day help me keep up my strength. Now tell me more about Robin. I know you two started off on the wrong foot."

"Robin still gets upset with me, but Katie keeps telling me over and over it's because she cares. That's hard to tell sometimes, but I can see Katie's point. I guess if Robin didn't care, she'd probably just ignore me."

"What is it that she complains about?"

"Well, she's a major neat freak and I don't keep my things tidy enough for her. At first, she wouldn't help me with my laundry, but now she does. We do our wash together, and then we fold our things on the tables in the basement because Robin says if we bring them up in the laundry basket to fold in the room, everything will be wrinkled. She showed me how to fold everything so it all fits in my drawers."

"How nice of her to be so helpful. That doesn't sound like complaining."

"Two things she gets all snippy about are studying and my boyfriend." As soon as the words were out of her mouth, Frannie's felt like her heart had stopped.

"Obviously she cares about you, or it wouldn't matter to her if you passed or failed. I can understand her concern about studying, but what is that bothers her about Stephen? He's the boy you're sweet on, right?"

"Oh, nothing. She doesn't even know him. It doesn't make sense to think someone is a bad person when you don't even know them. You've always told me never jump to conclusions about a person until I've gotten to know them. Robin needs to take your advice."

"Robin doesn't sound like a person who would dislike someone for no reason."

"Well, she doesn't *have* a reason. She says that she just *knows*. How silly is that?"

"You said he took you to the Christmas formal. What did you call it?"

A wave of despair washed over Frannie when her mind refused to forget what had happened that night. She smiled just in case Nana's extrasensory perception picked up on her anxiety. "It's the Christmas Gala and it used to be called the Hanging of the Greens. It's a formal event, but it's a concert, not a dance. They have fabulous entertainment and so many people from the community come that Blakemore Chapel is the only place big enough for it."

"What did you wear?"

"Katie said that I looked like a princess. I wore a long chiffon gown, a deep blue almost purple with an empire waist. Stephen wore a tux with a cummerbund and bow tie that matched, and he brought me a wrist corsage. We were the nicest looking couple there."

Nana waited for more.

Frannie hesitated, then continued. "After the program, there was a reception in the ballroom. We had refreshments, visited with our friends, and it was over before I knew it." Frannie prayed Nana couldn't hear the frantic drumbeat of her heart."

The first semester is over and I'm going to concentrate on getting better grades. The interim session course is right up my alley. That should be an easy *A*. Then when the second semester begins, I'll study more with the girls, but I'm still gonna spend time with Missy and Stephen."

"That sounds like a good plan. Everyone needs to have some fun, but Robin's giving you good advice when she reminds you to concentrate more on your studies than on your social life. I'm not sure that this Stephen you're dating should be your top priority." Nana said.

She KNOWS! I just knew she'd figure it out. Nana's never told me what to do, but she's always made it clear that she expects me to use my head and make good decisions"

"Nana, I'll study hard this coming semester, I promise. I want you to be proud of me."

"If you just use good judgment, you'll be fine. Go help your Mom in the kitchen now, while I rest a little. Then hurry back. I want to know more about Stephen and your classes."

On the way to the kitchen, Frannie resolved to focus discussions on her academic challenges and deflect everything else. She knew that Nana suspected that she was keeping a secret, but the Braun family was too respectful of each other's privacy to challenge anyone outright. She resolved that, for the rest of the vacation, there would be no further mention of Stephen. She couldn't risk letting the conversation come anywhere close to her dirty little secret.

"Mom," Frannie asked, "Is Nana doing OK? She just seems more… well, more tired than I remember."

"Nana's doing as well as can be expected," her mother assured her.

"You take such good care of her. There's no reason to think that she won't be okay for loads of years, right?"

"We hope so," her mother said.

"When I'm a nurse, I'll be able to help, too. I'm going to be a good nurse for Nana."

"Of course, you will."

Chapter 16

"Frannie, you OK? Robin asked. You're awfully quiet."
"I'm OK… just tired from the trip. Thanks for asking. You would think a one-hour time difference wouldn't matter that much.

"How was the holiday? I thought you'd be gushing about being home with your family."

"We really missed Petey. This was the first holiday ever without the whole family together. It was rough telling my folks that my grades weren't as good as they'd expected. After all, I read the assignments, it's just the tests that don't ask the right questions."

Robin started to comment, but Frannie continued, "The interim session is right up my alley. *History and Philosophy of Science* will be interesting and the tests won't have problems to solve. I'm going to enjoy it and get a good grade."

"You'll still have to study," Robin said. "You can't keep pretending that your grades will magically improve without your having to do a speck of work."

"Of course, I'll study. I just don't have to spend my life in the library to do it."

Robin bit back a retort.

"I'm going to study with you *some*," Frannie retorted defensively.

"Some?" Robin echoed. "Frannie, just listen. It's more about how you prepare for the tests than what you remember from reading. You don't just get to read and repeat. You have to apply the information. Study with us and we'll discuss the material. I think that will benefit all of us."

"OK," Frannie answered.

"I'll enjoy writing the papers," said Robin. "We don't often have a class where we can think independently, and I enjoy defending my opinions."

"I'll get more study time with this interim course, even with a longer athletic schedule," Leslie added. "I'm going to enjoy the interim semester, too."

Katie suggested, "Let's go for dinner. I'm hungry, and I want to spend some time in the library afterward."

"Uh... maybe tomorrow I'll go to the library with you."

"Busy tonight?" snapped Robin. "A Stephen night trumps study night. No surprise there!"

❧

Missy waved from across the cafeteria where she was sitting with J.R. and Mike. The four girls joined them.

"So, tell us about your vacations," J.R. suggested, letting the girls decide who would answer first. Stephen's loud voice captured Frannie's attention. She couldn't hear everything he said but caught *Mexico* and *amazing*. She hoped he'd tell her about his vacation when they met in the Game Room later.

"I was so glad to see Gram," Robin said. "She looks wonderful. I thought having me out of her hair would be a vacation for her, but she really missed me. I was a handful my last two years of high school and I tried to apologize for being such a shit, but she wouldn't let me. She said she didn't have time for ancient history and was only interested in school, my friends, and Dallas."

The Wake-Up Call

"Did you run into any of the *losers* while you were home?" Katie asked.

"Not a one," Robin said without missing a beat. No way was I wasting a minute of my vacation on trash. I spent the whole time with Gram, visiting, cooking, and shopping. It was wonderful!" Robin smiled at the memory. "Oh, and Katie, Gram said to tell your folks thanks for inviting me for Thanksgiving. I think she feels bad about my not being able to get home as often as you guys do."

"Mom said you are welcome any time you can't make it back to Chicago." She continued, "Christmas was great. Even Naomi was home most of the time. She'll start college right after we graduate and she's starting to ask me about Crestmont. I'm surprised how quickly she went from spending all her time babysitting and with friends to thinking about what she wants to be when she grows up. She's talking about nursing, but that can change in a nanosecond."

"We missed Petey," Frannie interrupted. "The house was so quiet without him. We're all worried that something might happen to him. I spent a lot of time with Nana. She understands how scared I am for him. Petey says I'm his good luck charm, but I wasn't lucky enough to keep him from going in the first place."

"Did you tell your family about your Prince Charming?" Robin asked. "Somehow I imagine they'd be less than impressed with a guy who has the manners of a billy goat!"

"Katie," J.R. said before Frannie could respond, "Go on about your Christmas vacation."

Grateful, Katie continued, "John and Mr. Brown spent a lot of time with us. Robin, John asked when you'd be coming back to Atoka. I think you made quite an impression on him!"

"He's such a refreshing change. I've ever met a guy that nice. Well," Robin said, winking at J.R., "present company excluded. But, then again, I haven't met many nice guys. You're lucky, Katie. You need to hold on to that one."

Katie inhaled, about to protest, then realized that she wasn't sure how she felt.

Mike asked, "How about you, Leslie; how was your Christmas vacation?"

"Lively, as always. Mama prepared her usual feast and Daddy had to put an old door on trestles in the living room to add seating. Mama invited a family of four who just moved to town, so we had 18 people, including all the kids. I'd hate to have to relocate over Christmas and miss all the festivities. My mom sure knows how to do Christmas. When I wasn't helping in the grocery store, I hung out with friends."

"What about Paul?" Frannie chimed in.

"Paul's at basic training somewhere. I'm not sure where. He just made the decision and left. He didn't even say goodbye to my parents." Pensive, Leslie remarked, "This was the first Christmas in a long time that we haven't spent together. I'm surprised that I didn't miss him."

"Some things, including people, are best left behind," said Robin.

Missy jumped in, "I love Christmas. "My mother decorates our whole house and it looks as nice as a department store. One year our house was in the Sunday paper. Oh, and the New Year's ball at the country club was glorious. Frannie, you would have loved my dress." They continued their wardrobe chat while the others went on with their tales of Christmas vacation.

At the first lull in conversation, Katie gathered her dishes onto her tray and announced, "I'm heading to the library. Anyone coming?"

"Me," said Leslie, followed by Robin's "Me, too." The three girls looked at Frannie.

"I'll try to meet you there later… if Stephen doesn't take me out. He said to meet him in the Game Room after dinner."

J.R. said, "Is anyone else invited to the library?"

Katie smiled, "Oh, I think we could make room for one more… or two… or three." They all left together, leaving Frannie alone, watching Stephen's animated conversation with his friends.

Eventually, Stephen rose and left the cafeteria without a glance in her direction. Frannie sighed, then followed, but before she reached the Game Room, a cramp sliced through her abdomen. She grimaced and doubled over, collapsing into a chair. The cramp subsided, and a smile spread slowly across her face. She hurried to the bathroom, grateful for the sanitary napkin dispenser on the wall. She couldn't remember ever being more relieved to get her period.

※

With anticipation, Frannie unfolded the first paper she'd written for the interim session. Her face fell.

Robin leaned toward her and whispered. "Trouble in Paradise, Roomie?"

"There's no way, I got *a* C. I read the assignment. I knew that material."

"Join us in the library tonight. Don't wait until it's too late. We care about you, you Nitwit... even if you *are* impossible."

Bewildered, Frannie said, "Really?"

"Really," whispered Katie from her other side.

※

At dinner, Stephen passed behind Frannie's chair on his way to the Game Room. "See ya downstairs," he said and continued walking toward the door.

"Sorry, Stephen. Not tonight," Frannie called after him, resolute, though disappointed.

"Suit yourself," he called over his shoulder, not slowing his pace.

"A real gentleman," Robin observed. "All boyfriends should be that concerned."

"He's just disappointed," insisted Frannie, not sure that she believed the excuse herself. The four girls dropped off their trays and left for the library.

Settled into their conference room, Robin suggested, "Frannie, read us your paper and see if we can figure out why you got a *C*."

Reluctantly, Frannie spread the paper on the table in front of her and read aloud softly. After only a few paragraphs, Katie interrupted, "I think I see the problem. You're describing the reading assignment. The paper was supposed to explore the influence that Louis Pasteur's germ theory had on the future of health. Frannie, instead of thinking, *What did I learn?* ask yourself, *What difference did it make?* "

Frannie thought a moment. "So, I should have written about how the discovery changed the way people lived. That's not hard. It's just a different way of looking at things."

"You're catching on." Robin grinned. "There's hope for you yet."

Chapter 17

Frannie had not been alone with Stephen once since Christmas. When she entered the Game Room, Stephen was engaged in an animated conversation with Greg and James. He looked up when she approached and asked, "You up for a date tomorrow night?"

She ignored the jibes from Greg and James. "Yes, of course. Where are we going?"

"I thought I would take you to a fancy restaurant."

Greg couldn't resist. "Ooooooooh, FANCY restaurant."

"Shut up, you Blockhead!" Stephen hissed. "Just listen and learn."

Frannie was pleased that Stephen tried to teach his crappy friends some manners.

The rest of that evening and all the next day Frannie thought of little besides her upcoming date. "I can't make it to the library today. Stephen's taking me out to dinner and I need to get ready," Frannie explained to Katie and Robin when the class was over."

"Of course, you do," said Robin, and rolled her eyes.

"It's just one day," Frannie insisted. "We're going to a nice restaurant."

"Of course, you are…"

Katie cut in before Robin could finish. "Study with us for a little while. We're all going to quit when Robin leaves for work. Leslie and I are going to hook up with J.R. and Mike to shoot some hoops. You'll have plenty of time to get ready."

"Thanks, Katie, but I'm not even sure what I'm going to wear. I need time to put an outfit together."

Exasperated, Katie said, "Then have a good time, but do plan on joining us tomorrow. Our next test is coming up soon."

She selected her paisley print shirtwaist dress with white cuffs, tied a scarf at the neck, and completed the outfit with red go-go boots.

Frannie was nearly ready when Katie and Leslie got back, red-faced from the cold, and laughing. "Sounds like you two had fun. You look frozen."

"We beat the socks off J.R. and Mike. It was awesome!" Leslie reported. "You look super, Frannie."

Beaming, Frannie twirled, her full, short skirt flaring around her.

"Where is he taking you?" Asked Katie.

"All he would say was a fancy restaurant. Isn't that just too romantic."

"Exciting," Leslie replied. "I've gotta clean up a bit. Katie, we've got to hustle so there will still be food that's edible."

"Have a great time, Frannie. Be safe," Katie said and disappeared into her room.

Puzzled, Frannie thought, "*I wonder why she said be safe?*" Then she shrugged, grabbed her coat and a small purse, and hurried to meet Stephen.

He arrived promptly at 6:30, wearing a suit and tie.

The Wake-Up Call

"Your paisley tie matches my dress, and we didn't even plan it that way." She pirouetted in front of him, showing off her outfit.

His gaze was more of a leer than a smile. "You look sumptuous. I could eat you up right now."

Frannie grinned with delight, then noticed Sally at the desk frowning. "Stephen, I absolutely cannot be late tonight. I can't imagine that Sally would cover for me twice." She took Stephen's arm and thought about nothing but the magical evening ahead. Stephen opened her door and settled her into the red Mustang.

The restaurant was superb, with white linen and formal place settings. The waiter flipped their napkins open and placed them in their laps. Frannie laughed with delight when the waiter poured a taste of white wine for Stephen to sample. "This is just like a movie. I've never tasted wine before."

Stephen allowed her to make her own dinner selection. She chose white fish in a cream sauce and a salad. She ate slowly while Stephen consumed his steak and baked potato with gusto. "Drink your wine, Frannie. It's expensive."

Frannie found the wine sweet and pleasant. The waiter filled both of their glasses twice before the bottle was empty.

"This restaurant is to die for," Frannie gushed, a bit flushed, already tipsy from the wine. "I've eaten way too much." Frannie put down her fork and sat back watching Stephen finish. *This would be a perfect setting for a proposal. Stephen would get down on one knee, and everyone would cheer when he said, "Will you marry me. Then someone would propose a toast to the happy couple."*

The waiter interrupted her reverie. With a flourish, he placed a soufflé in front of each of them.

"Soufflé! I didn't hear you order soufflé?"

"Surprise!" he said with a Cheshire cat grin. "I ordered them when you went to the bathroom."

"What an elegant ending to a perfect meal." Frannie reached for her wine, but the glass was empty. "Could we have a cup of coffee?" Frannie asked

"Nah, I'm full," Stephen replied and signaled the waiter for the bill.

Frannie's disappointment with Stephen's abrupt response disappeared when he helped her on with her coat and held the car door for her for the second time.

"I'm glad you liked the wine," Stephen said. "We have another bottle in the car, and we're going somewhere we can enjoy it together."

"I love being with you, Stephen," she said, slurring her words.

Frannie bolted upright when they pulled into the motel parking lot. "What are we doing here, Stephen? We can't go to a motel."

"Of course, we can Frannie. It's just a quiet room where we can talk with no one to interrupt. Our room is in the back so no one will even see our car. No worries. It's cool."

Frannie nodded, still unsure, but impressed that he'd gone to such trouble to ensure that they could have some uninterrupted time together. She had to admit that comfy chairs would be better than the Mustang.

Stephen opened Frannie's door and pulled her into a hug. "Frannie, I want to be with you. You're my girl, aren't you?"

"Of course," she confirmed, transported by his first acknowledgment of their relationship. Before closing her door, Stephen reached into the back seat and snagged the large, screw top bottle of wine.

The room was cold and Frannie pulled her coat tightly around her. "I'll keep my coat on until it warms up a bit."

Stephen adjusted the thermostat impatiently. "There, it will be warm as toast in just a minute. Let's get comfortable." He threw his jacket and tie onto a chair and kicked off his shoes. He filled two plastic cups with wine and set the bottle on the nightstand. "Warmer now?" he asked, handing one cup to Frannie.

She wandered around the room. "Not yet," she replied, clutching her coat closed with one hand and sipping wine with the other. "This is good," she said. "It makes me feel like I'm floating on a cloud."

"Then come sit with me on the bed."

She glanced at the two chairs and then at the bed. "Let's sit in the chairs and talk."

"Relax," he said. "This is our special night, Frannie. It's just you and me. We're safe here."

She sipped her wine, then shrugged out of her coat held it out to him. "I'm warm now; it didn't take long." Stephen tossed her coat onto the chair with his jacket.

"Come sit by me." He patted the bed next to him. She glanced again at the chairs. "Stephen, I'm not sure about this," she finally managed to say aloud. "People might get the wrong idea."

"What people? We're finally alone, and what's the good of being together if I can't put my arms around you? We won't both fit in one chair. Come sit where I can hold you."

Frannie giggled, picturing them squeezed into one chair, then frowned. "A motel room just doesn't seem right." She perched on the edge of a chair. "We shouldn't be here until we're married."

"Married?" he exclaimed, then caught himself. "Oh, married, of course. You like being with me, don't you?"

"You know I do."

"Then we're good" he soothed.

Frannie emptied her cup. Stephen took her hand and she sat unsteadily on the edge of the bed next to him. He put her empty cup on the nightstand and lifted his to her lips. She drank, then he emptied the cup and refilled both.

"I'm glad you like wine," he said, handing a cup to Frannie. While she sipped, he knelt to slip off her boots, first the right, then the left. Stephen set Frannie's half-empty cup on the nightstand with his, then kissed her passionately and pulled her into an embrace. They sat on the bed, arms entwined, Frannie lost in a swirl of feelings from Stephen's kisses, his touch, and the wine.

Eventually, Stephen stood and pulled Frannie to her feet. She reached her arms around his neck and pulled his head down for a kiss. She was breathless, her heart racing and her discomfort with the motel room forgotten. He kissed her, lifting her off the floor, snaking his tongue between her lips, exploring her mouth.

Their lips locked in a kiss, Stephen slipped the scarf from her neck and let it slither to the floor. He undid the top button of her dress, placing a soft kiss on her neck. One by one, he unfastened the buttons, following each with a tantalizing kiss on the warm, soft flesh from her neck to her waist. Her body trembled with each kiss.

He kissed her lips and teased her with his tongue as he slipped her sleeves from her arms. Only Stephen's embrace held her upright. His caresses, his kisses, and the wine left her weak-kneed and trembling. As familiar, delightful sensations coursed through her body, her dress puddled at her feet and Stephen lifted her out of it. He laid her on the bed, kissing away her small cry of surprise.

"You are so beautiful, Frannie," he whispered, lying beside her and stroking her skin.

"I love you, too, Stephen."

Stephen reached for a cup of wine and held it to her lips. His face swam in front of her as she took several swallows. He emptied the cup and dropped it onto the floor. "Help me, Frannie," he murmured into her ear as he guided her fingers to his shirt buttons.

As she fumbled with the buttons, he unsnapped her bra, his fingers like feathers on her arms as he freed them from the straps. His shirt and her bra slid together to the floor. He hugged her close, their warm skin touching, eliciting twin moans of pleasure.

"Mmmm, Frannie, you are so soft… so beautiful." He continued to stroke her softly and she cuddled closer to him.

"You make me feel special." Her voice sounded far away.

"Frannie," he murmured, "help me with my pants. While she fumbled with his zipper, he stroked her side then slid his hands into her waistband and inched her panties and pantyhose together over her hips. When her legs were free, he wriggled from his trousers and he pushed them aside with her garments, onto the floor. They lay naked, side by side, his erection prominent, his fingers caressing her thigh and hip. He pulled her close and the hot skin of their naked bodies touched, their moans of pleasure mingling into a single sound.

Slowly he straddled her, one knee on either side, taking in the beauty of her slender body. "You are a perfect angel."

Frannie smiled at the out of focus, handsome face above her. She grasped his face between her hands pulled him towards her. "I love you, too."

Stephen murmured in her ear. "Being with you does wonderful things to me." She moaned and writhed with pleasure at his words and his touch.

He kissed one breast, then the other. When he ran his tongue around each nipple, then teased each one with a nibble, she let the explosions carry her mind and her body away. She floated on spasms of ecstasy and dreams of marriage, lost to the here and now.

Stephen checked the bedside clock. Not yet 9:30. A wicked smile flashed across his face. No rush. He still had plenty of time.

They explored one another, lost in the pleasures that their caresses unleashed. Stephen ran his hand lightly from her breast, across her abdomen, over her hips. As he stroked her inner thighs, Frannie's body trembled. His fingers inched higher and when he reached her warm center, she cried out then arched to meet him as a lightning bolt coursed through her body. He curled her hand around him. She tightened her grip as her hand encircled the hard, hot shaft. He moved up and down within her grasp. She purred, enjoying the silkiness and heat of his skin as her hand moved the length of him, back and forth. She cupped him with her other hand and it was Stephen who cried out at the jolt of pleasure.

Then Stephen slid from her grasp and kissed his way from her lips to her groin. She writhed and moaned as his tongue sent bolt after bolt of ecstasy through her body.

He balanced above her and slipped between her legs, moving back and forth, heightening the nearly unbearable pleasure for both. He was careful not to enter, and he slowed before he reached a climax. He wanted this adventure to last. He'd won the bet, but there was no reason not to enjoy himself as much as he could in the process. He was surprised at her responsiveness and admitted she made a great lay.

Frannie grasped his buttocks and moved with him as he gently stroked her, sending her into blissful spasm after spasm of delight.

In an instant of clarity, she pushed him away. "Stephen, wait!" she cried. "You have protection, right? We need protection."

"It's fine," he mumbled, pressing her shoulders to the bed and lowering himself to explore her again. "I'll pull out and you'll be fine."

"Promise?" she pleaded.

He teased with the tip of his hardened shaft and she moaned.

"Stephen! Do you promise?" she panted.

His urgency increasing, he replied, "Yea, yea… I'll pull out. Don't worry. You'll be fine."

Frannie relaxed, confident that she could trust him.

"Doesn't this feel good?" he panted.

"Mmmmm, yesss," she slurred, arching to meet him.

He slid into her moist center and Frannie mirrored his thrusts, both breathing rapidly as their speed increased. With a final plunge that pinned Frannie to the bed, Stephen climaxed. Frannie wrapped her legs around him and arched her body for one last explosive moment.

They lay together, spent and panting. Then he rolled to lie beside her. Frannie curled into the crook of his arm, sated, and fell asleep.

When Stephen's breathing returned to normal, he glanced at the clock. "Shit!" he exclaimed. "Not enough time to score again. We barely have time to make curfew."

Frannie didn't move at all when he pulled his arm from under her and went into the bathroom. Gotta say," he said to the sleeping nymph, "you were lots better than I woulda thought. I might keep this bet going on for a while longer. The guys owe me now!"

She lay, passed out, as he dressed, leaving his jacket and tie on the chair. "Frannie." He shook her. "Wake up. You're gonna be late for curfew if you don't get up now."

The Wake-Up Call

Frannie opened her eyes slowly, unable to focus. When she tried to lift her head a wave of dizziness washed over her. Stephen's face appeared as pixels on a screen, clearing bit by bit. "W-What? What time is it?"

"10:45. You need to get dressed."

"Oh... Oh, no!" she cried. A fleeting memory of divine sensations made her smile until she realized that she was naked with Stephen fully dressed. Embarrassed and confused, she searched for something to cover her nakedness.

"Don't bother," Stephen smirked. I've seen it all." He gathered her clothes from the floor and held them out to her. "You'd better hurry."

She slid from the bed, swayed, then sat on the edge to regain her balance. She took her clothing from Stephen and walked unsteadily to the bathroom, then closed and locked the door. She struggled with the buttons of her dress, leaving the cuffs undone, then shoved her pantyhose into her purse when she couldn't manage to get them on.

Dizzy and confused, she tried to reconstruct the evening. There had been a wonderful dinner, with delicious wine. She remembered the soufflés and smiled at the memory of Stephen opening the car door for her. Her smile faded when she couldn't remember how they had gotten from there to here.

Stephen was waiting with a satisfied grin. He stood holding her coat, shoved it over to her without offering to help. Shame and remorse overwhelmed Frannie.

Stephen got into driver's seat of the red Mustang and reached across the console to unlock her door. When he pulled the Mustang to the curb in front of Hadley Hall, there were three minutes before curfew. "Thanks for the night," He said, but made no effort to get out of the car. Bewildered, Frannie opened her door and got out, holding onto the door to steady herself. She pushed it closed and he pulled away before she'd turned to walk up the path.

Frannie was grateful that the door to Katie and Leslie's room was closed and her bedroom was empty. She closed her door quietly, then lay in bed, unsettled from the wine, queasy, and a little frightened. She remembered the dinner and Stephen's gentlemanly behavior, but she couldn't capture the details of the remainder of the evening. All that was left was a sense of foreboding. She turned her face to the wall and cried herself to sleep.

When Frannie awoke, Robin's bed was empty. She sat up abruptly, anxious, and grabbed her head. *"Oh no! My head hurts. Not again! Did I sleep through my alarm?"* She relaxed when she heard her suitemates talking in the sitting room. She remembered that she and Stephen had gone out to dinner, then… *then what?* As she concentrated, snatches of memory crept back, but the big picture remained elusive. Her sense of foreboding returned.

Saturday passed slowly as Frannie recovered from her hangover, her memory of the evening clearing bit by bit. Disheartened that Stephen had broken his promise, she remembered asking him about protection but couldn't recall his response. She consoled herself with the belief that she couldn't get pregnant the first time.

She gasped, *"But it wasn't the first time."*

Chapter 18

Frannie studied for *History and Philosophy of Science* with her suitemates, but she could not keep thoughts of Stephen and their tryst from intruding. Finally, she went to the Game Room. She found Stephen with Greg engaged in a heated game of foosball. As soon as Greg scored the winning goal, she said, "Stephen, I need to talk to you."

Without turning from the table, he said, "Later, I'm showing Greg how to play this game."

"Please take a break. I need to get to the library."

"Not now." He sent the next puck flying. "Tomorrow," he said, putting an end to their conversation.

※

"NO WAY," Frannie squealed, staring at her final grade in *History and Philosophy of Science*. "How could he give me a *C*? I described every historical event we read."

"That's the problem, Frannie," Katie explained. Dr. Miller didn't ask us to describe the events. "He asked us to describe how a historical event influenced a future scientific development. Remember that reading and remembering aren't enough at this point. Our professors want us to *use* what we learn."

"But…" Frannie began, but Robin interrupted.

"Listen to her, you Nitwit. You're getting crappy grades because you won't listen. The three of us discussed every single topic that ended up on the final. If you'd studied with us, you'd have done as well as we did."

Frannie burst into tears. "I told my parents I was going to get an *A*.

Frannie left for the Game Room at 8:30, but it was after 9:00 before Stephen pulled himself away from the dart board to walk her home. "So, what's got your panties in a wad?" he asked.

"I want to talk about last weekend. I know you thought it was OK to go all the way because you love me, Stephen, but it was wrong. We should have waited until we're married."

Stephen smirked. "You liked it. It's not like I had sex all by myself. You were into it as much as I was."

"That's not fair, Stephen. You know it was the wine we drank. It was wrong of you to make important decisions when you knew I wasn't thinking clearly. It's almost like you did that on purpose, but I know you wouldn't do that."

"You said you liked the wine. I didn't force it down your throat."

"That's not the point. Did you use protection? I remember asking you. If I get pregnant, we'll have to get married right away before anyone finds out. My parents would never forgive me."

"That's stupid. Your parents will get over it. Besides, you're probably not pregnant, and even if you are, you can abort the brat."

Frannie gasped. "What? Never. We couldn't kill our baby. We'd have to get married."

The Wake-Up Call

"Whoa, Girl, not so fast. The only thing you should be worrying about right now is being late for curfew. It's almost 10."

"Isn't Dr. Grosvenor just the dreamiest teacher you've ever seen?" Frannie gushed after their Organic Chemistry lecture.

"Yeah. Focusing on discussions in *History and Philosophy*, during Interim session wasn't easy when he was our breakout group leader," Leslie added. Too bad he has that gorgeous wife and those two precious kids."

"He doesn't do that much for me," J.R. retorted, "but, I do like the way he teaches."

"At least his lectures have nothing to do with a crappy jaguar," chimed in Robin.

"He makes good sense. I think I understood his lecture on saliva this morning, and lab this afternoon could be fun," Frannie said.

"Yep, if you like spittin' in a test tube," chuckled Robin. Students sitting at adjacent tables shot her disgusted looks. "Oops, better watch what we talk about over lunch." she reminded the group with a laugh.

Missy called out, "Hey, y'all. What're you talking about?" J.R. pulled an extra chair to the table and she joined them.

"Oh, hacking up spit and stuff like that," Robin replied, enjoying the aggravated expressions at neighboring tables.

"Gross!" Missy grimaced. "That isn't any type of lunch conversation. How about the weather, or shopping, or *anything* more appetizing?"

"Missy, according to dreamy Dr. Grosvenor, the ptyalin number is a quantitative measure of a saliva sample's ability to digest starch." Frannie winked. "Since everything on my plate is a starch, I hope my saliva is doing a bang-up job."

Katie said, "Right on, Frannie. That was a super interpretation of what we heard in class this morning. Totally slammin, Girlfriend!"

Frannie beamed at Katie's compliment.

"We gotta git, Guys, or we'll be late. We lost track of time bullshitting about spit." Robin said, gathering her tray of dirty dishes.

"Frannie, are you coming to the library with us after lab?" Katie asked as they left the cafeteria.

"I was planning to go to the Game Room…"

"Hey," Robin interrupted. "Remember the wise words of your brilliant roommate: *If you don't study, you don't pass.* You're starting to catch on and now's when you need to buckle down and study. Think about it."

"But I told Stephen…"

"Never mind." Robin interrupted. "Do as you damn well please!" Robin hastened her steps, leaving Frannie behind to reflect on her choices.

❦

Frannie finally got Stephen alone during the following week. "Sit here by the fountain, Stephen. We have to talk."

"For God sakes, Frannie. What's to talk about?

"I could be pregnant."

He remained standing and said sourly "Not likely. We screwed twice? Odds are against it."

"That's mean. We only did it because we're in love, and if we're going to have a baby, we'll get married right away and no one will know."

"Whoa! Who said anything about love or marriage? We had some fun sex, that's all. I seem to remember that you enjoyed every minute of it. That's what you should be remembering. We had fun. If you get pregnant, you get rid of it. No big deal, and not my problem."

He walked away and she hurried after him. "Stephen, you can't just walk away."

"If you wanna have fun, Frannie, you let me know."

"I thought you loved me."

"Sex isn't love, Frannie, it's fun. You're great in the sack, and I'm the best you'll find around here."

When they reached Hadley Hall, he kept on walking. "See ya 'round and let me know if you want to hook up again," he called over his shoulder.

Devastated Frannie stared at his back.

Chapter 19

Frannie counted the weeks on the calendar in her lap. *"January 30 to March 22 …one, two, three… Seven, …Seven? If Leslie hadn't run back to the dorm for a tampon this morning, I would never have realized… seven weeks. I remember having my period right after Christmas vacation. That was January. Good. I know I've had one since then… but when?"*

Her smile faded. *"February? I don't remember a period in February or March. Oh, NO! This can't be happening!"*

Twisting the chain that held Petey's locket, her dismay grew. *"Oh, my Lord! What if I'm pregnant?"*

She wound the chain once too many times around her finger. "Nooooooo…" she wailed as the chain snapped. Horrified, she looked at the broken chain, then clutched at her bare neck. "Nooooooo…" she screeched, jumping up, searching frantically for the locket. She moaned as she felt under her bed, then Robin's. She knelt on the floor, leaned against the bed, laid her head in her arms, and sobbed. *"I've lost Petey's locket. I could be pregnant. I failed the last chemistry test."* She crawled onto her bed and curled into a ball.

The Wake-Up Call

As her tears subsided, one thought began to crowd out the others. *"Robin was right about Stephen all along. If I'm pregnant, then Stephen lied to me."* She moaned. *"My family will hate me. Everyone here will say, I told you so."*

Exhausted, with no tears left, she took a deep breath. *"What DID I expect? How could I have been so blind?"* She could hear Robin asking her the same questions.

"An abortion, that's what I'll have to do. But, how? I can't go to the infirmary, or the hospital, or even a doctor without my parents finding out. It's the only solution, but I'd be killing my baby. Stephen won't marry me, so I have no choice. My parents will disown me." Frannie lay numb facing the blank wall beside her bed. She passed the next hour alternating between the crush of hopelessness and moments of resolve. *God, help me."* Her sobs weakened into hiccups as she fell asleep.

Robin stopped by on her way to the library and found Frannie asleep. She shook her head and mumbled to no one in particular. "That girl can sleep any time without a care in the world. I hate to see the day when all of this catches up with her. She'll be a basket case."

※

"I'll bet Frannie's still sleeping," Robin said to Katie and Leslie as they prepared to leave the library for dinner. "I'll go back and wake the princess. Meet you in the cafeteria."

Robin opened their bedroom door. "Sleepyhead, want to come to dinner with us?" She shook Frannie's shoulder, then stepped back.

Frannie opened her eyes and looked up, bleary-eyed, not yet alert. "W-What? Dinner?" she stammered. Memory washed over her as her mind cleared and she choked back a sob.

"You OK?" Robin asked, concerned.

Awake now, and determined to soldier through her problems, Frannie forced a smile. "I'm fine," she replied and reached for Robin's hand to pull herself up and off the bed. "I don't know why I was so tired. Thanks for waking me. I don't want to miss dinner."

"Did you get any studying done this afternoon?" Robin asked. "The three of us are going to tackle the next organic chem test after dinner. You really ought to join us."

"I will," Frannie replied with determination. Before following Robin out of the room, she glanced at her broken gold chain on the nightstand, then scanned the bed and the floor, hoping to spot Petey's locket.

After dinner, the four girls left the cafeteria and settled into a small conference room in the library. "Katie, you and Robin have the best grades in chem so far, so you two ask questions and Frannie and I will see what we know, " Leslie suggested.

"Good idea," Frannie agreed. "When I read the material, it seems to make sense, but when I look at the test questions, I don't know what to do. I understand now that just reading isn't enough for this stuff."

"Good catch, Einstein," quipped Robin. "Seriously, I'm glad that you're studying with us. Explaining things to you and Leslie will help Katie and me, too."

By the time they got back to the dorm at ten, they were all tired. Studying had kept Frannie's mind off her predicament, but the desperation returned as she prepared for bed. As she brushed her teeth, Robin came into the bathroom, her hand outstretched. "Frannie, your locket, the chain must have broken." Frannie stared at the locket in Robin's hand, looked up to meet Robin's eyes with gratitude, then burst into tears.

"What's wrong, Frannie?" Robin said.

"I'm OK," Frannie sniffled and forced a reassuring smile. "I don't know what I would do if I lost it, especially now that Petey's in Vietnam. I'd feel like it was my fault if something happened to him."

"You dope, you can't think like that. You don't have anything to do with what's happening there."

"I guess I know that. It's just that he said I'm his good luck charm. If I lost the locket…" Seeing Robin's concerned look she said, "Thanks, but I'm OK. I know that nothing I do can keep Petey safe. That was a silly thing to say."

Relieved, Robin said. "You need to concentrate on keeping *you* safe. If you fail organic chem, you won't be able to stay in the nursing program with us."

"Things aren't as fine as I thought," Frannie admitted, dejected. "Thanks a lot for the help tonight. I guess I'm ready to admit I'm wrong."

"No problem. I hoped you'd come around eventually. We'll study together from now on. Have you packed for your trip home?"

"Yeah almost finished." Frannie left for spring break at home right after classes on Friday.

※

Frannie spent the hours on the plane concentrating on masking her discomfort with a cheery demeanor. As soon as she entered the terminal, her father enveloped her in an embrace. "Let's get your bags and get going. Your mother and Nana can't wait to see you."

When her mother opened the door, Frannie hugged her, then rushed off to see Nana. "I've been away so long and I miss you so much," she said, hugging Nana close.

Nana's always been the first one I've gone to when something was wrong. She can fix anything, but not this time.

"I love you, Nana," she said, and leaned over and gave her a kiss. "I'm going to see if Mom needs help with dinner. I'll be back soon."

"Just a minute. is there something you want to talk about? There's something you're not telling me."

Frannie's heart stopped and she could barely control her voice. She took a long, slow breath and fixed a smile in place. "No, I can't think of anything."

"If you say so." Nana hesitated. "You know that you can always talk to me."

"Of course, I can. I'll go help Mom and be back after you've rested. Let me help you get comfortable."

Frannie pulled Nana's door closed and stood, shaking. *"I'll never make it through the holiday."*

Frannie stopped by the powder room to regain her composure, then walked to the kitchen counter where her mother was mincing onions for a casserole. "Mom, are you ever going to teach me how you do that?" Frannie asked.

"Teach you what?" she replied, surprised. You've been watching me fix dinner your whole life."

"How do you get the pieces all the same size? And how do you get all the food ready for the table at the same time? I've always wondered, but I figured it was just magic. You never say, 'would you do this while I do that; it's like the meal just happens."

"Well, in a way, it does…" her mother said, "I've been doing it so long, I don't think about it."

Frannie shook her head. "That's why Robin thinks I'm spoiled."

"Spoiled?" her mother questioned. "You're not spoiled. You and Petey are both delightful, well-behaved children who know right from wrong. I don't think that's spoiled." Frannie winced as guilt sliced through her like a knife.

"You and Dad are pretty amazing parents, that's for sure," Frannie said forcing a broad smile to mask her shame. "I'll gather my laundry," she said, knowing that she had to get away by herself.

On Saturday, Frannie's mother said, "Come with me to Pantry Pride. We need groceries for the rest of your vacation. They have the best selection of fresh fruits and vegetables." Frannie joined her mom, grateful for the opportunity to go somewhere that might take her mind off her dark secrets.

"Mom, this is enough food for the rest of the year," Frannie said as they each pushed a cart full of grocery bags to the car.

"Frannie!" came a voice from behind them. She turned to see a young mother pushing a baby carriage. "Frannie!" the girl called again. "I thought you were away at school."

The Wake-Up Call

"Marcie! Oh, my goodness." Frannie said, taking several steps toward the girl with the carriage. "Oh, your baby..." Frannie noted the pink blanket. "She's adorable. How are you doing? I haven't seen you..." she hesitated, "well, not since you left school."

"I'm OK," Marcie replied. "Lisbeth is such a precious baby. I did hate to miss graduation, but my parents have been wonderful. I'll take my GED when Lisbeth is a bit older, and I'll go to college after she starts school."

"What are you doing now?" asked Frannie. "How are you managing?"

"I'm living with my parents. They wouldn't let me marry Gary. He's Lisbeth's father. They said that one mistake was enough. Gary disappointed me when he agreed without an argument. I thought he'd want to marry me to be with his baby, but that turned out to be wishful thinking. Now I'm glad my parents insisted. I think they knew all along he wasn't a good guy. They tried to warn me, but I wouldn't listen. Eventually, I'll be a teacher like I'd dreamed, but in the meantime, I'm working on being the best mom in the world."

"Well, she's a gorgeous little girl," Frannie said. "I'm glad your parents were so understanding. Good luck, Marcie, and I'm glad we ran into you."

"A pity," her mother said, shaking her head. "What a waste. Marcie was such a smart girl and had a great future ahead of her. Such a stupid mistake. When her parents wouldn't let her get married, she wanted an abortion. Can you imagine such a thing? Of course, they wouldn't hear of it. It's fortunate for her that her parents have the means to take care of her. She'd have ended up on the street if they'd let her marry that boy."

Frannie found it difficult to breathe.

"Come along. I want to have dinner ready when your father gets home."

Frannie followed without a word. They drove home in silence. *"Just let me get my period. I can't have a baby, and I can't have an abortion, so I just have to not be pregnant."* With that resolution made, Frannie relaxed in her seat and said, "Mom, can I help fix dinner tonight?"

"I think your time would be better spent with Nana." replied her mother. "She misses you and loves every minute she spends with you."

As soon as she heard the front door, Nana called, "Frannie," come sit with me. I doubt your mother needs help with dinner, and I want to hear more about school and that boy of yours." Frannie sighed and joined Nana, wishing she were back at school.

≈

Frannie spent the entire flight from Philadelphia to Dallas in a mild panic, thinking about the challenges she faced. Her mind ricocheted between failing and being pregnant. Either one would be devastating; she couldn't endure both.

In the Dallas airport, a voice called from behind her, "Frannie, wait up!" Leslie was waving and hurrying to catch up. "How neat that we got in at the same time. We can share a cab back to campus. How was your vacation? Did you do anything exciting?"

Frannie relaxed a bit and said, "We couldn't have planned this better."

"It was nice to be home with the family," Leslie began. "I needed the break from studying and track. We had a great Easter dinner. As usual, Mama invited every person in town with nowhere else to go. How about you?"

"With Petey in Vietnam, it was quiet at home. Everyone is worried, but we didn't talk about it. I spent lots of time with Nana. Mom and I did some shopping, and that's about it."

The cab driver carried their suitcases into the Hadley Hall lobby and nodded appreciatively when Frannie handed him a generous tip. When he left, Leslie reached for her wallet and Frannie stopped her with, "No, don't worry about it. My parents gave me money for the cab, and it didn't cost a penny more for the two of us." Leslie nodded her thanks.

The Wake-Up Call

Dropping their suitcases inside the suite, Frannie called out, "Anybody home?"

"In here," Robin yelled from the bedroom. "Getting dressed. I'm working 6-10 tonight." When Frannie and Leslie plopped onto Frannie's bed, Robin said "Welcome home. Did you both have a good vacation?"

Before anyone could answer, the suite door opened and Katie dropped her suitcase by the other two. She stuck her head into the room. "I thought I heard you all in here. Robin, I'm so glad you're still here. Hurry and finish dressing. My parents and John are here and they'd love to see all of you."

In the lobby, John and Mr. Grayfox rose from their chairs. Mrs. Grayfox gave each of the girls a hug, then turned to Robin and scolded her for not coming to Atoka for the holiday.

"I would have enjoyed every minute, but I needed to work," Robin explained. "You spoiled me over Thanksgiving. By the way, Gram has told me more than once to thank you for taking such good care of me. She wants you to know that she's happy knowing that I've such wonderful people close by."

"Well, you tell your Gram not to worry. We're happy to be your home away from home," Mrs. Grayfox assured her.

"How long can you stay today?" Robin asked the Grayfoxes. "I have to be at work at 6."

"Katie," Mr. Grayfox said, capturing everyone's attention. "What if we all go to Rob Rory's for dinner before Robin's shift begins. We can hear about everyone's Easter holiday. We were planning to eat before leaving Dallas, and I would be honored to host an end-of-holiday dinner for my daughter and her friends."

"Dad, how sweet! Are you sure it's OK? There are seven of us."

"Of course," he assured her and ushered the group out to the pickup.

"Robin, you're dressed for work, so you should sit up front with us," Mrs. Grayfox instructed. The rest of you climb in back. We'll have time for a nice dinner before Robin's shift begins."

Frannie was grateful not to be alone with her demons.

Chapter 20

Dr. Grosvenor returned the chem tests in lab on Tuesday after vacation. Frannie held her test, folded lengthwise, for several long minutes before opening it. *"The test questions might as well have been written in Greek! I waited too long to start studying."* She unfolded the paper revealing the red "*F*" in the upper right corner. Devastation washed over her, and she hurried from the lab before she burst into tears. In the dorm, tears blurred her vision and a torrent of thoughts spilled over one another. *"I've only got six weeks left before finals and I'm failing."*

Robin found Frannie curled up on her bed, mired in self-pity. "C'mon," she said softly but firmly. "We need to fix this."

Frannie turned away and buried her face in her pillow. "It's OK, Robin. Go to lunch. I'll figure it out."

"No, *we'll* figure it out." Robin rolled Frannie toward her. "Sometimes it takes a wake-up call to bring things into focus. I oughta know."

"I don't know what to do," Frannie sniffled. It's too late anyhow." Another sob escaped when she realized that Robin was privy to only one of her two unsolvable problems. "My family will be so disappointed. I can't imagine letting them down like this. I'm NOT the wonderful person they think I am. You called me a loser, and you were right."

"No, Stephen and Jake are losers; you're just an airhead," Robin gave Frannie's shoulder a squeeze. "You're a smart person who's never had to think or do anything for yourself… and now you do."

Frannie stared at Robin, with no idea how to respond or what to do next.

"C'mon, Frannie. Come to lunch. Then the four of us will come back and figure this out. We are the Nurseketeers, after all."

At lunch, Frannie played with her food. She felt less vulnerable with her friends around but remained despondent, with no clue how to change things.

In the suite, Robin took charge. "There's no reason that any of us should fail a course. We're all smart people. There are two parts to learning and it takes both to pass a course. The first is knowing the material and the second is knowing how to apply it."

Katie and Leslie nodded in agreement.

Robin continued, "Frannie, two things got you in trouble. First," counting on her fingers, "you had your head up your ass. You put your social life ahead of your classes, and all for the biggest loser on campus, I might add.

"Second, you were top banana in the brains department in high school. You didn't have to lift a finger because you didn't have any competition. Well, this ain't Kansas, *Dorothy*. A university's reputation is based on the quality of their graduates. That means they need to get rid of the losers along the way. So…" she looked Frannie in the eye. "Are you a loser, or are you ready to act like a winner?"

"What are you?" Robin repeated, looking sternly at Frannie.

"A winner," Frannie stammered. But what can I do?"

Katie said, "Frannie, first you need to decide what you want. Then we can look at what it will take to make that happen."

"I want to pass," Frannie said without hesitation.

"Then, figure out what you need to do to make that happen. Think the problem through. We're here to help your plan succeed."

Frannie shrugged, "I think I understand, but I don't know what to say."

"One problem," Katie pointed out, "is that you've never had to plan before. You've been lucky enough to have everything turn out just fine without any effort on your part. That's what Robin meant when she called you *spoiled*. It's not your fault, but it IS your responsibility, it's time to do something about it if you want things to change."

"But," Frannie began. "If it's not my fault, how do I get unspoiled?"

"Frannie," Leslie said, "that question was the first step in the process."

Frannie began to feel less like the target of criticism. Her courage bolstered, she announced, "OK. I'm ready to act like a winner. I have no idea where to start, but I'm ready to learn, and I promise I'll do my best. I won't let the Nurseketeers down.

Frannie stopped by the Game Room after dinner on her way to the library. "I've gotta meet Leslie and Katie in a minute," she explained to Missy and J.R. "I just wanted to stop by to let you know."

From behind them came Stephen's loud voice, "So, where ya been Frannie? Haven't seen you around. C'mon over and watch me play darts. I'll save the next game for you."

Without turning, Frannie called over her shoulder, "I've got plans for this evening."

Silence followed as Stephen and his friends stood, amazed at the change in her attitude. Stephen forced a grin. "Aw, c'mon Frannie, you can play a game before you go," he cajoled.

"Don't think so," she said, without breaking her stride. To Missy and J.R. she said, "Gotta go. See you later." She walked out of the Game Room without another word.

In the library, Frannie joined Katie and Leslie in the reserved conference room. "Your seat," Leslie pointed to the empty chair between them. "Here are the study questions from chem lab. Let's see what we can do with them."

They spent the next two hours working on the Organic Chemistry problems. "Frannie, you need to look up the answers on your own. It's not your brain that needs exercise," Katie reminded her. "You need to develop better study habits."

"Sorry. I thought this would be a lot easier."

"Bingo!" said Leslie. "That's the point. It's only easy after it becomes a habit."

Frannie sighed and Leslie continued, "So get to work. Your chem notes await you."

The three had been working for nearly an hour when Frannie cried out, "I got it! It's the *bonds* that differentiate alkynes from alkanes. You can see here how the formulas are different. Look! When you said you'd help me learn to study, I thought you meant you'd help me understand the material. Now I know what you meant. It's exciting when something new starts to make sense. I used to think you either knew the answer or you didn't. Now I realized that you apply what you learn to solve problems."

Katie grinned. "I can't wait to share the miracle with Robin."

"So, THAT'S it!"

"Not so fast, Frannie," said Leslie "It's a great start, and I'm glad you're pleased with yourself, but the bonds are only *one* of the principles you'll need for the exam. There's lots more material to cover. You'll need good grades on two more tests and the final for this semester to pass the course.

Sobered, but not deflated, Frannie took a deep breath and turned the page.

Frannie was attentive in lecture on Thursday morning. She took notes, asked questions, and participated in discussions. After class, she approached Dr. Grosvenor. "Would you have time this afternoon to meet with me?"

At 2:30, Dr. Grosvenor faced Franny across his desk. "So, Miss Braun, what can I do for you?"

"I'm sorry that it's taken me so long to realize that being at the top of my class in high school didn't automatically qualify me for the same position in college. I kept thinking that I'd catch on and that my grades would get better. They didn't."

"I understand…" Dr. Grosvenor encouraged.

"It's late in the semester, but I *know* I can catch up. Can you recommend a study outline that will help me prepare for the last two tests and the final exam? It's asking a lot, but I'm a different person now and I promise you my complete dedication to the course."

"I'll admit, Miss Braun that you're cutting it close; however, I do believe that you can still pass if you apply yourself."

Frannie, surprised and pleased with Dr. Grosvenor's support, replied, "Thank you, Sir. I know that I can do it."

"You won't need any special outline or guidance. The course outline is quite clear and each lesson is intended to build upon the previous one. If you will review the material from the beginning, you'll find that, once you've grasped the foundational material, you'll have no difficulty mastering subsequent lessons."

Frannie nodded.

"If you're as committed to passing this course as you say, I expect that you'll go back and start at the beginning. It will take time, but it's possible. You asked good questions in class today and supported your responses during the discussion well. Ask questions of that quality of yourself as you study, and the material will be less daunting than you expect."

"Thank you very much, Dr. Grosvenor. I won't disappoint you.

Chapter 21

"Wow, what a week this has been," Frannie exclaimed as the four girls finished lunch. "I'll meet you at the library in a while; I need to lie down for a bit."

"You OK?" asked Robin. "You're on a roll, don't stop now."

"Yeah, I'm OK," Frannie answered. "Just cramps or something."

"We'll wait for you in the library. Come on over when you feel better."

On her bed in the room, Frannie drew her knees up to her chest as a severe cramp spread across her abdomen. "*Owwwwch*," she moaned. She relaxed when the pain subsided, intending to rest a little, then meet the girls in the library. Another cramp started to build and she wet her pants. She ran to the bathroom.

As she lifted her skirt to sit on the toilet seat, she stared in horror at the red running down her leg. "*WHAT?*" she thought, panic-stricken. The blood flow increased and decreased with the intensity of the cramps. She sat on the toilet, trying to sort her tumbling thoughts. "*Make the bleeding stop. I need to clean up this mess. I've never had a period like this.*" She tried to relax and think, but each cramp drove rational thought from her mind.

Frannie had no idea how long she had been sitting doubled over on the toilet, the room spinning. She whimpered, overcome by pain and terror. Robin found her there when she came back from the library to dress for work.

Horrified, Robin took in the scene. "Frannie, what happened?" Robin knelt in front of her and squeezed her shoulders.

Frannie raised her head, her eyes unfocused and a bewildered expression on her face. "I… I don't know." The pains had subsided, as had the blood flow. It hurt so much, Robin. I thought I was going to die. I need to clean up this mess." Frannie began to stand, teetered, and fell back onto the toilet seat as Robin grabbed for her.

"Don't move yet," Robin commanded. "Let me get your bed ready so that you can lie down. DON'T move. Just sit there for a minute."

Robin backed slowly away from Frannie. "I'm serious. Don't try to get up. I need the shower curtain and some towels so you can lie on your bed without ruining it. But first, a soak in the tub." Robin lay a towel in the tub, opened the faucet, and fiddled with the knobs until the temperature was perfect. "Frannie, give me your hand, then stand up slowly. We'll walk to the tub and you can sit on the edge so I can help with your clothes. You can lie on the towel in the tub so you won't slip."

Frannie took Robin's hand and stood unsteadily. "Slowly," cautioned Robin. "We'll wash away the blood and make sure that the bleeding has stopped. Can you walk with me?"

When Frannie lay safely in the tub, Robin picked up her clothes. "I'll soak these in cold water so they won't be ruined. Then we can figure out what to do next."

"Robin," Frannie's voice was weak. "You can't tell anyone."

Robin replied. "Frannie, we can't pretend nothing's happened. We have to get you to the hospital to make sure that you're OK and make sure that whatever happened won't happen again."

"I mean, we can't tell anyone but the Nurseketeers. Not my family, or Katie's parents, or…. ANYONE. No one would understand. They'd never forgive me," Frannie wailed and burst into tears.

Robin, glancing at the bits of tissue in the toilet, understood. "Oh... Frannie, don't cry. We don't have to tell anyone. Katie and Leslie can figure it out for themselves. They'll protect your secret. I need to go get them right now so that we can borrow Leslie's car."

"Robin, I can't...."

Robin interrupted. "Frannie, don't even say it! We *are* going to the hospital! I'm sure you're going to be just fine, but we're not taking any chances. So, right now, let's empty the tub and run clean water so we can be sure the bleeding has stopped. Then you rest on your bed while I get Leslie's car."

They emptied and filled the tub twice. "The water's clear, Frannie," Robin reassured her. "Let's see if you can stand."

"Slowly, Frannie," Robin cautioned. "We don't know how much blood you lost. You might be weak or dizzy."

Frannie held both of Robin's arms and pulled herself up. She was wobbly. "Sit back down for a minute," Robin commanded. "We'll do this a little at a time. I can't let you collapse between here and the bedroom."

Frannie smiled. I won't collapse. I don't feel as dizzy as I did." Frannie took a breath. "Robin?"

"Hmmm?"

"Thank you."

"Thank me?"

"Yes. I figured out you didn't hate me a long time ago, but I still resented you because you refused to be nice to me. What's worse was that I knew you were right. Sometimes I tried to prove you were wrong, but that just got me in more trouble."

Robin said, "I was furious when you wouldn't listen. I knew you'd get hurt, and I didn't want that to happen."

"You're smart, and so organized, and there's nothing you can't do. I was jealous, but I didn't want to admit it."

"Frannie, you twit, you're a wonderful, sensitive person who just needs time to grow up. I'm sorry you had to suffer so much, but you'll be okay."

"I couldn't have done without you today, that's for sure."

"The rest of us faced more challenges growing up than you did, so we learned little by little. You had to face your challenges all at once. I'll just bet if we added up our growing pains, we'd all be equal in the end." Robin gave Frannie's shoulders an affectionate squeeze. "C'mon. Stand up slowly, and we'll get this show on the road."

"I feel so stupid. Robin, I'm happy that you're here. Do you think this nightmare will ever go away? I just feel like I'll be paying for being stupid for the rest of my life."

"We'll see," said Robin. The nightmare might almost be over. But, if feeling stupid gets you to study and pass organic chemistry and ups your taste in men, then you feeling stupid is fine with me. Oh, add *make your bed* to that list, and *do your own laundry*, and *put your clothes away...*"

"Okay, okay, I get it!" Frannie gave Robin a grateful smile. "I promise all those things… but not all at once."

Once Robin had helped Frannie towel herself dry and get into pajamas, she settled her onto the palette she'd made on Frannie's bed. "Just rest until I get back. I need to get Leslie's car and I need to call Rob Rory's and explain why I'm not there. They'll be fine with covering my shift. Don't get up! I'll be back in a jiffy. I mean it, don't move!"

Robin walked purposefully down the hall and through the lobby, attracting no attention. As soon as she got outside, she ran as fast as she could.

"Bring everything," she instructed Leslie and Katie. "We need to get back to the dorm right now. I'll explain once we're outside."

On the way to the dorm, Robin explained, not mentioning the possibility of a miscarriage. She left that for Frannie to share. "I think she's okay for right now, but we do need to get her to the emergency room where they can figure out what happened and if there's anything that needs to be done."

"The only hospital near here is Parkland, the big one downtown. Do you think it's safe to take her there?" Leslie asked.

"They took President Kennedy when he was shot," countered Katie. I guess if it was good enough for the President, it's safe enough for Frannie."

"Leslie, Katie and I will get Frannie ready," said Robin, "if you'll run get *Nellie* and pick us up."

Katie and Robin, with Frannie between them, pajamas hidden under her raincoat, walked casually out of Hadley Hall. They chatted as if nothing were amiss, and no one interrupted them before they met Leslie at the curb. "Frannie, sit back here with me," said Robin. You can lie down if you want."

"Katie, there's a city map in the glove compartment." Leslie said, "The hospital is close enough so you should be able to fold it to see the campus and the hospital at the same time."

"Go to Central, Leslie, and then south toward downtown. It may not be the shortest route, but it's the least complicated."

"Good thinking," Robin commented from the back. "No sense wasting time getting lost."

"That didn't take long," Leslie said as she pulled up to the Emergency Room entrance. "You guys go with Frannie. I'll park *Nellie*."

"It's good that you got here now," the ER intake nurse told them. "It's Friday and it won't be long before this place is a zoo. We call Friday night the *Knife and Gun Club*. Frannie, let's get you taken care of before the fun begins." She turned to the girls. "The exam rooms are way too small for a convention. Sit over there. I'll take good care of her and let you know how she's doing."

"I need to find a phone and call Rob Rory's," Robin said. "Be right back."

Leslie was sitting with Katie when Robin returned. "I told them my roommate was sick and I didn't want to leave her alone. They said they hoped she'd be better soon. I think they hire more students than they need because they're so generous. It pays off when someone can't make it to work."

"I hope that whatever happened to Frannie is over and she'll be able to come home with us," Leslie said. "There's no way we'll be able to keep her secret if she has to stay here."

Robin realized that Leslie had figured out what happened. "It's important to Frannie that we keep it secret," Robin explained. "No one can know. She said that her family would never forgive her. I'm sure they would, but she thinks she's let everyone down."

Katie added, "It's best if Frannie gets to decide what to share and with whom. That includes us, too. We need to respect her privacy and not ask her any questions. I know that I'd be grateful if my friends let me manage a difficult situation in my own way."

The three sat in silence, then Leslie looked at her watch. "It's been more than an hour. I'm getting worried."

"I think the longer it takes, the better things are," Katie suggested. "If they had to do something drastic, like surgery or something, they'd be asking us for information by now, wouldn't they?"

"Katie, you could keep hostages calm during a bank holdup," Robin said with obvious appreciation. "How do you do that? If anything, horrible ever happens to me, I want you to be with my Gram, holding her hand."

The girls watched the clock. It had crept through two hours when the friendly nurse pushed through the double doors and strode toward them. They tensed and started to stand, but she waved them back into their chairs. "She's doing fine. Which one of you is Robin?"

Robin stood. "I am."

Nodding, the nurse said, "Thought so. Frannie said you'd be the one with hair the color of a robin's breast. Hard to miss." She continued, "Come with me." Looking to Leslie and Katie, "As I explained before, there's not room enough for a convention. We won't be long."

Robin followed her into a tiny room where Frannie, in a hospital gown, lay on an exam table, covered with a sheet. She looked tired, but her face had more color than when they'd arrived. "I'm going to be okay," she said, reaching for Robin's hand. "They didn't say it was a miscarriage, but they did say that there was *no indication of retained tissue*. I guess they were trying to spare me the embarrassment. The best part is they didn't have to do any procedures, so we can go home. We don't have to let anyone know we were here."

The nurse stood in the doorway. "M'Lady can go home now. Robin. Frannie told me what you did. She's lucky to have a friend like you."

To Frannie, she said, "You're fortunate, young lady, but only if this ordeal has a happy ending. I'm going to trust that you will put this experience to good use and consider getting birth control pills."

Frannie nodded, and Robin said, "Oh, she will! She will. Thank you for taking such good care of her."

"Robin, come with me. Frannie, I'll be back in a moment to help you dress."

Alone, Frannie wrestled with her jumbled thoughts, every moment from her first day on campus.

The nurse led Robin to a desk at the end of the hall. "I think it's best not to bother Frannie with financial details right now. Do you know if she has insurance?"

"I haven't a clue, but she comes from a good family, so I'm sure that she does. Can we pay for this now, or make a down payment, and take care of the bill later?"

"I'm sure that we can make whatever arrangements are necessary," the nurse assured Robin. Frannie is a student at Crestmont. Our Business Office will work with her on payment. Come with me and we'll see what we can do to get Frannie out of here."

The bill was reasonable and Robin wrote a check to show good faith. They'd figure out how to pay the balance so Frannie's secret would be safe.

"We'll be back at Crestmont well before curfew," Katie noted. "No one will ever have a clue. Frannie, this whole thing will be our secret."

Leslie dropped the girls at Hadley Hall and went to park Nellie.

"Whew!" said Robin as she closed the suite door firmly. "Frannie, you go straight to bed."

"Not yet," Frannie insisted. "Let's sit together for just a bit." Leslie walked in and they all dropped into their usual chairs. "Thank you for being the best friends anyone could ever have. I'm sorry for the trouble I've caused, and for how much I've frustrated you. I'm just lucky that you didn't give up on me. I promise that you will be proud that I'm a Nurseketeer."

Chapter 22

"*Too little, too late,*" thought Frannie, as the four roommates walked to Nursing Seminar where the day's topic was *Sex Education*.

"Frannie are you okay? You don't seem quite yourself" Katie asked as they climbed the steps to Montgomery Hall.

"What if Ms. Reynolds asks personal questions, like, *have you had sex?* I'm not sure what I'd say."

"She's too professional to embarrass a student in class. Besides, even if she asked, she'd question the whole class, not a specific individual. You don't have to say a word."

Frannie took a deep breath. "It would show all over my face, even if I didn't say a word."

Ms. Reynolds began, "Today our discussion topic is sex education. In your junior year, you will be teaching this lesson to a class of high school students, so you can understand why our focus is protected sex. We'll begin with a review of male and female genitalia. Then we'll address two important concepts. First, we'll review the registered nurse's role in prevention initiatives for high school students, and the second will relate to accessibility of prevention strategies, with or without parental consent."

While Ms. Reynolds discussed male and female genitalia, Frannie glanced at J.R., surprised that he showed no embarrassment at all, even though he was the only male in the room.

One student asked about menstrual cycles and the rhythm method of birth control. Ms. Reynolds explained that it was the least dependable choice to prevent pregnancy. Another student brought up the topic of *menstrual synchrony*, the concept that women who live or work closely together begin to have their periods at the same time. "That is a timely question," said Mrs. Reynolds. "Until this year, *menstrual synchrony* has been considered a myth or a coincidence, but this past January, a study by Martha McClintock about women in a college dorm suggested that social interaction can have a strong effect on the menstrual cycle.[1] If you wish to read the article, I can reserve it in the Library for the class."

After class, Frannie said to her roommates, "I learned more in that seminar than I did in my whole sex education class in high school. They taught in generalities and we got no specific information about condoms, diaphragms, IUDs, pills or practical information like the need for a spermicide in conjunction with some of the various prevention options."

Leslie agreed. "It was an impressive class session. I was glad they told us that we have access to prevention methods. I wouldn't have had a clue what to do next if I wanted to get on the pill or use a diaphragm."

"Would you guys help me get birth control pills?" Frannie asked. "Yes," chorused all three of her suitemates.

"I don't plan on having sex again anytime soon, but I never want to be that scared again. I can guarantee that there will be NO unplanned pregnancy in my future."

---

[1] McClintock, M.K. (Jan, 1971). "Menstrual synchrony and suppression." Nature 229 p244-245. doi:10.1038/229244a0

The Wake-Up Call

"You can borrow Nellie," Leslie offered. "Ms. Reynolds said it's a walk-in clinic and you don't need an appointment. You just have to be willing to wait a bit."

"I'll drive you," said Robin, "One cool thing about being on the pill is that you always know when your period is going to happen."

"Good point," Katie agreed.

"Who knows," Frannie announced. "We're the Nurseketeers. We just might wind up with menstrual synchrony!"

Chapter 23

"I need a break," Frannie announced after she and her suitemates had been studying for several hours. "Anyone want to go with me?"

Robin said, "You know, a break sounds good right now. My brain could use a vacation." The others shook their heads and returned to studying.

"Super! I can't remember a single time that you've gone to the Game Room with me."

"First time for everything, I guess," Robin said as they left the dorm.

"I got cash from my bank account to pay you back for the hospital bill. Thanks for taking care of that and you've never mentioned it once.

"I never doubted that you were good for it."

Frannie and Robin stood in the doorway of the Game Room, looking to see if Missy and J.R. were there. Sure enough, they were standing with Mike by the dart board, but they weren't playing. All three stared across the room. Tess and several other girls at the foosball table had also stopped playing to focus their attention in the same direction. Frannie followed their gaze and caught her breath when she saw Stephen holding court with Greg and James. His loud voice had captured the attention of everyone in the room. Around his index finger, he twirled a pair of blue bikini panties.

"…Yep, I won the bet! You guys owe me big time for scoring a home run with Frannie, just like I said I would. And lemme tell you, popping that cherry was EASY. Just act like you care a little, and she's down for the count."

The room remained silent as he boasted.

Tess frowned, then gasped when she saw Frannie standing, wide-eyed, and motionless in the doorway.

Time stopped and Frannie didn't breathe. Robin's face filled with rage. She clenched her fists and stepped into the room, all set for a *Chicago rumble*.

Frannie's breath returned in a rush. She grabbed Robin's wrist, jerking her to a stop. Their eyes met. Frannie shook her head and mouthed, "No, …HE'S MINE!"

"I'm good, Guys," Stephen continued, "but you wouldn't believe how slick it was. I just…" Stephen's satisfied smirk faded as the silence in the room crowded him. He followed the crowd's gaze and found himself face-to-face with a Frannie he didn't recognize.

She stood, shoulders back, seeming taller than her 5'2", and glared up into his eyes. "You Bastard," she hissed, "YOU FUCKING BASTARD!" The sound of her slap across his cheek echoed like a rifle shot in the silent room.

Stunned, Stephen looked around, desperate for support. "You BITCH! You WANTED it. You…"

"NO!" Frannie cut him off, glaring. "I wanted YOU. I hardly knew what *IT* was!"

"See…" Stephen looked at the crowd. "She…"

"SHUT UP, Stephen! I wanted a boyfriend so badly I couldn't hear all the people who tried to protect me. I made excuses for your rude behavior and convinced myself you were my Prince Charming. You took full advantage. You ARE the devil incarnate!"

When Frannie turned on her heel, the room erupted into shouts and applause. "Frannie STAY; Stephen GO! Frannie STAY; Stephen GO!" Frannie turned back to Stephen and said, "GO!"

Stephen looked around, but there wasn't a single friendly face. Greg and James had worked their way quietly to the door of the Game Room, leaving only menacing faces staring at him. Stephen shrugged, trying to look righteous then slinked out of the room as the shouts of "STEPHEN GO!" Increased in volume.

When he was gone, Frannie acknowledged the crowd with a soft *thank you*, then left to the sound of cheering.

Frannie marched toward the dorm, fists pumping, shoulders squared, head high, with Robin hurrying to catch up. In the suite, Frannie crumpled into a chair, weak-kneed and spent.

"Frannie?" Katie asked tentatively. "What happened?"

"She was awesome, Guys," Robin exclaimed as she knelt by Frannie's chair. "She neutered the scumbag and the crowd cheered."

Missy burst into the suite and squealed, "That was UNREAL, Frannie. You're famous! They're still cheering for you. I wouldn't be surprised if Stephen slithers away and Crestmont never sees that loser again. That's probably a good thing because I am positive that J.R. will pound him to a pulp if he stays. Are you OK?"

Still shaken, but resolute, Frannie said: "I'm alright."

Super, I have to tell J.R. you're okay cuz he's about to have a stroke in the lobby." She gave Frannie a hug and said, "You are just so COOL!" and darted out of the room.

Frannie took a deep breath. "Thank you," she whispered. "I know that you all tried to keep this whole disaster from happening. I can't tell you how sorry I am that I was too… well… too stupid, to listen. I just made excuses And I'm so embarrassed. It's not going to be easy to face the campus after this. But, I will. I'll be a worthy Nurseketeer."

The Wake-Up Call

Robin stood behind Frannie's chair and clasped her shoulder, then pumped a fist into the air and shouted, "THE NURSKETEERS ROCK!"

Chapter 24

As the girls left organic chem lab on the day after Frannie's momentous confrontation with Stephen, Robin put her arm around Frannie's shoulders and said, "So, *Frannie the Bad-Ass Loser-Slayer*, do you have enough energy left to kick the crap out of the chem test on Thursday? You have to pass or you'll end up a year behind us in the nursing program, and that would suck!" Robin said with conviction.

Frannie smiled. "I haven't left myself much choice, have I? I promised Dr. Grosvenor that I would succeed, and I will! Besides, I can't let the Nurseketeers down."

"Then let's hit the library before dinner and go back afterward."

"I'm in", said Katie."

Leslie added, "I'll meet you at dinner and go to the library with you afterward. I've got a 2:30 meeting at the Sports Center. Track finals are just around the corner and Coach Thomas is going nuts about practicing."

Sitting in their reserved conference room, heads bent over their organic chem textbooks, Frannie sighed, "I thought I'd catch on faster. Dr. Grosvenor said that if I started from the beginning, it would all make sense. I pray I didn't wait too long."

"You can't give up now," Katie encouraged. "He wouldn't have said you'd get it if he didn't think you would. Show me what's confusing you."

"Look here," Frannie pointed to the problem she was trying to solve. "If I use this formula, I'd have to know this value, but I don't."

Robin looked over at Frannie's book. "Yes, you do," she said. "Read the description of the problem again, and remember what values make up the number you're missing. They're right there."

"Of course!" Frannie exclaimed. "Why didn't I see that? I can't even blame it on being tired. We just *got* here." She grinned with satisfaction. "Thanks, you two. I'll just read a bit more carefully. What I need is more confidence in myself."

"Listen to her," Robin grinned at Katie. "First she has so much confidence she doesn't need to study; then she has so little confidence she can't study. What are we going to do with her? Just remember yesterday, Oh *Bad-Ass Loser-Slayer*, and let a little of that amazing performance spill over into Organic Chemistry."

Frannie, true to her word, used every spare minute to study. She feared she'd waited too long to buckle down. She unfolded her test to reveal a red *C* in the upper righthand corner. "I'm running out of time," She moaned.

"Not true," said Robin, hiding the A on her paper. "You still have one test and the final exam. You've done a great job so far. That was a lot to catch up on and you're nearly there. The next test and the final will be better. Remember the Nurseketeers. *One for all and all for one!* I know you can do it."

"Dr. Grosvenor reminded me that my lab grade is good, and it will be averaged in with the test grades. I'm still cutting it close, and it all gives me a case of nerves." Frannie's shoulders sagged as she pulled her notebook closer and prepared to listen carefully and take notes.

Robin came in after work to the usual mess in their room. Frannie's clothes were strewn about, and Frannie was sprawled on her bed, asleep, with her cheek resting on her open organic chemistry textbook.

Robin muttered, "I can't expect you to concentrate on anything but passing right now. You absolutely HAVE to pass! I know you've learned your lesson about… well, about everything. The next guy in your life is going to have to be one impressive dude or he won't get a second glance. And, I doubt I'll ever see a novel hidden behind a textbook in class again."

Robin worked the text from under Frannie's head and pulled the covers over her. Then she changed and got into bed.

Frannie stirred. "Robin, you awake?"

"I thought you were sleeping. You looked beat when I came in."

"I didn't mean to fall asleep. I was working a chem problem in my head. I think I'm beginning to get it, but I'm afraid to congratulate myself too soon, especially after the last test when I thought I knew more than I did."

"Don't be too hard on yourself. You're doing all the right things. Just stick with it."

"Robin?"

"Hmmm?"

"Can I ask you something?"

Robin chuckled. "You've been asking me lots of somethings for weeks. What gives?"

"I used to think you hated me… you were always on my case. What changed?"

"You did, Frannie. I never hated you. I've always known you were a good person… well, after I got over the mess you made in the room when we first moved in… I just didn't have patience with how *immature* you were and what crappy decisions you insisted on making. It made me mad to see what you were doing to yourself, and I couldn't do anything about it."

"I don't think things would have turned out well if you hadn't stuck by me. Katie and Leslie have always been supportive, but you're the one who gave me the strength to do what I had to do. Thanks for that…

"What you did at the Fair in Atoka," Robin continued, "convinced me that I was right about you.

"Atoka? What *about* the Fair in Atoka?"

"One of the nicest things about you is that you don't even know what I'm talking about. Do you remember the little boy whose ice cream fell on the ground?"

"Sure. Some lady bumped into him and the ice cream fell out of his cone. He couldn't stop crying."

"Right… Then what?"

"I gave his sister some money to get him another ice cream."

Robin smiled in the dark. "And you don't have a clue why that's so special. You are a good person, Frannie. When I was a little younger than that boy, my mother bought me an ice cream cone at the zoo. It might have been the only time I ever *went* to the zoo and it was probably the only ice cream cone I ever had… that is until Gram came to get me. Anyhow, my loser father was on a tear about something, and he swatted the cone out of my hand. The scoop of ice cream hit some lady, then fell to the ground. My father never said a word to that lady… no apology… no nothing… he just kept screaming at my mother. I just stood there staring at my ice cream on the ground and wailing. I think I was stunned, and maybe a bit scared, I don't remember.

"Then out of nowhere, a lady was crouching down beside me, smiling. She wiped my nose with a tissue, then asked if I wanted another ice cream. I don't know when I stopped crying. I couldn't believe what she'd just asked me. Anyhow, she walked across the path to the ice cream vendor and bought another cone. She came back, handed it to me, lifted me onto a bench, and sat next to me while I ate it. She never said another word.

When I finished, she wiped my mouth, hugged me, and walked away. I don't remember saying *thank you*. I've never forgotten that encounter. I don't know who she was. I don't have a clue what my father was ranting about, and I don't even remember leaving the zoo, but I'll never forget that lady. Frannie, I don't think that little boy in Atoka will ever forget you."

"I feel like I should be spending all of my time on Organic Chemistry," Frannie said. "My grades in English, Sociology, and New Testament are fine now since you convinced me to concentrate on applying the material instead of repeating it. I just wish chemistry was as easy to master. In Sociology, the influence of culture on behavior makes perfect sense, but who consciously makes a connection between saliva and digestion. I mean, who *knows* that saliva contains amylase that breaks down starches? There's just so *much* to remember."

"Just have faith in yourself," Katie said. "You've been working hard and you're smart. That's the perfect combination for success."

"Besides," Robin added, "if you don't pass, I'll kick your butt!"

Leslie and Frannie stifled their laughter when a *"Shhhhhhhhh"* came from the table just outside of their little room. Frannie whispered, "I need to pass. I wouldn't stand a chance against Robin."

"I'm not sure I'll survive today," Frannie moaned, sitting on the edge of her bed on the last day of class. "If I don't pass the chem final, I won't be in the nursing program anymore. I could get into the next class, but I'm not sure I even *want* to be in the program if I can't be with you guys."

"C'mon, Girlfriend, put a hearty smile on that gorgeous face," Robin commanded. "You need to believe in yourself. After all, we believe in you, and that has to count for something."

The Wake-Up Call

Frannie groaned. "You know, the worst part of failing would be letting you guys down. I can't bear the thought of not being a Nurseketeer after all you've done to support me."

"Oh, for god's sake," Robin said, "you're such a drama queen. We all believe in you. You've done a fantastic job. You've done a complete 180, and not everyone can pull that off, you know. You're smart and you understand the material. Don't let fear get in your way; just picture yourself in front of Stephen and give the chemistry final your best shot. You're ready for this."

From the other room, Katie called, "If you two want breakfast, you might want to consider getting dressed. Leslie and I are starving."

"I'll be ready in a jiffy," Robin called. "Don't know if I can make that promise for the princess here." Robin winked at Frannie who was pawing through her dresser for underwear. "It might take her longer to pick out something to wear than it takes me to shower and dress."

Frannie dressed in record time and joined them in the sitting room. "How's *that* for an Olympic style performance?" she said. "If I'm going to slay the chemistry dragon today, I figured it wouldn't hurt to start by setting a record for getting dressed."

The girls gathered their things and left for breakfast. "Gym class will take our minds off the final," said Robin. "We'll concentrate on pulverizing our opponents in volleyball. I, for one, have trouble worrying while I'm showing those stuck-up girls how volleyball is played. I can't beat 'em without your help, Frannie, so gut it up and let's kick some butt!" The Nurseketeers set off for breakfast, then the Sports Center.

<hr />

"Smile," Robin coaxed Frannie on the way to their last chemistry class. "Everything you said last night sounded like you understood the questions and answered them correctly. Give yourself a break and expect the best instead of the worst?"

"I'm afraid to think I passed, then find out I didn't. It's better to be prepared."

"Idiot!" Robin punched Frannie's arm. "The Nurseketeers are invincible… and you're a Nurseketeer."

Frannie slowly unfolded her final exam results. There was no grade in the upper right-hand corner. She took in a sharp breath, then realized that the top sheet of paper was a note from Dr. Grosvenor.

"Miss Braun,

It is unusual for me to communicate in this manner, but your dedication, commitment, and resolve to succeed merits a comment. Whether you passed or failed your final, you should be proud of yourself for rising to the challenge. It would be difficult for the brightest of students to overcome the deficit that you created by waiting until five weeks before the end of the term to begin your studies. The study of science is challenging. Principles must be committed to memory before they can be used, sometimes singly and sometimes in combination, to solve the problems of our universe. I am both impressed and proud that you were willing to undertake such a challenge.

Dr. Grosvenor

When Robin opened her test and discovered the red *A* in the upper right corner, she stifled an exclamation of joy and looked at Frannie. Before she celebrated her success, she wanted to be sure that Frannie also had reason to celebrate. Frannie was reading, and Robin saw no grade on the paper.

"Frannie? So…what did you get on the final?"

"I… I don't know," Frannie whispered. "Dr. Grosvenor wrote a nice note, but it doesn't say whether I passed or failed, and I'm afraid to look."

Frannie held the paper so that Robin could read the note. When she finished reading, Robin took the papers from Frannie and bent the top right corner of Dr. Grosvenor's letter forward so that she could see the first page of the test. When Frannie heard Robin gasp, she buried her head in her hands, trying hard not to cry.

"You idiot! Look at this!" Robin hissed, holding the test paper in front of Frannie's face.

Frannie's gasp was loud enough that others turned in her direction. "I… I can't believe it," she stammered. In the upper right-hand corner was a red *A*. Frannie burst into tears and hugged Robin, while Dr. Grosvenor stood smiling, watching from the lectern.

Frannie met his gaze, her lips forming a silent *thank you*.

"We have to celebrate," Robin said as they walked to lunch. "The Nurseketeers live on! Frannie, I'm so proud of you."

"We're all proud of you," Leslie concurred. "We didn't even want to think about moving on without you. How shall we celebrate?"

"What about dinner at Rob Rory's on Friday night before my shift begins? Robin suggested. "With my discount, it won't be expensive, and it's a special occasion."

"So what plans do you have for the summer, Frannie?" Katie asked, enjoying their meal at Rob Rory's.

"I have great plans. You guys will be pleased to hear that they include keeping my room straight all by myself and helping my mother in the kitchen. I'm drawing the line at ironing, at least until I master the basics."

Everyone laughed. "You, Sleeping Beauty, have surprised us all. It's hard to believe you woke up just five weeks ago and mastered a semester of organic chemistry… with an *A* on the final, no less. You are a whiz kid. I imagine you'll get straight *A's* next year, now you understand the magic of studying," Robin said.

"That is definitely my intention. I expect to *lead* the Nurseketeer study group next year." Frannie said. "If any of you need help, I'll be there for you.

"This summer I plan to do some volunteer work at the children's home near where we live. That darling little Karen from the Halloween party made me realize that just by spending time with those children I can make a difference. I hope that they all don't make me want to cry like she did."

"Frannie, what a great idea," Robin said. "I know that little girl got to you. Like that little boy at the fair in Atoka, she'll never forget you."

"So, what about you, Katie?" Frannie asked.

"I'm hoping to work at the clinic in Atoka. They told me last year that they'd be happy to have me cover for employees on vacation. Not the nurses, of course, but I can manage the front desk and whatever else they'll let me do."

"Cool," said Leslie. I might check out something like that in Abita Springs. I don't have anything lined up except helping in the store, but they've gotten along without me all year, so Mama and Daddy might not mind my doing something different. I'll have to make my own fitness regimen, too. If I show up next semester out of shape, I won't have a shot at varsity. That leaves you, Robin. What do you have planned?"

Two things top my list. First is working and socking away as much money as I can. The average pay in Chicago is better than Dallas. If I build up my account, it will be easier to take time off work during the semester to do cool stuff with you guys. Second, but more important, is spending time with Gram. The two years before I left home, I was a real bitch. I hung around with losers that Gram didn't like and didn't pay much attention to anything she said to me. Sound familiar, Frannie? She knows that I've turned over a new leaf, but I want her to see for herself that I've outgrown that bad girl stage. She's the neatest lady, intelligent, well-read, and funny. She's more like a best friend than a grandmother, and I wasted two whole years of that great relationship.

"Okay now…" Robin lifted her glass of *Coke*. "A toast to us, the Nurseketeers!"

The suitemates raised their glasses in unison and toasted, "To the Nurseketeers!"

Their waitress arrived with a tray of hot fudge sundaes. "Mr. Davis said that a little bird told him there was a celebration going on here. Somebody got an *A* on a chemistry final or something. He said that a celebration requires ice cream, so here you are, on the house. Ladies… Our house specialty… a zillion calories each!"

The girls looked over to the hostess station where the Davises were and raised their sundaes in acknowledgment.

Acknowledgments

Our sincere thank you to consultants Diane Gries and Charles Seawater who assisted us with Indian culture. We are grateful to Stacey Kuhnz, Marcia Crosthwait, Katia Goodman, Daryn Herrington, Amy Clark, and Chelsie Gable whose valuable insights contributed immensely to the final manuscript of *The Wake-Up Call*. In addition, the tremendous support of our families and our nursing friends who encouraged us to move forward with this story of Frannie and the *Nurseketeers*.

Authors' Note

We hope that you enjoyed *THE WAKE-UP CALL*. Ratings are instrumental to the success of a novel. We would appreciate it if you took the time to leave us a review.

Visit our website at, https://www.bakergoodman.com/ and join our mailing list for notification of new releases. *Friend us* on Facebook at Baker & Goodman Authors, https://www.facebook.com/jt.bakergoodman and follow our Author page at https://www.facebook.com/bakergoodmanbooks or email us at admin@bakergoodman.com

About the Authors

Joy Don Baker and Terri Goodman were nursing students in the '70s like the characters in their books. They are both published authors in professional nursing literature. They met in the 80's and have remained friends for years. Both authors reside in the Dallas/Fort Worth Metroplex where Baker is a Clinical Professor in the graduate nursing program at The University of Texas in Arlington, and Goodman is self-employed as an Approved Provider of continuing nursing education.

Frannie, Robin, Katie, and Leslie represent the rich diversity found among nurses. The suitemates provide exciting challenges for the *Nurseketeers Series*.